FOR PARIS~
with Love & Squalor

FOR PARIS~
with Love & Squalor

M. J. Moore

 Heliotrope Books

New York

This is a work of fiction. Names, characters, places, and incidents either are products of the author's imagination, or are used fictitiously. Any resemblance to actual events or persons, living or dead, is coincidental.

Cover Design by M. J. Moore and Naomi Rosenblatt
Thanks to Deborah Clove Lilienthal, Lorena Raynor, and Diana Rosenblatt
Typeset by Naomi Rosenblatt

For my late, great father: James Joseph Moore.
And for his father too, the quietly gentle grandfather
I never knew: Maurice Anthony Moore, Sr.

For my son, Daniel, my son's mother,
And our granddaughter: Evelyn Meadow.

Also for my three sisters:
(Colleen Marie, Laura Anne, Kathleen Therese).
Plus our Uncle Kevin. And also Aunt Dee Rosenblatt.

A slow salute offered here for
Richard M. Daniels and Clove Lilienthal
(Godfather and Godmother extraordinaire).

And especially for my mother,
Mary Ann Moore (*nee:* Fabish).
With inexpressible gratitude for a
lifetime of love.

SOUNDTRACK

"Flying Home" ~~

BENNY GOODMAN SEXTET
(featuring Charlie Christian and Lionel Hampton)
https://youtu.be/gn0hDIkvl0Y

LIONEL HAMPTON & HIS ORCHESTRA
(featuring Illinois Jacquet and Ernie Royal)
https://youtu.be/Pm8zT35WqNM

GLENN MILLER & THE ARMY AIR FORCE BAND
(featuring Bobby Nichols: trumpet)
https://youtu.be/CDSjCwJ3JYU

"I'm Getting Sentimental Over You" ~~

TOMMY DORSEY & HIS ORCHESTRA
https://youtu.be/lCDQqXHifCw?list=PL4264FE8D7F0C8B5C

"Loose Lid Special" ~~

TOMMY DORSEY & HIS ORCHESTRA
https://youtu.be/zCsyUSJh-jk

"Amapola" ~~

JIMMY DORSEY & HIS ORCHESTRA
https://youtu.be/UcFNRGsDQ1s

"Tangerine" ~~

JIMMY DORSEY & HIS ORCHESTRA
https://youtu.be/q-JDUnZv1N0

The Concert for Bangladesh ~~

GEORGE HARRISON & FRIENDS (full concert performance)
https://vimeo.com/66413717

"Fascinating Rhythm" ~~

TOMMY DORSEY & HIS ORCHESTRA
https://vimeo.com/72531299

How to Tell a Love Story

There is a story that I must tell, but
The feeling in my chest is too tight, and innocence
Crawls through the tangles of fear . . . If only

I could say just the first word with breath
As sweet as a babe's and with no history—but, Christ,
If there is no history there is no story.
And no Time, no word . . .

If only the first word would come and untwist my tongue!
Then the story might grow like Truth, or a tree . . .

Perhaps I can't say the first word till I know what it all means.
Perhaps I can't know till the doctor comes in and leans.

Robert Penn Warren

1

My time is up. But I won't let go until it's finally told. All of it. At last. Okay?

Dexterity is gone. (It's also a Charlie Parker tune—"Dexterity," that is—but now's *not* the time for Bop; besides, I was a Swing Kid, most of the time).

Just holding a pen at this time is like trying to balance on one toe.

So, talking into this gadget is the only way to go. The aide who got me started with this thing won't be back for a while. Yakking at this gizmo is something I can manage, but I'm too weak to press on Pause or Stop and . . . oh, God, I may as well just start in.

All right. I'm going soon. And that's that. At 92, it's been a long and winding road. And believe you me, that won't be the last time I echo one of my son's favorite songs.

Hemingway put it so well when ending *Death in the Afternoon*. Let me try to paraphrase: *Some practical things have to be said.* That was his gist. Thus he ended that book. Which is as good a place as any to start. Because that was the first book that ever hit me. Actually, it was the principal who hit me, for just having the book. Well, not just *hav*ing the book, but also bringing it to school.

For "having it on your person," as Sister Therese Ellen said.

I should have expected trouble. C'mon, it was 1938. A Catholic high school in Chicago. And Hemingway was controversial. Not like later on, when he ended up on Mount Rushmore. Not like now, when he's canonized. He was a hot potato then. So, how the hell did a 12th-grade girl who was barely sixteen get a hold of that book?

Long story short: It was thanks to Pop. Who never *really* liked being called Pop, by the way. He preferred Dad, and I suppose I don't blame him. But, by the time I was en route to senior year, he'd gotten used to being called Pop. What he never got used to, that summer before I entered my senior year of high school, was my innate ability to be happy "doing nothing." That's how they put things. Ol' Mom had much the same problem with me, and between the two of them the questions persisted all summer long. "How can you be so happy just sitting there?" "What do you day-dream about all the time?" "Are you doing anything today, or are you *just* reading?"

That's the kicker right there. I wasn't actually all that idle. I *was* reading. And it was weird that it annoyed them, because they loved to read. When they had free time. Which they hardly did. They both worked. That was more common than you might think. But it's how they kept their mortgage during the Great Depression.

What happened was I'd turned into a reader at the end of 7th grade, against all odds. Mostly due to discovering a special edition of a book left behind in my classroom at St. Rita's. That's the name of the school I attended. The grammar school. Where I'd never been much of a reader, despite the best efforts of the nuns to get us going on that. But it changed overnight one day after I picked up this nifty special edition of the Sherlock Holmes tales that somebody had left on a shelf in Sister Rose Cecile's classroom. It was just *there*. Waiting for me.

I reacted right away not just to the iconic images on the book's dust jacket—an Edwardian pipe and a deerstalker hat, of course—but I also got caught up in the two stories. Like I said, it was a special edition and the publisher had glued together in one book the first long stories (they were short novels, in fact) that put Holmes, Watson, and Arthur Conan Doyle on the map. I loved those titles: *A Study in Scarlet* and *The Sign of Four*. Maybe that's where all of my varied "four" obsessions began.

It wouldn't surprise me. Long before I was assigned to the Fourth Infantry Division years later, when we all got caught up in the war, my hang-up on "four" was chronic.

Fast-forward: So, for most of June, July, and August in 1938 all I wanted to do was read and reread my favorite new books. Sister Ann Damien, the high school librarian, had let me take four books home for the whole summer; and I was enthralled. Two were by Edith Wharton, and the other two by guys: William March and Jack London. March's *Company K* told the truth about poison gas. Bayonets. Trenches. World War One's madness. In France. It was considered violently grim. But our school library had the book. The same with Jack London's *Martin Eden*. Sister Ann Damien said that both writers were akin to Zola, their books representing "the apex of Naturalism." *Martin Eden* even had sex. And suicide. We whispered about that in Sister Ann Damien's English classes.

Otherwise, all I ever wanted to do was stick my head near the radio and hear Benny Goodman on his weekly "Camel Caravan" program. I loved his band and the singer was all right, too, but what I prayed for each week was that he'd feature the Quartet on his radio show. Like I said, the "four" thing was entrenched long before the war.

But right before senior year started up, Pop decided that my endless days of reading and rereading needed to change. I needed "projects." That's the word he used.

Projects. As in . . . cleaning the garage for the umpteenth time (hauling out every last thing, properly sweeping, using the hose to wash the floor of the garage, and so on). Then: Cleaning up the basement yet again, even though it was always spit and polish. How could it *not* be? We cleaned it together once per week when he was home on the weekends. But suddenly I was ordered to clean it on my own, even more, on some of those few remaining weekdays before school started up.

And that's when Pop got the bright idea for "a new project." One day on the phone (he usually called in the middle of the day just to "check on things") Pop said: "Empty out the basement cabinet of books and then reorganize them: neatly."

There was no question involved. It was a task. Period. But instead of turning out to be a chore, it became a joyous discovery. I'd never really known that many years earlier, before his life got swept away by long hours at work and sports on the radio, Pop had been a serious reader. Avid.

That cabinet in the basement that I was ordered to sort out, dust, and reorganize "neatly," had great stuff. I knew Pop had gone to college (which no other father on our street had), but I was still both startled and annoyed by my discovery. Startled, I say, because right off the bat I saw there were books by other controversial writers: Whitman's poems, novels by Dreiser and Crane, plus a handful of Hemingway titles. Why annoyed? Well, I said to ol' Mom: "If Pop could read all *those* books, what's wrong with me reading William March? Why won't he tell me?" Pop didn't like the idea of me reading March's *Company K.*

Most of all, though, I was irked that he hadn't opted to toss all of his books at me.

And that's how I got my hands on *Death in the Afternoon* by Hemingway.

2

One month later, that's how Sister Therese Ellen got her mitts on me. It was all about the book. Not its "disturbing title" (as she put it), which I still think is a real grabber. Nor was the problem the wide variety of photographs in the book. I was surprised by my curiosity about something as alien and as exotically foreign as bullfighting, which is the core subject of *Death in the Afternoon*; and the array of photos selected to illustrate the text was pretty damn impressive. But to echo the good Sister, the photos were "unwholesome." Other than that, I don't recall her saying zilch about the pictures in the book. The language? *That* infuriated her.

What happened was one day on the playground, before the eight-in the-morning bell rang, four of us girls were in a circle. Utterly transfixed by *Death in the Afternoon*. We were looking at the photographs of bullfighters in various scenes of bullring mayhem. Our predictable symphony of exclamations ("Holy Moses!" and "What is *this*?") were gassing up the air like the smokestacks of the Rheem factory over there on Kedzie Avenue. Then: As she made her morning rounds to ensure the moral rectitude and the good manners of the Irish-Catholic lassies in the old neighborhood, the mere sight of the four of us entranced by a book (I don't think she could hear the quasi-blasphemous "Oh, Jesus!" wailers) was mysterious enough to turn Sister Therese Ellen into Sherlock Holmes. But she needed nothing as royal as "the science of deduction" to get her dander up. All it took was a quick one-two-three of flipping through the pages and . . . *"Outrageous!"* That's the next thing we heard. Sister had more than once used her eagle's eyes to hone in on the pages where dashes galore replace missing letters, yet the first letter was always there and it was "f" and the dashes that followed weren't diminishing the impact for her at all. Hemingway had clearly meant "fuck" this or "fuck" that, even though on the page what the reader saw was "f" (dash-dash-dash) and there it was: "f---" on several pages. She demanded to know who had brought "*such filth*!" to her school.

Of course my goose was cooked.

By the time she hauled me up to her Principal's Office and called ol' Mom and told her that she and Pop had to personally retrieve the book from her office—"I will not brook allowing any child to carry such a book *any*where, and neither should you!" was the way she tried to shame ol' Mom on the phone—the whole thing became a blur. With one exception. Before my folks arrived to retrieve Pop's book and also to endure the wrath of the good Sister (our house was scant blocks from the school and it was early enough in the morning for Pop to still be at home; he always took the streetcar to his office and never left the house before nine in the morning), she smacked me. It was way more than a slap. Hell, I'd been hit by other kids in typical scraps and all like that, but her smack hurt worse than being slugged closed-fisted by one of my tomboy pals. Maybe it hurt more because she was supposedly holy and that gave her something like an aura. Neither she nor the other nuns had the remoteness of the parish priests, because the nuns really ran the school; they did all the hard work and the priests were sort of like mysterious dictators or something.

Anyway, before ol' Mom and poor, embarrassed Pop finally got to the Prinicpal's Office that day, the good Sister made me just stand there. "No sitting down!" she insisted, when for a moment I almost took a chair. "You should be scrubbing floors in church for the next month, as far as I'm concerned. On your hands and knees!"

You get the picture. She was dressed of course in her full habit (black garb from head to toe, with a rosary-like belt from which hung a wooden cross with the weight of a street cop's billy-club), and all of a sudden she started interrogating me.

"This book!" she hollered. "I should have you suspended for having it on your person." To her it was like a used condom. "How did you come into possession of *this*? Such *filth* certainly doesn't belong on school grounds." Now she was hitting the cover of the book with her rigid index finger, poking Hemingway's name as if she were stabbing him, and bellowing: "Did you know this man is *divorced*?" And she looked stricken as she harshly whispered the word "divorced."

Then she went in for the kill: "He is a sinner!" she declared. Dummy that I was, I meekly replied: "But he seems to have an exciting life, Sister." And then: *Smack!*

She let fly with one monumental whack across my face and I saw stars. Truly.

Then I saw my parents, fortunately. Which opened another can of worms. I'd done a really good job of organizing and "neatly" rearranging my father's cabinet full of books in the basement. Actually, I'd even alphabetized his collection according to authors' names. But I conveniently forgot to ask permission to walk off with a book.

They made me stand out in the hallway as they spoke tersely in the Principal's Office. I could hear the first question that my folks were peppered with: "Don't you think you ought to pay *more* attention to what your *only* child reads?" That in itself was a zinger. It was not only rare to be an only child in our neighborhood; it was almost unheard of. Catholic families were not just encouraged to breed like rabbits, but, the women were threatened with eternal damnation in the bowels of Hell if they practiced any type of birth control. Yet my birth nearly killed ol' Mom, and her "female problems" (as Pop softly said) made more kids impossible.

Chances are, Sister Therese Ellen knew zilch about ol' Mom's hysterectomy, but to me that didn't matter anyway. Our family being a trio was none of her business. So, standing there, overhearing more of her shrill questioning ("What kind of book is *this* for a youngster?" and "How can such *filth* be in a good Catholic home?") got me good and steamed up. She was really jabbing at Pop and ol' Mom. Then it ended.

I was ordered to return to my classroom. Later that afternoon, back at home, ol' Mom was silent. When I checked the basement cabinet, I saw that *Death in the Afternoon* was back in there. In alphabetical order. But there was still an empty space where the Hemingway titles were "neatly" on display. A book was missing.

But a piece of paper was there. It was a note from Pop. In his manly block-print style, he wrote: "We'll talk about this one in your room, when I get home."

3

Upstairs in my room I saw on my bed the book he'd withdrawn from the basement cabinet. It was *A Farewell to Arms*, by You Know Who. I sat there and stared for a while at the book's title page. There was no dust jacket. It had been removed.

For a minute or two I tried to recollect the sequence of actions from earlier, in an effort to recall precisely why I'd decided to walk off with *Death in the Afternoon* instead. You see, thanks to a really popular movie version of *A Farewell to Arms* with the youngest Gary Cooper you'll ever see (along with a sweet old babe named Helen Hayes that you probably never heard of), *that* was the famous book to have.

It was one of those big-deal, in-the-air cultural things. Everyone at last *knew* about it, even though, like most of the time, hardly anyone had time to read it or see it. But it was famous. You could tell how popular it was because even though the movie had been released when I was barely ten (no jive: I recall hearing my parents say to each other that they'd better not speak freely to the neighbors about how much they wanted to see that film, because it was "scandalous," just like the book), way back in 1932, it was periodically brought back to the movie-houses for what we called "a revival." No kidding. At least once every other year, it was presented again.

"You actually remember hearing us talk about that?" Pop asked me. He'd come home from work right on time—he always did—and as we sat side by side in my room upstairs, I saw how perfectly his tie was tied. He never loosened it after work. In his view, you wore a tie the right way. Or not. He looked ready for inspection.

"I do," I said. "You two didn't want to see it with others, but by yourselves."

"That's five or six years ago," he said. "Why in the world would you recall that?"

"It sort of ran through my mind when I was cleaning the cabinet," I said. "But the pictures in the other book really got my attention. So, that's the one I borrowed."

"You're better off having a look at this one," he said. "But the book stays in this house. Preferably in this room. Your mother's not too thrilled about this idea."

I rifled the pages and the first thing I noticed was that there were some dash-dash-dashes (once again) in place of the words that could not be printed. Before I had the chance to ask any questions, Pop explained a few things in his quiet way.

"This one's a novel. Not like the other one. But this kind of novel is not for everyone. It's not meant for what they call entertainment. Not really. It's a love story, but it's also a war story. Or I should say it's a war story that turns into a love story. But the language issues that infuriated your Principal, they're in there too."

"How's it going to be okay if I'm reading this one instead of the other one?"

"Because you're reading it at home, for starters," he said. "And now you have my permission, which you should have asked for when you took the other one."

"What about mother thinking it's not okay?" Whenever I spoke with Pop, I called ol' Mom "mother." Funny, he corrected me if I called her "she," so, "mother" it had to be.

"Your mother knows that I'm suggesting this to you," he assured me. "Sometimes your mother also suggests that I talk to you more about what's going on in the news, the bad news from overseas. And I know that you have asked her—more than a few times—about my service in the Great War. Well, this book is part of that whole era."

Then it started all over again. It was a repeat of the Sherlock Holmes experience. I read and reread the same book, the same chapters, the same favorite passages for months in a row. Again and again. Time after time. It became like my new gospel.

"Don't say that," Pop corrected me when I referred to *A Farewell to Arms* that way, calling it something like a gospel. "That's one of the reasons that your principal reacted with such fury. In the Gospel according to St. John," he softly instructed, "we're told: 'In the beginning was the Word, and' . . ."

I could tell he was waiting for me to finish that. "And the Word was God," I said.

"That's one of the reasons why newer books are sometimes called blasphemous," he reminded me. It was getting close to Thanksgiving when we had this talk around the kitchen table, and then Pop asked me to turn up the radio. I loved listening to the news with them. And he adored my "encyclopedic memory," as he put it.

Ol' Mom sighed, of course. Heavily. She always did.

It was more bad news. We're talking the middle of November 1938. By that time, toward the end of that year, Hitler had already waltzed into Austria and they loved him. Then he chopped up Czechoslovakia that autumn. Ol' Mom was frightened. I turned up the radio, the way Pop asked me to, and we listened to more bad news.

On one dreadful night in November, only twenty years after the end of World War One, a savage outburst of Nazi-organized violence in Germany led to the burning of 400 synagogues and the destruction of more than seven thousand Jewish stores and homes and businesses. First on CBS, we heard Edward R. Murrow report that 100 were killed and more than 25,000 German-Jewish civilians were being "dragooned" into concentration camps. Thanks to Sister Ann Damien's literature classes, I knew what "dragooned" meant. But I had to ask Pop and ol' Mom to explain about concentration camps. They weren't able to say a word.

4

Boyfriends and all somehow seemed unimportant—even to me—in the shadows of all the bad news that month. We heard those radio reports about the Night of the Broken Glass in Hitler's Germany; and awful news about the Japanese rampaging and raping in China and also Mussolini's Fascist armies running amok in parts of Africa.

We sure as hell took note of the Spanish Civil War, too. Ol' Mom wasn't really a Hemingway fan (whereas Pop admired him, always reminding me that "he grew up not too far from here, over in Oak Park, before he went off to my war"), but ol' Mom was a chronic reader of John Dos Passos. And both Hemingway and Dos Passos were writing for the magazines about Spain and "the good fight" (both my folks loved that phrase) against General Franco's fascists.

That's another way in which Pop and ol' Mom went their own way. When we sat in church on Sunday for the Mass at ten in the morning (no questions about attending Mass; it was a must), there were periodic sermons about how and why and with small donations all Catholics were "duty-bound" to help General Franco's forces, who had the Church on their side and the blessings of the Pope and the support of Rome. End of discussion. Except it wasn't. Not in the privacy of our home.

The drift in the neighborhood and the sole opinion of the Church added up to supporting Franco because those against him made room for Communists. And the singular opinion in the air was that most of the writers who were cheering on the anti-Franco crusade were Communist Leftists. Or "those Reds."

That's why Pop and ol' Mom kept quiet about their appreciation of Dos Passos, Hemingway, and others, too. I was intrigued, a bit amazed, and somehow moved by the very idea of writers being so caught up in the history of the times. But in our neighborhood, loving books was not exactly up there with baseball, boxing, money, and the usual American nonsense. And it was books and all those up-to-the-minute dispatches from Spain that made my folks quite sure that the Church had it wrong in its support of Franco. "He's another bully, another dictator," is what my folks said.

Five years later, just a couple days after my 21st birthday in June 1943, that's when I enlisted in Uncle Sam's Army. No hesitation on my part. No joining the Navy on the assumption that the WAVES might be easier (which it could be, but not always). And no effort on my part to get into the Nurse Corps—or what they'd started to refer to as the Army Nurse Corps. I'd exited nurses' school after one year.

"I hope you'll reconsider," Pop said one night, "even at the very last minute, you can select nursing assistant as an option because you're enlisting. Maybe they'll send you back to school. That's a benefit right there. You have some choices. But to volunteer for Communications right off, well, why be so adamant?" It was a rhetorical question. He knew why. So did ol' Mom. I'd brainwashed myself reading Martha Gellhorn's first novel and her journalism. Martha topped all that by marrying Hemingway, after he dumped wife Number Two.

By the time I had my 21st birthday on June 4, 1943, our usual family tradition of not just appreciating certain books, but, reading and rereading them, had been amplified in a major way. Odd but true: As far as writers, books, culture, and the temper of the times were concerned, Hemingway finally won over ol' Mom. All three of us had star eyes about *For Whom the Bell Tolls*, which came out in 1940. Then the incredibly ambitious, long, and richly-colored movie version of that new novel hit screens right around the time I turned 21 in 1943. It was majestic.

Our last outing as a family took place when on the weekend right after Halloween in '43 we all went together to the Hi-Way Theater and saw *For Whom the Bell Tolls* in all of its three-hour Technicolor glory.

I was already in uniform. Sharply pressed. On furlough after basic training at Fort Des Moines in Iowa (which was pretty much like an intensive eight-week physical fitness marathon; all the gals who'd enjoyed gym in high school did pretty well, but others struggled; somehow, though, even the smokers huffed and puffed their way through it all; my secret weapon was the "proper breathing" methods taught to me by Pop). Ol' Mom cried through the second half the film. But it wasn't the story of the star-crossed lovers that got to her; nor was it the way that Gary Cooper (he seemed to be born to inhabit Hemingway scenarios) played to the hilt his role as the American volunteer who goes to Spain to fight "the good fight" against Fascism.

By the time we huddled in the theater together and saw *For Whom the Bell Tolls* in the early autumn of 1943, the Spanish Civil War seemed like a distant memory. It ended badly with Franco's victory back in 1939. But when my 21st birthday rolled around in '43, Spain was out of the picture (neutral, supposedly) and the world was aflame damn near everywhere else.

The folks couldn't believe that I was joining the fray.

5

"But it wasn't all doom and gloom." I can hear ol' Mom saying that right now. In my mind (what's left of it, anyway) I still hear echoes of some of her favorite bromides. "It wasn't all doom and gloom" and "Put one foot in front of the other" or "That guy could foul up a one-car funeral" and all the others. Almost always, she was right.

The aide who appears at the same time each day in this here Hospice Suite, in order to make sure I'm settled as comfortably as possible, is a bit of a wizard. She's got a gift for all the wacky and, to me, wondrous toys that makes the world go 'round these days. Nothing fazes her. She can figure out *any*thing. And that's why I'm now the proud owner of what they call a "stylus." OK. That's a weird word for a stick that I can use to poke here and there and Press Play or Press Record or Stop, and make this gadget work on my own. It's been liberating.

And to give credit where credit is due. This amazing aide over here, her name is Lorena and everyone calls her Rena—right? Right. Well, it didn't take long for my usual wordplay to kick in and because the nickname Rena-Bena is already used by others—everyone loves a goofy rhyme, right?—I've officially anointed her Beansy. And she also asked what ol' Mom would've asked: "It wasn't all doom and gloom, was it?"

Hell *no*. That's the only answer. And that's the damnedest thing. All along the way, no matter what ghastly stuff was in the headlines, we were still aware of the nicer things going on. Or the happy things that somewhere, somehow, gave us joy. New movies—a few were in color! That was quite rare back then. New dances, of course. Great new looks in hats and hairstyles, especially for the ladies. That's no joke about Irwin Shaw being spot-on regarding "the girls in their summer dresses."

Sure, the newsreels blared at us with all the war news that unfolded month after month and year after year between my exit from high school in 1939 and my enlistment in the summer of 1943 (and during those years the war news was relentless: from Hitler's invasion of Poland to France's fall in 1940 to Pearl Harbor and our catastrophe there in 1941 and then more and more and more with Europe crumbling and the Brits holding out until we joined them in the North Africa battles really late in '42, and things began turning around a bit in 1943, while at the same time the war in the Pacific was an island-hopping crucible in its own right, chewing up the Navy, the Marines, and the Army altogether, but nothing was going to stop those guys). Yet there was also an astounding amount of great-good stuff going on. I mean with life in general.

In my case, and I know this was true for Pop and ol' Mom as well, the radio music of the times was a balm in many ways. Not the usual mediocre stuff that was always on the air, but the special programs featuring the slew of great bands who took over the culture and raised the bar in popular music back then.

My aide here, Beansy, in all of her effervescent youthfulness (she's bright as a Westinghouse light bulb and full of all the right questions), she asked if what her grandparents told her is true—and what her grandparents told her is that Glenn Miller's band was the biggest thing going at that time. Odd but true: It's the right thing to say and yet it's also the wrong thing.

"What you wanna take into consideration," I reminded Beansy, as she was putting a fresh plastic bag into the trash container in the corner, "is that so much was going on just in popular music alone that there was no one single band that took over the world." Yet I understand what she was getting at. In a funny way, it's like the way the Boomers lined up later on, always comparing the Beatles and the Stones and the Doors and the Who (thanks to my son, I actually learned a lot about all of them through the years; and some of their milder stuff always appealed to me).

After decades have passed, it seems like one band topped all the others. But at the time, when things were all new and happening all at once, it was different. There were simply *so* many great new players and top bands and fine singers. All at once!

"You should talk more about your favorite music someday," Beansy then said, just before she had to go off on other rounds.

That calls for a one-way ticket to 1943.

6

Beloved Beansy, bless her heart. She got me 90-minute cassettes to use now.

And so, here goes. One night in 1943 (after completing WAC basic training and after my two-week furlough back home and just after I was temporarily parked in New York City while waiting to go overseas), I had a weekend pass and one thing led to another and I ended up in the audience of a "Live!" radio broadcast in Manhattan.

And it was no soap-and-cereal show, as far as the music went. It was one of those special broadcasts we lived for—at Radio City Music Hall.

That night was one of the final stateside performances of Glenn Miller's Army Air Force Band. And believe me when I tell you that there were a dozen differences between Miller's Army Air Force outfit and that civilian band the public loved. For those of us who really dug big band jazz, Miller's civilian band was merely OK. He streamlined everything. His singers damn near took over. But the public ate it up. Something went haywire in a fantastic way, though, because once Miller enlisted (he was already 40 or so!) he staffed his Army Air Force Band with an ass-kicking, all-out crew of musical heavyweights. Real jazzmen. And when I heard them make a miracle of freshness out of an older hit like "Flying Home," I went right to heaven.

Radio City's auditorium was like a vortex that night. Everything came together. And we were so young that a well-known song only four years old (there I go again with my "four" thing) seemed like an old favorite already. That's how young we were. And that's how it is when you're barely twenty or under twenty-five. Something that hit like the biggest thing going when you were a high school freshman can seem really long gone and off your radar screen by the time you're a high school senior.

That's the way it was with "Flying Home" that night. At least when its title was announced. You see, by the time that the most-most-most important version of that tune got recorded in the summer of '42 by Lionel Hampton and his band, the song had already been a huge favorite for three years. Lionel wrote it with Benny Goodman, they recorded it with Benny's sextet, and they performed it everywhere starting back in 1939. (Don't even get me stated on how important 1939 was.)

And so, OK, we'd heard it on the radio, it was a 78 record almost everyone had a copy of at one time or another, and then Lionel waxed that ultimate recording of it in 1942, with the legendary tenor-sax solo that went on and on. Gotta give that tenor-man credit: Illinois Jacquet was his name.

And Pop was a major fan of the multi-chorus solo that Illinois Jacquet played on that record of "Flying Home" that Hamp and his band made into a sensation. Not that he had much choice. I must've played that record a thousand times. But Pop was quite the music fan, you see, in addition to being a bit of a bookworm.

In fact, on a whim back in the eighth grade, I talked him into dusting off his clarinet (something else that was tucked away in a basement cabinet) and giving me enough rudimentary lessons to actually produce a sound. That's no small feat with a clarinet. It's a tough instrument. And I learned it the hard way. Pop said I'd be better off—if I really wanted to learn an instrument and all—studying the alto saxophone, for example, or the tenor saxophone. And then, after a year or two, he said I could learn "to double" on clarinet and that way "be an asset to the whole woodwind section in the school band." But I wanted nothing to do with school bands. There was no question about that. I just wanted to be close to Pop.

Still, I had a secret weapon. An ace up my sleeve. Without brothers or sisters to draw their attention, and with my single-minded interest in the clarinet (thanks to my radio addiction to Benny Goodman), ol' Mom did a fine job of persuading Pop to not only let me toodle and experiment with his old clarinet, but to teach me. Slowly.

And I mean teach. Formal lessons were underway before I started high school. In our own way, we found our rhythm and made it work. Pop knew what to do. The mystery of developing an embouchure (that's the placement of the mouthpiece and its reed into the pie-hole of the player) and the importance of scales. Tone and the most fundamental technique issues: You can't be*lieve* how subtle a clarinet is and how precise and me*tic*ulous you have to be with your fingers and your breathing.

That was a major lesson right there. The breathing thing. Each time Pop wanted to demonstrate something for me, he stopped talking and took hold of the clarinet. He had an extra mouthpiece and his own reed was wet and warmed up (that's another thing about Pop: he had this picky thing going on about "the perfect reed" and all), so, he could swiftly take hold of his old clarinet, talk to me about what he was about to demonstrate as he switched the mouthpieces, and then . . . I would *see* the magic.

Forget about what I heard. Pop was merely showing me—literally— the how-to of one small detail or another. Or illustrating "how you want it to sound," as he said.

But it was something else entirely that I witnessed. This came in handy in the war.

It was the transformation that came over him when he took a deep breath and with a slight nod began to play anything. Even a scale. Even the simplest melodic line. Whatever he was playing took second place to *the way* that he played it. And I don't mean that he had the chops of a Benny Goodman or the artistry of an Artie Shaw. Those guys were virtuosos. They played like visitors from another planet. What I mean is that the way Pop took a deep breath and centered himself was the key. He'd learned a lot from his brother, who'd originally owned that clarinet.

You could *see* it. I certainly saw it. And for the first months of our at-home lessons throughout 1935, during the spring and summer before I started high school, he made a big deal all of the time about the breathing thing. "Proper breathing requires that your stomach enlarge, " he reminded me a hundred times. "Your shoulders are not supposed to rise and your chest ought not to heave. Yet, your belly enlarges."

He made me place my open palm on my stomach for weeks, in order to really feel how the deep breathing process makes the gut grow out. It wasn't easy at first. Hell, as a kid back then, after seeing all those bathing suit ads in the magazines, we all assumed that sucking in our guts and puffing out our chests was the right way to go.

No way. I finally got it. And mostly from watching Pop. Not just seeing how his own shoulders remained still or how his own chest did not puff out, but, from marveling at how his deep breathing routine made his stomach expand. And changed him. In a moment.

It *really* changed him. His focus was more intent. His concentration, intense. And then he'd demonstrate the musical lesson, in that moment, with hypnotic focus.

That's the real deal. Pop's music lessons taught me most of all about the need to practice "proper breathing" (he never called it anything else). And aside from anything about the music or the horn, what I really got was how it changed him.

His total concentration. Real focus. It's like he became one with the instrument.

And later on, that night in 1943, when I was lucky enough to be in the audience of the Radio City Music Hall and Glenn Miller's Army Air Force band opened its show with what the announcer bellowed as "their rocket-gun version of 'Flying Home,'" once again I saw that hypnotic concentration.

Maybe it's because it was Friday night. No kidding. Maybe that had something to do with it. I'm sure it was a Friday night because it happened only hours after I wangled a weekend pass at the last minute. That's another story for another time.

But something was in the air that night. It was Friday-night energy. No doubt.

By that I mean all around me the mood was up, up, up. The auditorium was filled to capacity (no surprise there; attending a radio show was a big deal back then, just like later on when people got jazzed about being in the audience for a TV show), and lots of sailors and soldiers were in the crowd. Along with older folks and kids, too. It was a "most peculiar mishmash," as Jerry liked to say. That's the night I met him.

But before I met anyone that night—things started out with me on my own; little did I know how that would change—there was nothing but the music on my mind. And it all began with the total surprise that seized my spirit when the program began.

Seeing Glenn Miller himself was an unexpected thrill. I mean, of course, I expected to see him. He was leading the damn band. Everyone knew he'd be out front, as usual. But it was different. Yes, indeed. It had all changed all right. And seeing Miller in uniform was part of it.

In a funny way, Glenn Miller was more hip in his Army Air Force uniform than he'd ever been in a suit when leading his civilian band. Before he enlisted, he was the kind of guy who looked (in pictures) and sounded (on the radio) like a banker or a dull insurance salesman. And it hardly mattered because neither Miller nor his trombone playing was the main event. We all knew *that*. He was no virtuoso like Harry James on the trumpet or Benny and Artie on clarinet and never-ever could he compete as an instrumentalist with Tommy or Jimmy Dorsey. It was different. The gift of Glenn Miller was in his way of arranging those charts of his, like "Moonlight Serenade" and all the others. The band's *sound* was defined by his arranging.

And that was the beauty part. Tons of Miller records and most of his radio shows and, of course, the way his civilian band had conquered America's theaters and ballrooms all boiled down to the unique sounds that were written into almost every chart: the brass players using plungers like crazy to get their "Doo-Wah" effect time after time. The sax section with the famous "clarinet lead" element. All that stuff. It was as easy to identify Mlller's band in a blindfold test as it was to identify drummer Gene Krupa, who sounded like no one else. Anyone truly listening could tell.

Anyway, that's another reason why I ended up with goose bumps, a palpitating heart, and a dizzy spell on that Friday night. Because everything expected by me, and that audience in the RCA auditorium, well . . . *everything* was a surprise instead.

I certainly never expected the show's opener to be a red-hot, aggressive, brand new arrangement of a tune that was four years old. But "Flying Home" was made new.

And the biggest surprise of all was that none of the predictable Miller tricks were in the chart. Not only did the band sound heavier, gutsier, freer, and way jazzier than Glenn's civilian band ever did, it sounded more *serious.* Jesus, I hope that makes sense. I don't mean serious like Mozart or Bach. I mean serious as in: *Look out!* When Miller counted off that opening number (and I'm not kidding: there was a peculiar something about the way that that guy, on the edge of being 40 or more, looked so suddenly hip in a military uniform, even though we all knew he was kind of a square from Iowa), there was no gradual introduction or anything. No one-at-a-time instrumental entries. No incremental introduction of themes or motifs. It was a monumental *blast-blast-blast,* and a riff and a kick and a crash of the drummer's cymbals that instantly raised high the roof, because everyone played all at once and always at top volume. They also played with intense focus. They *breathed* together. Beautifully.

You gotta remember that with most of the charts by the bands of my era, you'd have a gradual accumulation of sounds. Things started a little bit at a time. All building up to the point where the whole band would play together at the end. But now it had all changed. Miller's AAF version of "Flying Home" started out in fifth gear and it hit hard, right off the bat, and somehow managed to build from there.

I wasn't alone in reacting to this. You could tell from the whiplash way that folks looked at each other and from their instant clapping along and their howls and whistles that everyone's batteries were being recharged. And the familiar melody—which after that blasting fanfare of an introduction came at us like a locomotive—allowed the sax section (without the predictable "clarinet lead") to sink into a groove that was the musical equivalent of a hot bath, a cigarette drag, and sex.

And then this kid trumpet player—and I mean he *was* a kid: after the show, when I first met Jerry, he told me this kid trumpet player was only 19 years old—blew an extended solo that did more than cause other band members to shout; it also gave the audience permission to holler and wail and cheer him on. That *focus*. I could see it from my seat in the fourth row. The trumpet player did more than just concentrate, wholly commit and blow like a madman. He did his "proper breathing."

The effect was extraordinary. And watching and listening and all from the fourth row gave me not only a bird's-eye view of the stage and the musicians and even Miller's reactions (a small grin eventually gave way to a wide smile and then he nodded his head with a gesture of total affirmation), but made it easy to turn fast and see how the crowd all around me was affected.

His volume had a lot to do with it. The kid trumpet player, I mean. This skinny little guy was nothing to look at. His uniform was too big for him, and even his trumpet seemed oversized. But the way he *set* himself . . . his focus . . . that stance he took, just a moment before he started to blow like Gabriel. He was *really* something. And his volume, like I was saying, *that* was key. After he took his first deep breath—and I could tell he knew what the hell he was doing because his shoulders did not rise up, but instead his elbows extended outwards a bit as he raised the horn to his chops, and I knew—I absolutely *knew*—that his gut was enlarging the right way.

Then the trumpet-playing kid cut through the whole damn auditorium with a tone and a volume and powerful solo as robust as the band at large. That had everything to do with why the crowd got crazy. It sounds exaggerated, I know. But the volume attained in that solo by Bobby Nichols (later that night, when I met Jerry and we took turns talking about all this, he told me the kid's name; he'd already been written about in *Metronome* and *DownBeat*, and the guy was barely nineteen) was nothing like a typical horn solo in any of the bands. He set that place on fire, he did.

Within seconds I could see how he made it happen. His elbows gave him away. I knew as it happened that he was taking a proper deep breath before every four-bar phrase that he improvised and blew in his jazz solo. If you don't know a thing about music and all that business about "bars" or "measures" (which are the same thing), something like this is no less effective. But it helped me to be able to see right away that the trumpet player's deep-breathing pattern was the gateway to his pacing of the whole solo. And he started out hot and heavy and (like the arrangement itself) managed to dial it up and build and intensify his solo with each four-bar passage.

Behind the trumpet player's wailing interval, the rhythm section just kept up a solid swinging pattern of support. And as a Swing Kid who'd spent the past several years with both ears glued to the radio and often with my eyes locked onto pages of both *Metronome* and *DownBeat* (those magazines were to our generation what *Rolling Stone* and *Creem* became for my son later on in the late 1960s and the 1970s), my excitement was enough to make me dizzy when I saw that in this hot new AAF Band there were players who towered above the OK-but-not-that-great players in Miller's old-time civilian band. Right *there*, rocking the roof as Bobby Nichols improvised passage after passage of fiery swinging jazz, the rhythm section alone was stupefying: Mel Powell on piano was running lines and adding "fills" that he comped with total confidence, and why not? He'd become a star player in the 1941 Benny Goodman band, which was for a while as trailblazing and as innovative as the BG outfit that made history back in the 1930s. And right *there*, right in the moment paying close attention to the cadences and phrases that Bobby Nichols created on trumpet, drummer Ray McKinley kicked, accented, cymbal-crashed, and rebounded with much more drive and finesse than his predecessor ever did back in the Miller's civilian band, which also made sense.

We all knew Ray McKinley from his years in Jimmy Dorsey's band, which was steeped in everything from Dixieland to Swing. The drummer in Miller's civilian band was mighty fine, but Ray McKinley took charge. And the same applied to the bassist. They nicknamed him "Trigger" for his chops. Anyway, speaking of chops—that's a funny word in music circles; it means ability to play and how good or great or lousy you are (as in, "Gerry Mulligan's got great chops on baritone sax," but for horn players in particular, it also means their mouths) the other best thing about this gut-busting chart of "Flying Home" was that after Bobby Nichols ended his full two-chorus solo, the band and Mel Powell took over for a bit and each time the band finished roaring through a four-bar passage, Mel would come back at 'em with four measures of jazzy piano. It was call-and-response time. Then I looked behind me again. I mean, I could not see Mel's hands at work on the keyboard; not from my seat, and not from the way he was tucked back there in the rhythm section. So, as I heard his dizzying melodious riffs toward the end of the arrangement, I just naturally looked sideways and turned around and then laughed. There were more than a few couples making out. I mean it! And I laughed because this wasn't a dark movie theater. This wasn't a dive bar. The lights were not low. But the music was hot and the intensity of the performers set off a chain reaction. I thought I was seeing things at first, but I rubbernecked each time piano notes filled the air for a four-bar riff, and couples were smooching and making out all over the place. Most of them were couples with guys in uniform, so they got way with it.

And then I saw one unusually tall guy, standing alone. We looked at each other.

7

Then it wasn't long before the program finished. And we sort of inevitably met each other. Radio shows in those days were often 30-minute episodes. Sometimes they were 15 minutes, but not always. Especially music programs. They were scheduled in 30-minute blocks (or an hour) every day and every night. I know that sounds a bit crazy, but with brief verbal remarks and rapid rotation of the tunes, a popular band could play lots of numbers in 15 or 30 minutes and make everyone happy.

I slowly made my way up the aisle to the Exit Door at Radio City Music Hall that night. My being there alone felt like a bit of an oddity. Almost everyone else seemed to be coupled off. Guys and gals (the temptation to say "guys and dolls" overwhelms me) were not only in the majority that night, but they radiated a Planet Romance kind of mood. And I'm being polite to a fault by using the term "romance." Sex was in the air. And the band's performance had played to it. The tall guy said so first.

"What's your guess?" It was the unusually tall guy standing alone behind the back row taking the lead and asking me that as I got near the door. "Looks like you and I are the only ones here stag tonight," he said. "So I figure I'm not holding you up."

He extended his hand and automatically I shook it. That's the way we were. A handshake always initiated things. We'd been raised that way. You offered a handshake or you accepted one, but either way you looked everybody in the eye and made a proper introduction. None of this lazy, slack, modern-day, eyes-down bunk.

Anyway, he was in uniform and so was I and our nearly identical Army garb was enough to hold my attention, especially when I noted that he had an extra stripe. I was a Private, barely out of basic training, but he was a Corporal and looked a few years older than I was.

I'd saluted of course, but that happened so fast that my mind was already at work on the question he had posed. "What's your guess?" he then repeated. And sensing my confusion, he smiled and expanded on his question.

"My guess," he said, "is that within two hours of the show that just ended, more than ninety percent of the young folks here in the audience tonight will be pretending they're on a honeymoon together. With green lights flashing and the whole world's OK to act accordingly. Those tunes tonight were like gas on fires. So, what's your guess? Did they love the jump tunes more? Or the four-song medley?"

To allow the heavy crowd traffic to keep moving toward the Exit Door, I'd had to step aside and reposition myself adjacent to the tall guy. And he *really* towered. I was exactly five-feet-ten with my shoes on. For gals, that's above average.

If you want a specific yardstick to measure that by, here's the truth, the whole truth, and nothing but the truth: My son thrilled me once by telling me that Robert Redford's also five-feet-ten. I was amazed to learn that. On screen, he always looked taller than that. Same as Paul Newman, in fact. But neither of them had the six-foot-two thing going on, ever. On the other hand, looking up, I realized that Jerry had all that.

I also realized that I had no choice. To talk to him, I had to look up at him. And before improvising an answer to his question, I blurted: "How tall are you, sir?"

He cracked a smile and for a moment rose up on the balls of his feet. "Six-two in stocking feet, and six-three in shoes. Especially these shoes. Thank you, Uncle Sam. And you can call me Jerry. We're old pals by now. Don't let these stripes stifle you."

"Sorry to sound like a teacher," I said. "But you could be Lincoln in a school play."

"Funny you mention that," Jerry said. "I was a classroom disaster in high school. Military school. Both, actually. Not every class, but most. But I loved theater. That was my world, in a way. The readings. The rehearsals. Performing. Loved it."

One thing led to another, and by the time the crowd thinned out and the aisles were cleared, the two of us just naturally drifted from our spot behind the back row out to the lobby. And, just as naturally, we both reached into our pockets and plucked out our packs of cigarettes. Much to my parents' chagrin, I completed basic training with a new appreciation for free (or at least excessively discounted) cigarettes. They plied us with those goddamn things. Threw them at us by the carton at first, and then made them a nickel a pack at the PX. Tops. They knew exactly what they were doing. Nothing bonds strangers faster than sharing smokes. Old Gold for me. And Jerry had a pack of Chesterfields. I fished in my pockets for my Zippo lighter.

"Allow me," Jerry said. And he fired up something more impressive than a lighter.

He quickly opened one of those classy little boxes with sandpaper sides, and retrieved a small wooden-stick match. Striking the match with expertise, he lit my Old Gold as I cupped my hand around the flame for a second. Then he lighted his Chesterfield. What killed me was the calligraphy on his box of wooden matches.

The Stork Club. Yowza! Even a gal from the South Side of Chicago knew what *that* meant. Fame. Class. Fancy photos in *Life* Magazine. And the anecdotes in *Collier's*.

That's how the whole crazy business began. Right then and there when I gawked at Jerry's matchbox from the Stork Club. He noticed. He picked up on *every*thing. My self-consciousness kicked in when I realized my eyes bugged out à la Harpo Marx.

"Ever been?" Jerry asked me. He tossed the matchbox in his free hand as expertly as actor George Raft flipped a coin. "We can't zoom through the big town without a pit stop at the Stork Club."

"You ever read *Collier's* magazine?" I asked him. I still didn't know exactly who he was or what he did. So his answer went over my head. "I read 'em, and I argue with them all the time. Not face to face. Only when they return new stories to my agent."

I figured he was talking jive about this or that. And like the yokel I was, I asked him: "Did you see the photo of Ernest Hemingway in *Collier's* last summer? Right around the time *For Whom the Bell Tolls* had its premiere? The film and all? *Collier's* ran a photo of Hemingway standing there at the Stork Club with the owner or the top manager or somebody big—Stanford Helmsley or Stanley something . . ."

"You mean Sherman," he corrected me. "Good old Sherm. Man about town! The estimable Mr. B. Friend to anyone, save the impecunious proletariat. Billingsley."

"*Billingsley!*" I confirmed. "That's it. They had this photo in *Collier's* of *that* guy and Hemingway at the Stork Club with an anecdote about how that's where—"

"Say no more," Jerry interrupted. "I'll tell you right now. It's a true story. Really. That's where Ernest the Lion-Hearted brought his check from Paramount Pictures after they paid him a lump sum for all the rights to make a movie of *Bell Tolls*. And it's true, my curious young friend, that that *was* a check for about a hundred grand."

"And it was cashed by Sherman Billingsley out of the safe at the Stork Club?"

"That's the way the story goes," Jerry said. "Why don't we go there right now?"

Before I took another drag on my Old Gold, the wheel turned.

Actually, everything turned. Fast.

8

To this day I can't decide what's crazier. The fact that I next found myself at a table in the Stork Club, where it seemed that Jerry felt ridiculously at ease. Or, the fact that we rode there in one of the Army's official, newfangled, wildly popular wartime vehicles: a jeep. This is no jive. While I was cooling my heels that month at Fort Dix in New Jersey, waiting with innumerable others for orders that'd set me on my way, it turns out that Jerry was in a similar state of limbo at Fort Holabird in Maryland.

"Aside from everything else going on there," he explained at the top of his lungs while driving us through the noisy nighttime streets of New York, "Holabird is the Army's depot for jeeps that'll eventually be sent *over there*." He sang the last two words and no explanation was required. The anthem of World War One—"Over There"—had been revived for the duration. It really caught on again after James Cagney played the daylights out of the part of George M. Cohan and that film of his in '42 made the song new all over again. That's another thing that needs to get across: We knew that a movie like *Yankee Doodle Dandy* was corn and syrup and apple pie all combined. But it really did give us one hell of a lift. But, let's all remember this: When that film was packing theaters all through 1942, we were losing the war on all fronts. That's not bunk. The Nips and the goddamn Nazis had all of the advantages. I get the feeling nowadays—I've had this feeling for decades—that most Americans raised on television and Hollywood nonsense and then computers and all ended up with this cockamamie notion that after Pearl Harbor, we were in it to win it, and just somehow leapfrogged to victory in 1945. But it wasn't like that at all. Not *ever*.

It took *for*ever to start getting back at those bastards. And it seemed like eternity to us at the time, because when you're barely twenty you're a lot closer to fifteen than you are to thirty, and just like with high school kids, a few years is like forever. And we needed a few years to get traction all over the world. I've asked Beansy here if any of this stuff connects with her generation (she hates when I ask her about her age, but finally she admitted she's "fat and forty"). Beansy was born in 1975. So, she was ten in 1985, the year of "We Are the World" and "Live Aid." She grew up (the poor kid) thinking that Michael Jackson, Madonna, and "Rambo" were national heroes. "We learned nothing about World War Two in school. Nothing I can remember, anyway. Sorry," she now says.

No wonder everyone thinks that we magically fast-forwarded to Normandy, the Bulge, Iwo Jima, and two atom bombs. Hell, I've got Beansy here saying that in her eight years of elementary, her four years of high school, and all of her college time at Loyola University (that's a good school, too), she and her crowd never heard a word about Midway or Guadalcanal, North Africa or Sicily, Burma, Saipan and Salerno for Christ's sake, not to mention Anzio or Monte Cassino. It's like it all never happened.

Anyway, what happened was that Jerry not only wangled a pass for himself that weekend but because he'd just been bumped up upon acceptance into a special training program for new guys in the Counter Intelligence Corps—the CIC—he got another stripe, and that helped with his crazy request to have authorized access to a jeep for that weekend. We got looks of wonder and awe from people on the streets.

Remember, the jeep was a fairly new thing. It looked great. Everyone considered it cool. "Even Glenn Miller has blessed it," Jerry joked as we parked around the block from the Stork Club. "The same guy who wrote *A String of Pearls* just knocked off a new tune called *Jeep Jockey Jump*. We are officially in style!"

I hadn't heard that tune yet, so for all I knew it might've been blarney. I decided to test him. "OK," I inquired: "Help me remember. Who wrote *A String of Pearls*?" I was a total music geek, but I long ago learned that most folks don't care for details.

"Jerry Gray," he answered. "Who the hell wouldn't know that?"

We were kindred spirits. Even though we came from two different worlds. But that fact that we hailed from separate planets is maybe why we hit it off so well. Right?

I mean, he came from a Park Avenue family, and I swear the brash confidence that he had was partly due to the financial armor that goes hand in hand with being the only son in a wealthy family. That was another thing. He, too, was the one son. And in the natural course of making the usual introductory small talk admissions—and he liked that both of us knew what he meant when he said that such exchanges were like the piano man and the trumpet player "trading fours" at the end of that "Flying Home" arrangement, where each one took a took a turn, time after time, playing four measures of improvised riffs and having sort of a musical dialogue—we compared notes on life. Easily.

But we were worlds apart. When he was younger, his family wouldn't have hesitated to browse at Tiffany's. In my youth, in our neighborhood on the South Side of Chicago, it was considered a cultural event to browse at Sears, Roebuck. There was a Marshall Field's store, of course, but that was downtown and not really where we felt at home. But if we were downtown, we stared at the front windows.

On the other hand, I could tell from the way he displayed his manners at the coat check counter (Jerry knew what to say, how much to tip, and it was effortless for him to steer us through the crowd and right on up to the *maitre d*, who seemed to know him; and I mean *know* him-know him, he wasn't just doing his job and being polite and all), well, I could just tell that Manhattan was a playground for Jerry, and the Stork Club merely featured in it. That's how unfazed and nonplussed he was.

Me? I was transfixed. The candles on the small tables (with their beautiful tablecloths and shiny silverware), complemented by the soft lights above that were countered big-time by the spotlights beaming at the small stage, where musicians and a slew of singers took turns that night—nobody really big, just solid New York pros all around—in addition to the roving Cigarette Girls and the waiters in their classic black-and-white uniforms (mostly older men, just like the musicians were older, too, because all the younger ones were caught in the draft)... I was in awe.

Jerry ordered a cocktail for himself (it was an Old-Fashioned), but I insisted on a plain tonic water with a lemon twist. I learned that from ol' Mom. Being careful.

Out of the blue, with a half-spoken and half-musical lilt in his voice, Jerry began to sing: "*It's a long way . . . from Tipperary,*" and then his mind drifted, and he stopped.

I knew the song. It was extremely popular during the First World War, according to Pop. And thanks to Pop, I knew the title and corrected Jerry: "*It's a long way . . . TO Tipperary,*" I said. But I said it nicely. "That's one of my father's favorite songs. He was in the first war. You know, the one that was supposed to be the last war."

"How could I forget?" Jerry said. "I was born one year after it ended. And it's something I've missed ever since." His quirky humor appealed to me.

For a moment we were quiet. But it was noisy all around us. Chatter went on even as the musicians and the various singers performed. Glasses clanked. Chairs were moved hurriedly. It was a smoky, boozy atmosphere, but also hectic and strained.

"That's how we talk these days, isn't it?" Jerry remarked. He was thinking out loud.

"The lines have been drawn. And 1939's the new dividing line. Or, for Americans, maybe it's 1941. But now you hear 'the first war' and 'the second war' all the time, and pretty soon the last one'll be so forgotten that everyone'll just call this mess 'the war.' How can it be possible that the last one ended only twenty-five years ago?"

"If not for my father," I admitted, "I'd never think about the first war at all. He still calls it the 'Great War.' But he was caught up in it, at the end, like most of the Yanks."

"I'd kind of like to hear more about that," Jerry said. "Was he a Doughboy?"

"Sure was," I said. "Drafted in 1917. And he was a boy in France in 1918."

"And here we are a mere quarter-century later," Jerry said. "On our way back."

This was the early autumn of 1943, and nobody knew exactly when the Allies would again land in France. But it was the big invasion everyone assumed would happen. Meantime, the year was ending with gratitude for the victory in North Africa, some amazement at how quickly Sicily was liberated, and then there was dread about the Italian Campaign. It seemed like it was taking forever to get from Naples to Rome.

"Remember that scene in *The Wizard of Oz* when it all turns into color?" I said.

"Judy!" he exclaimed. "You are a soothsayer. I was just thinking about Judy Garland's new film. Have you seen it? Say 'no.' It's called *Presenting Lily Mars.*"

Everything's changed, of course, and that's the way life goes, but in some ways I'm sure that one thing hasn't changed all that much. The excitement in a young man.

I mean, the way a young guy gets when all of a sudden he realizes that he can let loose and truly share his hot coppers about something (or someone) without any self-conscious embarrassment over what he's fired up about. Witnessing that kind of unbridled enthusiasm—Beansy tells me that this still happens, when she learns that a new friend of hers is "a wonk" or "a word nerd"—can be remarkable.

And there's no other way to describe how Jerry went from here to the moon, when he realized that I, too, was a big fan of Judy and wanted to see her new film with him.

All of a sudden, everything else around us dissolved. We were at the Stork Club? So *what*. It was just another place, all of a sudden. There were bigwigs or rich people or somebody famous in the crowd? So what! We had notes to compare about Judy. And we had a bona-fide Stork Club ashtray to fill.

It was just a few years after the release of *The Wizard of Oz* in 1939, but already she had a following that was unusual. Or, just the opposite. Which is what baffled Jerry.

"There's a girl I knew," he told me, "bright and young and aware of who's who. But other than the role of Dorothy, she didn't ever see Judy in anything. Not *any*thing!"

"That's a mystery to me," I said. "But my situation is a bit cornball, I'm sure. My parents and I made sure to see every new film she's been in ever since 1938. So we've been following her at the movies ever since *Love Finds Andy Hardy*."

"But she also makes records and comes across really well on the radio," he said.
"I know," I replied. "Sure. Of course. But my mother teaches in a public school and my father's an office clerk. We hardly ever bought records. Movies are cheaper."
"Speaking of records," he said, "her new film also features Tommy Dorsey's band."

That sealed the deal. Jerry wanted me to jump in that jeep he had for the weekend, and zoom off to the Capitol Theater, where a ten p.m. show of *Presenting Lily Mars* was set to begin in less than an hour. But I wouldn't risk all that trouble. My hotel reservation was already made, and it had a check-in time that you couldn't fool with. Otherwise they'd give the room to someone standing in the lobby and praying for such an opening. Hotel rooms—especially on weekends—were at a premium in those years. Besides, there was curfew and the blackout to deal with.

"Tomorrow," I said, "Let's meet there for the first afternoon matinee. But first I want to hear your story. How did *your* grand crush on Judy Garland ever get started?"

It was like putting nickels, dimes, and quarters into a jukebox.

"It didn't really hit me until last year," he started. "But I've been hitting the movie theaters for as long as I can remember. Except when I lived in

Europe," he said.

"Lived in Europe?" I interrupted. That, to me, was like hearing he could levitate.

"Before the war," he quickly said. "Just before the war with the Eskimos."

I almost swallowed my cigarette, but then realized his quirky humor was at work again. Quickly, he amended: "Oh, wait. We're not fighting the Eskimos. Not yet. What was I thinking? Just before the war with the Nazis and all things Nipponese."

"Are you making this up?" I asked. My sense was that he was *not* putting me on.

"Seriously," he said. "In '38, right before the war. After I left college. My father sent me to Austria. He's in the import and export rackets. I was supposed to learn that."

"Good God Almighty," I said. "You were living in Austria in 1938?" That stunned me.

"Anyway," he interjected. It was a verbal pivot. I could tell he wanted to steer clear of the subject. "When I was back here in 1939—" That's when I interrupted him.

"Are you a native New Yorker?" He mashed out his cigarette and lit another.

"I am," he said. "Be it ever so phony, there's no place like home." Too much was going on all around us to examine subtleties, but years later I'd certainly discover (along with half the world) how much mileage he'd get out of the word "phony."

Then he summed up quickly: "What happened to me was, well, you see: I love music. Okay? Yes, indeed. I think we've established that tonight. And after I saw her in the musicals she made with The Mighty Midget—"

"I assume you're referring to Mickey Rooney?" Mickey's height was always a joke.

"Indubitably," Jerry said. "Those musicals with him were fun. But last year, when I saw her with this new guy—the Irish guy who dances like a god: Gene Kelly!—my heart did more than leap up. Apologies to

Wordsworth. I fell in love. Just *like that*."

His face had changed. He wasn't putting me on at all. He looked stricken. In love.

"My folks and I saw that together," I told him. "We all agreed that she had really grown up. I think she made that film right after she got married to David Rose, the composer in Hollywood. Older guy."

That's when his face *really* changed. For the worse. He looked furious. Not at me. But at something else. Something private. It was spooky in a way. Alchemical.

"Let's not talk about fast marriages or older husbands," he said. "Let's talk about Abbott & Costello."

And that's how we ended our outing at the Stork Club on that Friday night in the fall of 1943. We instigated the first-ever academic colloquium on the phenomenon of Abbott & Costello. It sounds dopey, but it wasn't. Not at all. And I don't mean that we got around to the silly effort to recite the "Who's On First?" routine that everyone else tried to pull off. Turns out we both had too much respect for the team to try to emulate that kind of long-form, rhetorical stunt. We actually analyzed the phenom.

Isn't that the right word? "Phenom"? Believe me, that's what they were when America entered the war at the end of 1941. And they still were in 1943.

"Although they've run of out service branches to play for laughs," Jerry noted. "Unless they try to get funny with the Marine Corps, which isn't recommended."

I knew precisely what he meant. You see, out of nowhere (even though they'd had some success on radio), the Abbott & Costello phenom exploded in 1941. As my son would later say about movers and shakers in the Sixties and Seventies, they were "on *time . . . right* on time." And that's the way it was. It all happened in 1941.

"What I remember most is seeing *Buck Privates* by accident," Jerry told me. "It was a Sneak Preview and the crowd was informed by an usher in a snazzy coat with his little hat up front before the scheduled film began . . . he told everyone that they could stay for free—kind of a big deal on a weekend night—and see a brand new comedy after the end of *Honky Tonk*, the Gable and Turner picture."

Clark Gable and Lana Turner in a film together were really hot stuff then.

"But the deal was," Jerry recalled, "that, to stay, we had to fill out Preview Cards after the show. It was not a task. The audience ate that film up, from beginning to end."

"It happened in Chicago, too," I said. "*Buck Privates* caught on like mad. It was the perfect blend of current events with the draft and all, plus slapstick, and the verbal shenanigans with the sergeant and the soldiers—plus music and a romance, too."

"Whoever wrote it deserves a prize, Jerry said. Packing every possible cliché into a new Army comedy, and somehow making it fresh. I mean, it *really* worked. It *did*."

"You're preaching to the choir, Sonny Boy," I replied. His expression startled me. But it wasn't until decades later than I learned his boyhood nickname was Sonny.

I went on to say: "More amazing is that in a row, they managed to make that formula work three times over in only a year's time. Think about that. Both *Buck Privates* and *In the Navy* came out in '41, and then the one about the Air Corps—"

"*Keep 'em Flying*" Jerry clarified.

"Right, right. That came out in '42. And everyone loved all three. Or so it seemed."

Actually, that's not true. There were plenty of folks—especially the ladies—who did not care that much for Abbott & Costello. But guys loved them and kids in general got a big kick out of Lou, in particular. Being short and fat was always a winning combo when it came to comedies. But the phenomenon was a very real thing, even if lots of folks thought they were overrated, or over the top, or just plain obnoxious.

We touched on that. "It's the leftover vaudeville schtick," Jerry said, using one of the few Yiddish words that everyone understood. "Which is part of their magic, but also part of their mystery. Bud and Lou are really vaudeville guys who come across well on the radio because they're so verbal and all. But what they figured out in the films is how to combine that verbal dexterity with the visuals needed for a storyline. So, then the whole package works: Physical stunts, music scenes, some diversionary romantic angle, topped by their rhetorical patter."

"Hands down," I said. "Nobody's made better use of popular music in their new films than those guys." Abbott & Costello's three most popular films (the ones set in the Army, the Navy, and the Air Corps) had all featured the Andrews Sisters and the swinging bands that each branch of the service conjured up. We knew right off the bat that "Boogie Woogie Bugle Boy" would be a smash hit; and when it became a big hit all over again, when my son was young in the early 1970s, I couldn't get over it.

We talked some more about how the Marx Brothers had stopped making movies and the Ritz Brothers had been eclipsed in popularity by Abbott & Costello, and I see now how this pattern has been the same forever and ever. When people meet and start getting to know each other—at a party, or on the job, or in school or anywhere at all—they usually end up talking about the movies. Or TV shows. Stuff like that.

My fondest wish was to carry on with such a dialogue when we met the following day at the Capitol Theater's matinee to see Judy Garland's new film: *Presenting Lily Mars*. I would have loved to talk more about music with Jerry, especially because Tommy Dorsey's band was nicely featured in the movie, and I had a whole theory to share about the ways in which Tommy's outfit differed from his brother Jimmy's equally famous band. They were ferociously competitive for two brothers, yet managed to share the spotlight.

But I ended up seeing the film alone. Jerry never showed. He stood me up.

The next time we crossed paths, it was August 1944. Over there.

9

It's every damn thing that's left out—*all* of the time—that's what bothers me now. More than ever. Because in a crazy way, it's all been deliberate. Since whenever.

I don't know who'll ever hear these tapes or whatever might become of them, but I don't really care anymore. Time is running out. I'm running out of energy. As for time . . . nobody here can pinpoint anything. All we know is what we don't know.

Having said that, I want to get back to every damn thing that's left out. And always was. Okay, o*kay*. Yes, yes, *yes*. Seventy years ago *is* a long time ago. That we know. But what's always bothered me is that the entire story of our whole epoch—not just our war, but the years before it and the years right after it, and then the decades that followed—somehow ended up packaged and sold like Coca-Cola.

I mean, just forget about the obvious and at least somewhat familiar fact that at least one hundred and fifty thousand women were in the WACs. Sure, that number is minor compared to the fifteen million men who served during the second big one. That's understood. And yet, wait! We're still talking about more than one hundred and fifty thousand women who saw the same hardcore pitch in the 1942 newsreels that I saw: the speech from Lionel Barrymore that was played in every American theater as a special newsreel recruiting women for the Army. You don't hear about him now, but he was famously famous then—by which I mean we didn't just know his name; we recognized his voice alone from the radio and we knew his face from the movies and being part of America's royal family—so to speak—in drama, he really got through to us.

My decision to enlist was a reaction to his clarion call.

But I'm not the issue here. Not really. The thing is like this: Except for a throwaway line of two in those dreadful textbooks that high-schoolers use to cure insomnia, it never got across just how bold and brave a woman had to be to step forward and volunteer to serve her country. In uniform. As more than a nurse. And while the nurses were angels and amazing and true miracle workers in the field, they also got a dose of serious respect just for being nurses. Which was fine. But it wasn't fine that those of us who enlisted, even though we weren't nurses, caught holy hell. Did the WAVES and WASPS catch hell as badly as WACS did? I wonder.

And this is a part of what's bothering me about all that's been lost. It always *was*.

Even during the war, at the height of the whole crazy-making thing, all that we did was somehow sidelined, and the wackiest kind of misrepresentations took over. I can't begin to tell you how mad this makes me now. And even *then*, I was livid.

I remember the clashing newspaper articles. The resistance to women in the ranks turned into a great debate fought out in the newspapers. The power of the press back than was like the Internet today. Everyone fell back on the "if it's in the papers" line the way that everyone now assumes that if it's material found on the Internet, it *has* to be true. Or valid. Or worthy. Or credible. Crazy as it sounds, with so many newspapers on a daily basis back then, their authority was unassailable.

And while everyone from President Roosevelt to Lionel Barrymore was seen in the newsreels calling on America's women "to free a man for combat" (I'm not kidding; that was their sales pitch) by enlisting and declaring a specialty in communications or any number of non-combat essential duties, the backlash was downright swift.

One of those big-big-big newspapers owned by the Hearst family (in Chicago their claim to fame had plenty to do with the *Chicago Herald-Examiner*, but they had untold numbers of newspapers all across America) poured gasoline on all of the fires later in 1943, right around the time that I signed up. They were shameless. I'm not making this up. To add fuel to the fire that was already raging, thanks to a cabal of ass-backward

Southern senators who were ranting against the WAC recruiting efforts and howling about how American society would be injured or destroyed if so many women veered away from marriage, motherhood, and all the homey and very traditional ways of comporting themselves—well, you can imagine what they said.

Or maybe you can't. One thing I know is that it never got across in the textbooks or for that matter the major magazines that were also in every home decades ago. But it sure got into the newspapers in the middle of the war. How could it not? Those stories in the Hearst papers about how we were being issued a hefty supply of condoms before shipping out for overseas duty? Those stories set off a firestorm. It wasn't true, of course. But that counted for nothing. Once the story was printed and reprinted and syndicated here and there, the public really soured on us. I mean it.

We could feel their eyes on our backs. Wherever we went. In uniform, of course. That's a fact. We wore our uniforms as loyally as the men, but something shifted after the debates got nasty in 1943 and 1944. We were suspect. We were looked upon as being sluts. All of a sudden there was something in the air and it was not clean. Which is a damned hoot because almost every one of the women I met in the Army had enlisted, partly, from an exalted sense of ethics. And duty. And honor.

But it all got twisted around and misrepresented, and what you could ascertain from certain looks or remarks and all the innuendo that was palpable . . . what we picked up was the assumption that women in uniform (except for nurses) had to have decided to enlist because we were nymphomaniacs or lesbians. Plus, the other sales pitch was for WACS "to release a man for combat." Some punch line!

I remember how, many years later, way later in the 1970s, I startled my son by telling him about this business. He was actually shocked.

"I never thought you used those words back then," he told me. Like so many young people who grew up in the 1960s or the 1970s, he and his crowd thought they were the first ever to discover *every*thing. But it wasn't their fault at all. The simplified, minimized, sanitized, all-American Hollywood horseshit that passed for history in their schoolbooks and their classrooms and the culture all around them—all bunk!

But that's the way it was. Right after Pearl Harbor, all throughout 1942, there was a fierce national campaign to recruit women for the Army. And everyone who had eyes to see was so used to all the ads, that hardly anyone noticed when WAAC (for the Women's Army Auxiliary Corps) got shortened to WAC (for Women's Army Corps). All that mattered was the recruitment drive. It was a national emergency. And even a math-impaired dummy like me could understand the numbers. In the Army, a full combat division consisted of fifteen thousand men. So, when we tallied up at more than one hundred and fifty thousand strong in the WACS, we were doing the jobs that allowed for the creation of *ten* more combat divisions. Major numbers.

And guess what? In a crazy way, that ended up working against us. I mean, it came as a surprise at first, but then it made more and more sense. Lots of the guys were *re*ally angry at us and plenty were downright resentful, because having answered the call of duty (and having done so mostly because FDR and Eleanor, too, made all of their great speeches) it was inevitable that our presence to perform our duties meant that *they'd* be assigned to far more dangerous duty. They were pissed!

Many of them, anyhow. And how could they not be? That's something else that's never been made clear. It never gets across that plenty of the guys wanted safe duty. Or duties that were many miles behind the lines, if not stateside. All of this movie nonsense about everyone just dying to "storm the beaches" and being full of blood lust and wanting to kill, kill, kill? That's the ultimate Hollywood fantasia. I know for a fact that most of the guys were *not* gung-ho infantry wannabes, and when they ended up in the infantry divisions they were mighty grateful not to be riflemen. But *that* never got across either. I mean, the plain truth is that in a combat division of fifteen thousand men, you'd have three thousand or so as riflemen. The guys *way* up front. But the vast majority? They were performing other essentials.

10

Speaking of essentials. As far as we knew, up until a sudden change of plans at the last minute, Paris wasn't *really* considered a top priority or a strategic essential. I was as surprised as anyone else—and all around me, there was a mixture of awe and a wondrous kind of giddy bewilderment—when Ike and his staff turned on a dime (or "turned on a *franc*" as several of the girls joked) and made the decision to have us lend a major presence to the days of liberation in Paris at month's end in August 1944. It was more than a surprise. It made us delirious. Something . . .

Something more than language is needed here. The words I am speaking are hardly sufficient. Phrases seem paltry. Sentences anemic. The images overwhelm my mind. Still. After seventy years! But the same problem comes back again. Through the years, anything resembling the truth has been lost. Smothered. Manipulated and revised and used for lots of simpleminded agendas. But we know better. We who were there. It was unlike any other ecstasy in the history of the world. I know.

Let me latch onto the most obvious example. You still see this newsreel footage. Even now. On PBS flashbacks or in special documentaries. Sometimes inserted into new movies for dramatic effect. Even though it's black-and-white film footage. No amount of computer gimmicks or big budgets could re-create the old newsreel films with anything comparable to what really happened. And what *really* happened?

Magic. That's what it was, on the one hand. It was magical and majestic and simply beyond our wildest dreams. But it was also practical, expedient, and logistical. I'm not getting to the point here, am I? Sometimes I want to throw this gadget away.

But I can't. Our story was never properly told. Not as far as I'm concerned.

All right. First things first. The entire summer of 1944—from D-Day on June 6th at Normandy all the way through the end of August in liberated Paris—was one bold move and one damned obstacle after another. Nothing happened smoothly. All the plans were forever upended by the war's realities, the unpredictable weather, the feral resistance of the Germans, accidents galore, and a thousand other variables.

Good Lord. Did I just say "variables"? Listen to me. Still a schoolteacher's kid. But maybe that's the best way to try to get some of this across. What would ol' Mom do?

Well, these days ol' Mom would be smart enough to know that words alone won't do. Apologies to Tolstoy, Hemingway, and Jerry too, but ol' Mom wouldn't hesitate to crank up the audio-visual components and then use her words to talk it all out.

Which is impossible, of course. That's the thing. Anyone truly in the war found out through personal experience that talking about it went nowhere. We could *not* find the language. Civilians who said they wanted to hear about what it was *re*ally like "over there," well . . . we were on separate planets. And that's something else that got twisted around and misinterpreted and ended up used for others' agendas.

Our silences. Our remoteness. Contrary to the goddamn clichés that I heard for decades about my generation going off to fight "the good war" and then "putting it all behind us" (that's the expression that always infuriates me), the truth was that it was im*pos*sible to talk about it. Besides, no one wanted the truth. They wanted all sorts of patriotic romance and Hollywood endings. So, the men who actually went overseas said nothing whatsoever for most of their lives about all of that—not even to their wives or children—while the fortunate ones who were in uniform but never overseas (and millions of GIs were lucky enough to remain stateside) mostly joined the American Legion and became barstool generals. At least the men had that much.

But getting back to ol' Mom and how a teacher of her caliber would tackle this.

If you remember it was something like twenty years ago that once again, thanks to the movies and all, the Second World War was suddenly in fashion. That's the only way to put it. All of a sudden, it "trended" (as Beansy likes to say about whatever is popular or "hot" these days). And that film *Saving Private Ryan* had a lot to do with it.Right off the bat, the long opening scenes that used computers and every other gadget to re-create the D-Day landings at Omaha Beach . . . the public ate it all up. I read in ten magazines and heard on all the TV shows that "*this* was the way it was." And that the agony and mayhem and suffering in the war were being truly shown.

Maybe so, up to a point. *Saving Private Ryan* was certainly an improvement on the old-time, gung-ho bloodless movies about the war that came out back in the day. Up to a *point*. But then it just went off the rails and became another Spielberg sudser. And don't get me started on what noble goals he achieved with *Schindler's List*, because to me that was just a way to finally atone for the vulgarity of using Nazi characters for laughs in those Indiana Jones films, which in my less than humble opinion was as unfunny as playing the whole war for laughs in that stupid so-called comedy of his called *1941* (which apparently hardly anyone recalls, thank God).

But around the same time back in the late 1990s, there was another film about the war, and Spielberg had a producer's hand in it and it played on cable, where he probably had it tucked away to minimize competition at theaters with *Saving Private Ryan*. Not that competition would have ensued. This other film was too much of the real deal.

And I can imagine what ol' Mom would do in our time. These days, she'd get a hold of the DVD of that other film (if I'm not mistaken, it's called *When Trumpets Fade*, and with a title like that you know you're not lined up for any happy endings). And then she'd use the magic of the Pause button on the remote to get some of the truth across. Sort of like what she did with slide projectors and filmstrips way back when.

How so? All you have to do is start with the opening credits. You see, it's one of the films where the newsreel footage of the American soldiers marching in Paris at the end of August 1944 really gets shown in *all* of its glory. Most of the time, in documentaries or in still-life photos in textbooks, all you see is a massive bunch of GIs marching with the Arc de Triomphe looking splendid in the background. There is never any context. It all looks so easy. You'd think every soldier had a fine day.

But it's different during the opening three minutes or so of that little film *When Trumpets Fade*. Even though there are other distractions, the truth seeps out a bit.

The other distractions are inevitable. A narrator speaks quickly as the credits begin, while the newsreel footage shows the Parisians going absolutely wild with glee, and gratitude and celebration as the GIs join in on one of the Liberation Week parades. I remember nearly falling off my chair when the film was first broadcast, because for once that legendary newsreel footage was allowed to go on and on. No quick cutaways.

But as the narrator speaks quickly and sums up the rapid progress made by the Allies in France during the summer of '44, there's also the soundtrack music. Which is crucial, of course. But that also knocked me for a loop when first I saw all this. It's a recording of "Over There," which is still a song that belongs to the First World War, but it's a recording made during the Second World War by Glenn Miller's Army Air Force Band. The same band I saw that night when I met Jerry. And it was made new and spiffed up and speeded up and once again it was *right on time*. No matter how corny the lyric might sound, that song had a magical effect on people in those days.

But here's the truth. You hold your remote in hand as you watch the opening credits of *When Trumpets Fade* and refuse to let yourself get too distracted by the spirited music or the narrator's summation . . . and wait for those brief seconds when the newsreel cameras zoomed in for close-ups on the faces of the American soldiers in the parade that one day in Paris. Then: Use your Pause button. The truth emerges.

Faster than you think. That's how quickly the truth can emerge. Faster than I ever thought possible. Especially thanks to Lorena (my Rena, the one and only Beansy), who was in top form very first thing this morning.

Her energy level was A-OK right off the bat, even though today is Saturday. That means she didn't stay out late drinking too much with her friends last night. We've talked about her dialing down on all that.

This morning, she deftly whipped through the usual business with my meds and my food and then what she calls my Lady Bits Care. The worst thing about this goddam illness is the dreadful paralysis from top to bottom; but I'm one of the luckier ones, because my hands (though weak) and voice and eyes are still in the game. I could tell Beansy was pondering. We'd been listening to yesterday's tape.

"Let me look for something," she said. Then she got *that* look on her face. Once she hauls her iPhone out of her pocket and begins the thumb-happy boogie-woogie they all perform on their phones these days, I knew she was on the case. A bomb could explode across the street and she'd not look up. Her techno-focus is a marvel, even though it's kind of scary. I mean, in front of any screen she's in another world.

"I think I've got it," she happily announced. Then she came around to the other side of my bed, where it's easier for me to turn my head, and sure enough she had it. All the way. In spades. Thanks to YouTube, of course, which never ceases to amaze me.

"Out there in the wider world," she said to me, "somebody somewhere uploaded it. No surprise. Everything you can imagine—or remember—is probably on YouTube."

She's so savvy with this brave new world and the only thing that fazes her is that I'm still surprised. It's not like *any*one's life flashing before your eyes—in addition to your own—but it's more like *every*one's life flashing before your eyes on YouTube.

To think that such a free and wide-open wonder is there for *all* the world to see.

"*That's* the one!" I exclaimed. Beansy had turned up the volume after adjusting my glasses and within seconds I heard it all as we watched the clip together. The music was instantly identifiable: the special swinging arrangement I knew of "Over There" that was recorded back then by Glenn Miller's Army Air Force Band (I wonder if the muted trumpet solo during the intro, right before a crackling drum solo and then the band jumping into the melody—I wonder if that kid trumpet player was at it a*gain*).

And the narrator's little speech over the opening credits . . . explaining this and that about the wildfire progress made by the Allies toward the end of the summer of '44, and how expectations were higher and higher that the war would end by Christmas. Indeed, that's what we were led to believe. "Home Alive in '45" was our slogan. It was all right there on YouTube, just as I remembered from seeing *When Trumpets Fade* on HBO eons ago, and just as I recall from when I'd check out the library's DVD years ago (when I was still out in the world on my own). The whole damn movie is available on YouTube in ten-minute chunks, thanks to some kind soul uploading the whole kit and caboodle. I forced my mind to focus and tested Beansy on my theory.

"Can you make it pause, like on a remote?" I asked her.
She nodded.
"Pause!" I said.

Her timing was impeccable. She had hit it *just* in time. And there, frozen in time, was one of the GIs in the 28th Infantry Division marching down the Champs-Élysées back on August 29th, 1944. I'll never forget the date. Or the division. But most of all I'll never forget seeing it happen. Because I was there. In person. On that day. But I kept that to myself until just now—it's on the record, now, on this tape. But I didn't even tell Beansy this morning. There was something else I wanted her to focus on.

"What do you notice?" I said. For a moment she stared at the black and white film.
"Well," she said, "it's grainy. Kind of fuzzy. But you can tell it's a parade. And all those guys are marching past that famous landmark—the Arch of Triumph, right?"

"Right," I said. "The Arc de Triomphe. An Army photo of this moment ended up on a Victory Stamp in 1945. But, look *closer*." She held the screen up to our bulging eyes.

"I'm going to poke this to look again," she said. And before I could even ask her how it was possible to do so much on a gadget as small as a paperback book, she again had the first few minutes of *When Trumpets Fade* playing away on her trusty iPhone, and together we watched the newsreel footage that plays on and on as the opening credits appear and disappear while the narrator explains X, Y and Z . . .

"Pause!" we bellowed together. That's another thing about Beansy. Her memory is like Velcro. Everything sticks. She'd remembered precisely where we'd paused on the first go-round. This time, she *really* nailed it. You see, it was that magic moment right after the Army Signal Corps guys filming the march during Liberation Week in Paris at the end of August 1944 went from a wide-angle view—where all the guys look like one identical mass of marching humanity; a regimented congregation of GIs looking sharp and moving like some gargantuan unified living-breathing force—to the first of the close-ups. And I mean ex*treme* close-ups. "Look at that!" I said.

"Do you mean the guy with the flower in his lapel?" Beansy asked. She saw it, too.

"Bingo!" I said. "That's what I'm talking about. I think it might be just a daisy, for goodness sake. But he turned it into a *boutonniere*. Chances are, one of those lovely, cheering, grateful, hollering *Mademoiselles* handed him that single little flower, and he stuck it in his buttonhole there. Look! And go forward just a few seconds."

She pressed whatever and the clip continued. Just two or three seconds later I said: "Pause!" And once again, she caught the moment. Back when my dexterity was aces high, I used to sit with my remote and work it like that with the DVD.

You could see that the GI marching right next to the soldier who'd placed that tiny flower into the buttonhole on his left lapel was being looked at askance by the soldier marching right beside him, whose expression seemed to say: "Uh, buddy. You know that's against regulations, right?"

And it *was* against regulations.

"But that was his way of rebelling just a little," I explained to Beansy. "That was his way of retaining some of his individuality. It mattered to him."

Truly.

11

Individuality? That's a big one. More important than I'll ever have the time to say. Retaining just a bit—even a speck—of one's individuality in the midst of a massive organization. Any organization that's huge. Whether it's a corporation or the Army.

Or even a smaller organization. Like a sports team. That's all I'm hearing about today. Everyone here is in the doldrums. Last night, the local team blew it at the NCAA championship game down in Indianapolis. Even I stayed up much later than usual, because the game didn't begin until eight-thirty last night. But our guys lost and today this place ought to change its name from Village Oaks to Fallen Oaks.

You can feel that everyone's down about the big game being a bust. Even Beansy.

She just went off on her next mission and I won't see her until this afternoon. But I'm glad it was her on duty today. Sometimes they shuffle their schedules here. It was not, however, Beansy at her usual vibrant best. She had "serious blues" (those are her words for whenever she's way down). I tried to share an insight with her.

"Sure, I'm sort of disappointed," I admitted to her. "This whole place has felt different ever since they stormed out of the Elite Eight and then managed to win that Final Four game big-time last weekend."

"That's what I can't believe," she said. "Three days ago, they're on top and we're all feeling like the world's been conquered. Then: last night they lose and it all fizzles."

I asked her to stop for a minute. Not stop talking. But to stop *all* activity. A pause. "Hold on, sweetie. For one minute just skip the duties and answer me this: What has fizzled? Think about it. I mean, what's really changed or been lost?" I waited.

"Okay, I know what you mean. It's only *a game* and all. But still. Out there all over town, in recent weeks, it's like their March Madness victories changed everything."

"How so?"

"People were talking to each other more. Strangers and all. It felt like an early spring. Even when the weather got cold again. Even after it snowed again. Nobody seemed to be all that bugged. I don't know—it was just *dif*ferent. We felt better."

I mimicked an old line from the Westerns that we saw when I was a kid: "What do you mean '*we*,' white man?" Beansy was flummoxed by my ancient one-liner.

And since she's been elsewhere, I've had time to think about the one aspect of last night's game that got to me. It was mentioned on the radio and, of course, on TV, but I don't think others were hit by it the way I was. They're simply not old enough.

For me, though, this was the killer-diller about last night's NCAA showdown between Duke and the Badgers—it was the very first time since 1941 that the Wisconsin team made it to the final. First time since 1941. No kidding.

And I may very well be one of the only codgers here—even in this museum of human remains—who clearly recalls and vividly remembers the 1941 games.

Yesterday, when spirits were high (as Beansy said: "The vibe is electric all over the city, even here!") and the radio loudmouth once again mentioned the UW team had not been this far along since 1941, I watched as Beansy did a double-take and said: "Jesus, that's seventy-four years ago. That's like, three quarters of a century!"

"Welcome to my world," I kidded her. "Seems like only yesterday!"

But it doesn't.

It seems like what it is: Three quarters of a century, indeed. And yet, at the same time, to me, it's like any other memory. It seems like it just happened. Surreal. That's the way memories of everything affect me. I'm not out of my head. The calendar on my wall is clear to me and easy to read. I know it's April 7, 2015. And I'm fully aware that it's a Tuesday. And now that last night's game is over and done with, I can feel the letdown and the disappointment others are speaking about. But the damnedest thing is, well, just take the big game last night. Okay? It's not yet even twenty-four hours in the past, but, in my memory, it occupies the same space that the 1941 game occupies. Isn't that crazy? But I'm not. At all. It's just that in the privacy of my mind, the game that ended badly for us last night is just somehow out of time now—and simply in the past, generally speaking—and, as such, it's really not all that different from the win our team enjoyed when they *did* win the big game back in 1941. Both games concluded. Differently. But they're equally in the past.

The thing that stood out for me, though, as I watched last night's game, is that I noticed how in one way the guys on both teams were doing the same thing as the beautiful soldier in the old newsreel of the American march through Paris back in 1944. That GI who put a flower in the buttonhole of his uniform and by doing so created his own *boutonniere* (and also broke a regulation about properly wearing the uniform *sans* any *accoutrements*—*oh la la,* I'm using my French again), well, he was making a little statement there. He was *still* an individual. And something as small and seemingly irrelevant as all that meant the world to him, at that time. It was kind of like the kids in last night's game, who had their identical uniforms and their identical colors (just as the GIs had identical everything—almost—as you can see from studying any newsreel film), but then again one of them wore his hair in a style so wacky that his individuality stood out. Others found other ways to retain a dose of their individual selves, even as they blended in with the team. I liked that.

And I like how watching last night's big game conjured up memories of seeing Pop and ol' Mom sitting in their big chairs back in 1941, leaning in closely to listen to the radio as the Badgers of Wisconsin played like the blazes and won that year's NCAA tournament. "That was only the third year of the tournament," I explained to Rena. *Ha!* I hardly ever think of her as "Rena" anymore. She's my beloved Beansy. Maybe I'm still a seventh-grader at heart. Nicknames give me such a kick. They always did.

All that probably started around the big radio in our living room when I was a kid.

Pop really loved sports and his enthusiasm was contagious, so ol' Mom would get fired up too (about Notre Dame football games, in particular, which to Pop were like some sacramental ritual; he'd place his ear so close to the radio that ol' Mom would joke about him breaking his own neck; but it pleased her to see him so engaged). By the time I was in high school, I'd learned to love all the nicknames that went along with the great sports figures of that time. I thought "the Fighting Irish" sounded terrific and calling Joe Louis "the Brown Bomber" was perfect, just as calling Joe Di Maggio "the Yankee Clipper" made total sense. And you don't hear enough about her anymore, but there was a remarkable woman back then nicknamed "Babe" and it's a real shame that these days Babe Didrickson Zaharias isn't still a famous name.

She sure was then. A household name. Everyone knew about her. Not just for her record-breaking wins at golf and all, but for other sports achievements too. "Babe."

I loved her nickname as much as I loved seeing her in the newsreels: Not just tall, but unusually tall. Statuesque. Like some of those human sequoias in last night's game. And she was graceful and confident and moved with real purpose. "Babe."

My first thought back in 1944, after our mail call included a copy of a recent issue of *The Saturday Evening Post* (sent loyally to me by ol' Mom, of course) was that Jerry named one of his characters "Babe" Gladwaller as a tribute to Babe Didrickson Zaharias. My second thought was: "Holy Moses! Jerry's story is in the *Post!*"

What hit me right between the eyes—even now, in my mind's eye, I can see it all on the Contents page—was how Jerry's name and the title of his story were *right there* in *The Saturday Evening Post*. It took a moment for me to recall his remark from our dialogue that night when so much happened so fast (hearing Glenn Miller's band at Radio City, meeting on the way out, talking at the Stork Club, of all places). And though it seemed to be a quip at the time (that remark about being "annoyed" by the editors at Collier's) I did learn that he was writing and publishing.

Of course he told me that much. Actually, when I pressed him to tell me about the new Counter Intelligence Corps training that he was to be immersed in, he tossed off my questions with a couple of witty replies ("I'll be a spy for Uncle Sam, spying on my cousins" he joked; and then he added "I requested special training as The Invisible Man, but H. G. Wells sold the secret potions to Claude Rains," and that gave me the biggest kick because Pop and ol' Mom and I were all big fans of the actor Claude Rains, and the way he played the lead in *The Invisible Man*). So after he told me not to be fooled by his being in uniform and that he was—"the war be damned, which it ought be anyhow, even though now we have no choice but to win it"—he then bounced off my question about what he did, or had done, or wanted to do after the war, and his adamant words were: "I *am* a professional short story writer."

That really caught my attention. Unlike most young fellas and just about all the young ladies I knew in the first years after I graduated high school in 1939, he had not hemmed and hawed and said "Maybe I'll do" this or that; nor had he floated any dubious notions or get rich quick schemes, so there was none of that "If I could just figure out how to" get here or there. No. His ironclad statement was intact. "I *am* a professional short story writer," he said that night. And yet, when I asked him to name any stories that he'd published, he demurred. "Trifles," he said. "Done with."

I was no dummy. I sensed that he didn't want to be peppered with questions about any of that. And thanks to growing up in a house full of modern magazines and also to finally being able to talk more and more with Pop and ol' Mom about books and who their favorite authors were. Until I enlisted in 1943, my life after high school was evenly split between working as both a switchboard operator and postal wizard for Illinois Bell, and later enrolling in some night courses at DePaul University.

I learned from them that in press releases or in brief autobiographical blurbs for their books, writers from John Dos Passos to Hemingway kept quiet about their writing. Most of the time, anyhow.

So I wasn't too surprised by the "end of discussion" hints I picked up from Jerry.

But believe you me, when our latest mail call came through at the end of August in 1944 and I saw that ol' Mom had sent me the *Post* from earlier in July of '44, well, the first thing that occurred to me was that ol' Mom must've just packed it off right away, without even reading it. I mean, there we were, newly reassigned to Paris just days after its liberation at the end of August in 1944, and suddenly I'm turning the pages of a July issue of the *Post* thanks to ol' Mom's generosity and swift footwork.

Nothing, however, startled me more than seeing Jerry's name listed after a short story title that was, to me, *right* on time: "Last Day of the Last Furlough." One hell of a title, I'd say.

And it was one hell of a story, believe you me. I used a bathroom break as an excuse to go sit in private and look at that story. I wasn't able to take all the time I needed to read it slowly, word for word (that would happen later), but I was able to sit for as long as it took to give it a solid once-over. And getting the gist of it was enough.

Like I said, one of the main characters was named "Babe" and that zinged me. The kicker was that in "Last Day of the Last Furlough," it's John "Babe" Gladwaller in the red-hot center. I thought it was clever for Jerry to use the same nickname the most famous female athlete of our generation had; a nickname shared with Babe Ruth.

But for me the killer issue in the story was the way it broke down into five distinct sections; it was *really* clear and easy to see on the pages of the *Post*—I mean, they used the formatting and all to make the five sections easy on the eyes. And right off the bat, as usual, my eyes were drawn to dialogue sections. That's when I teared up.

In the first of the dialogues that I read quickly as I sat in the stall, pretending to be indisposed, I caught the essence of a family scene where on the final day of the furlough for this John "Babe" Gladwaller character, a conversation at home is the main event. A talk with his folks at the dinner table. It was like being home again.

Except in my case, unlike what goes on in the story between "Babe" and his father, I had no conflict with Pop. In Jerry's story, he's got "Babe" sitting there getting more and more steamed up because his father is waxing sentimental about his time in the Army in the First World War, and the father's tone of wistful "I remember when" goopy talk really does not appeal to "Babe." All of a sudden, in the story, "Babe" launches into a dinner-table speech, going on and on about how the ultimate duty of any soldier who survives the new war is to never-ever talk about it. To *any*one. The line that shocked me is when "Babe" insists that it's more honorable to ignore the dead. And he goes on about how repulsed he is by phony "Lest We Forget" rhetoric.

Well, the last day of *my* last furlough (after concluding our basic training at Fort Des Moines in Iowa), it was just the opposite. As usual, although I asked some questions, and even ol' Mom chimed in, I really could not get Pop to talk about his time in the Great War. We still used that expression. Lots of folks held on to that expression. But except for sharing with me the specific names of places (Chateau-Thierry and Meuse-Argonne) where his Division had fought (and Pop didn't have to remind me of his favorite passage from *A Farewell to Arms*, the one about how the names of places were all that had any dignity; I'd memorized that one), he stayed silent. "Do your duty, but don't volunteer for anything," he instructed. The other dialogue in "Last Day of the Last Furlough" that caught my eye was toward the end, when a lot of conversation goes on between "Babe" Gladwaller and his kid sister. I still recall her name in that story: "Mattie." She really gave me a kick.

But nothing gave me a bigger kick than knowing that I knew the writer. Not that I *knew* him well or anything. And I certainly hadn't "known him" in the Biblical way. Believe it or not, my bunkmates actually asked me about that later in the evening, when I sounded off about knowing the author of this newly published story in the *Post*. "Well, didn't you go from the Stork Club to . . . *you know!*" they all giggled.

But I tried never to lie and I disliked tall tales. That was that. "No!" I insisted. "We were supposed to meet the next day for a matinee, but he never turned up. At *all.*"

That's all the more reason that I nearly fainted when I saw him again in Paris.

12

Today is Saturday. That changes everything around here. Well, not *everything*—but lots of things. You can tell it's a Saturday by the total absence of familiar faces. Almost all the aides who zip in and out of my room here—what they grandly call a Hospice Suite—throughout the week, well, they have their weekends off. But it's been almost two months since I arrived here, and I pretty much know all part-time weekend staffers too. Still, it's different. There's less activity in the hall outside my room. My suite, I mean. And because the weekend staff is so skeletal, it takes a lot longer for anyone to respond to my requests. But I still get the help I need. *Amen.*

I confess: What I really want someone to do today is *not* going to happen. It'd be too weird to ask, and I don't have the energy to explain. But I wish that oversized 2015 calendar on the wall right there was not reminding me that today is April 11th. Not that there's anywhere else to hang the calendar in a sensible way. It's tight in here. Usually I pay more attention to the gorgeous photos on the calendar: birds, trees, and flowers galore, of course, thanks to the Madison Audubon Society and their free calendars for those who donate. Good Lord, I miss those field trips and excursions to the Arboretum and most of all beautiful Olbrich Gardens. Even in a wheelchair or back in my scooter days, those magical places worked wonders for my soul. Before the past year's disintegration, I'd probably have been able to find someone to agree to help me get back onto one of those paths. It's the main reason I migrated to Madison years ago. Three lakes and many beautiful sites abound here.

But now it's quite different. Field trips are off my agenda. Right now I'd settle for having that calendar removed. There's a gorgeous photo of a finch up above the April page, but it's still impossible not to see the numbers and April 11th always made me sad. I'll bet on CNN today or in the newspapers (the few that are left) or whatever it is people are paying attention to, I'll bet that there's some of the 70th anniversary attention that's been going on periodically in the last year. Actually, this past year or two has been a dizzying series of overlapping anniversaries. It's enough to make Beloved Beansy crazy: "If it's not the 50th anniversary of *some*thing from the 1960s," she huffed one day, "then it's nothing but news and flashbacks and blah-blah-blah about the 70th anniversary of what-*ever* from World War Two. No offense! But, it's kind of wack, the way everyone is always looking backwards."

Maybe she's right. Maybe it is a bit crazy, with the Boomers recounting and recapitulating each successive year of the Sixties. Even I was annoyed by the wall-to-wall saturation coverage of the 50th anniversary of JFK's murder back in 1963, and I'm one of those sleuths who never stopped trying to figure out what *re*ally happened in Dallas. Of course all that anniversary coverage ignored the grim questions and never dared to question the innumerable holes in the official story.

And then, the obsessive Boomer focus in the following year about how the Beatles shook things up in 1964—I mean, the media overkill was embarrassing.

But it's been a thing—how do you like that? I'm using Lorena-Rena-Beansy's pet expression: "It's a thing!" She'll be so proud of me. I wish she were here today. Anyway, like I was saying, it's a thing that's been constant ever since Reagan's big speech at Normandy back in 1984, when that 40th anniversary of D-Day suddenly caught on with John Q. Public and lo and behold a trend was born. Before that, I can't for the life of me recall this thing that now goes on and on. Like perennials. That's what it reminds me of. I swear to God. Just like perennials in my garden.

For the past three decades: First there was all that 40th anniversary hoopla in 1984 and 1985 about the D-Day landings at Normandy, and then the Battle of the Bulge, and finally the end-of-the-war anniversaries. Okay. In a funny way, I was grateful. Because there had not been *one* iota of such attention back in the mid-1970s, when so many of us who had lived and served and survived the war woke up to realize that somehow 30 years had flown by since the whole damn thing concluded. God, *that*

awful year. Don't get me started on what a pot of shit 1975 was. Our
exodus from Vietnam and those humiliating images all over the news as
we abandoned our embassy in South Vietnam and equally abandoned
the vast majority of those South Vietnamese who were left behind to
be abused, tortured, starved, "re-educated" (and that belongs in larger-
than-life quotation marks) and oftentimes killed in a hurry by the sons
of bitches who marauded through that country knowing full well that
Uncle Sam wouldn't be back; not after we fucked up every aspect of that
war between the early days and the so-called "peace with honor" that
Nixon talked about when the end was supposedly negotiated in 1973;
which I can't forget because right at that time my son was staring down
the road at his eighteenth birthday and I was so incredibly relieved that
his birthday fell later that year and he didn't have to be registering, once
Nixon shut that damn thing down and ended the draft.

But, I digress. And the noon hour is almost over and the aide who
helped set me up will soon be back to help me with . . . never mind *that*.
What I *really* need to say is that T.S. Eliot spoke volumes with one line in
"The Waste Land," about April being the cruelest month.

That's what it felt like in April 1975, when every dream we ever had
the audacity to dream thirty years earlier was tipped overboard with the
helicopters dumped off of those American aircraft carriers. And that's
what it felt like in April 1968, when the murder of Martin obliterated
not just his dream, but also destroyed our hopes. No wonder there was
such adoration for Reagan's simpleminded speeches and all of the D-Day
40th anniversary business in 1984. The younger folks devoured such rich
quantities of Hollywood scripting. I was still teaching my adjunct classes
at Ignatius College down in Chicago, and even now, three decades later,
I can recall with almost frightening detail the sheer childishness of the
new students in the 1980s and how they genuflected with gratitude over
Reagan's paternal, comforting fantasies.

I'm sounding like a crank. Don't get me wrong. I was as grateful as any
other member of my so-called "Greatest Generation" (a term that royally
infuriates me, I'd like to say) that those 40th anniversary respects were
paid. But, it all soured in April of 1985 when Reagan stumbled into his
Bitburg snafu and because he was such a dunce who depended wholly on

his handlers, he actually ended up visiting and then standing in a posture of memorial honor at that German cemetery loaded with the remains of Waffen SS officers. Even now, that's enough to make me sick. It just *is.*

Ten years later, of course, the media's binge over the 50th anniversary of the end of World War Two was nothing but big business. A marketing fiesta. The ultimate capitalist bonanza. And all that "Greatest Generation" hokum spelled fat profits.

What killed me about that razzmatazz was that it was mostly savvy Boomers with MBAs who figured out that there were zillions of dollars to be made by indulging in latter-day hero worship for my generation, which was derided, patronized, and more or less dumped on for so long by the movers and shakers in Boomer culture.

How crazy *is* this? I cannot remember what was on the news two weeks ago or what I saw on a magazine cover last month. But the calendar near to me is a reminder, moment by moment, that today is April 11th. And that distresses me. Even now.

I've decided not to tune in to CNN or Sky News or anything else, because I'm sure that today's 70th anniversary stories are about what the American soldiers saw at Buchenwald when it was liberated by our guys, seventy years ago today. I'll bet that all of the networks make sure to broadcast not just the ghastly films that the Signal Corps was ordered to make (Eisenhower was criticized for being ghoulish, but good ol' Ike ordered that everything be filmed for posterity; he was old enough to recall that most of the atrocity stories of Pop's war—the First World War—ended up being disbelieved, thanks to denial and the lack of incontrovertible evidence), but also the famous radio broadcast made by Edward R. Murrow. He was there with the GIs at Buchenwald, and what he reported about what they saw . . . unspeakable.

And that's when our hearts broke, if you really want to know how it was. Despite dancing in the streets, the waving flags, the worldwide celebrations and every other image you might have about the winning of the war back in 1945, ours were young hearts sobbing.

Our hearts broke in April and May of 1945, when the concentration camps were liberated and the photos, the films, and the eyewitness accounts made a mockery of the bliss we allowed to consume us in liberated Paris, less than one year earlier.

13

The women of Paris hurried to have the liberating troops hold their babies. They hurried toward the jeeps, half-tracks, and any other vehicles that'd paused. They bustled onto the boulevards of Paris. They stood on tiptoes and then with complete confidence and total trust, raised high the little ones—toddlers, mostly, but also some babies—and the soldiers reacted with glee, joy, and beatific smiles. I saw that. I saw it all with my own eyes. And I saw it again in my dreams this morning.

It doesn't take a psychologist to analyze this. The act itself: Mothers of little ones suddenly waving, cramming onto crowded avenues, holding their little ones aloft for strangers to embrace. To hold dear for a second. To love on a higher level. But they knew it was safe. There were no strangers that day in liberated Paris. The women who joyfully asked the Allied soldiers rolling through the city to take a moment and behold (literally) their little ones, to cradle their babies in newfound freedom, they trusted those guys. The guys were an angelic presence, with grit, heart, and Lucky Strikes, plus their expressions of wonder, awe, and absolute exhaustion. I'm grateful beyond words for my dreams this morning. Such reminders are just like prayers.

That's another thing—here I go again—that never-*ever* got across. Not in any way that *I* thought was true. And I looked everywhere—for years; even decades—after I returned from the war and paid close attention to the books and the magazines, the television shows and the movies, too, of course, as trite as they could be. Usually.

But I'm not kidding at all. I don't think that it ever really got across how impossibly spiritual we all felt about peak moments like what happened in Paris late in August of 1944. There was too much else going on. And whatever they always selected in order to show what the war was "really like" (I wish I had a buck for each time that cliché was coughed up in an ad campaign or a documentary) missed the essence of what I know to be true: There *was* a sacramental element. I saw it. And felt it. In the middle of wartime degradation, liberated Paris was sublime.

I know, I know. I'm all hung up on certain specific days. Selected hours. Mere minutes of unconditional, ecstatic human communion. I know, I know, *I know.*

And I should know. Because even as we stood there (a handful of us were always ordered in right behind the troops who were soon setting up temporary command and control HQs, and we who were communications specialists had front-row seats to astounding episodes of overnight transitions from the Nazi occupation to all the baffling new days of liberation), even as we witnessed quick, fleeting, evanescent, and ineffably beautiful moments of being (merci beaucoup, Virginia Woolf), even as the seconds of boundless transcendence gave way to minutes of stupefaction and then hours of hazy anxiety (liberated wine cellars and fear about catastrophic food shortages make for a dicey combo), it was clear that all hell was breaking loose.

That's all the more reason to treasure this morning's dream images. Because the women of Paris really did scurry onto the Boulevard Saint-Germain and of course the Champs-Élysées and other extraordinary avenues we'd read about in books, and they truly did cry out and wail with wet, shameless tears while making clear what they really wanted: And what they wanted was for the GIs and the Free French soldiers, allied with us, to offer the benediction of embracing their little ones. Such blessings from the liberators superseded priestly rites that day.

Yet you didn't have to look too far to know—or to see—that plenty of trouble was in the mix. Here's something else that never got across. Plenty of gunfire was still exploding, day in and day out, that week. Believe you me. That last week of August 1944 has been mighty whitewashed in some ways. Not that there was anything like Warsaw or any other awful destruction going on. But that's just it. Thanks to a big book that became a bigger movie that was hugely popular in 1966 (I can remember that because I asked myself if taking my eleven-year-old son to see it was

A-OK), the whole wide world got the idea from *Is Paris Burning?* that it was like a cakewalk.

But even though that German general really did surrender the city and not set off all the explosives and bombs and mines and whatnot that Hitler ordered him to use (of course Adolf's mandate was to destroy everything with a scorched-earth retreat), it wasn't at all like a peaceful segue from occupation to liberation. Snipers who were die-hard loyalists to Hitler and cadres of SS who refused to follow orders ran amok throughout that whole week. I mean, even as de Gaulle led the grand march down the Champs-Élysées, which was the liberation parade for the ages, just a few days before the 28th Division of the American Army had its day in the sun on the same boulevard, there were chronic outbursts of sniper fire and civilians were killed and injured and maimed; now and again, thousands hunkered down for cover, hundreds were killed and hundreds more wounded, and no matter what de Gaulle stood right out there, as tall as Lincoln and just as majestic. I still can't get over how de Gaulle refused to duck and run. He stood right out there! He was resplendent.

And what I really couldn't get over—no kidding, I wondered if someone spiked the coffee I'd had that morning; or if something crazy was in the bottle of wine I'd sipped from—it was impossible not to be handed a bottle to chug from that day—what I absolutely couldn't believe was that despite this kooky hat he was wearing, I recognized Jerry as he stood there speaking with a number of smiling Parisians.

It wasn't just his height that made him easy to see. Although that helped. A man who is more than six feet tall has advantages in many ways. But it was more than his height. And it was even more than the snazzy hat that was perched on his head. Talk about non-regulation! It wasn't exactly a pork-pie hat like Lester Young made famous, but it was the same sort of jazzman's headgear. It looked terrific on him.

Most of all, it looked contrarian. I mean, he was in uniform. No mistaking that. His 4th Infantry Division insignia was there for all the world to see. I knew what that meant. Those of us in Communications just naturally tracked the progress of the Army divisions that'd landed at Normandy back on June 6th. And in the privacy of my mind, it took all of two seconds to register that the 4th ID patch on Jerry signified that he'd somehow survived everything between the Utah Beach landings and the ghastly fighting in the hedgerows and the bloodbath at Saint-Lo, and more.

Which is all the more reason it not only startled me, but, downright pierced me to see him standing there in the midst of a pleasant conversation with his new friends in the City of Light.

14

Paris. *My* Paris.

I made the mistake on several occasions of trying to share all this in conversation. It never worked. Listeners assumed that I was out of my mind. It all sounded too surreal. How could it not? It *was* surreal. And that day surreal was the coin of the realm. The norm. But of course *none* of it was normal. Not a bit.

Once, when I tried to tell my story to a fellow who was about my age (just a few years older, actually), he more or less accused me of "talking through the wine" and you can safely assume that I swiftly off-loaded that knucklehead. It was for the best. By that time I was well into my fifties, and except for the oddly wonderful interlude with Sheridan O'Neill, later, when I was sixty, I'd written off men for the duration.

Anyway, the plain truth is that for the rest of my life—and believe you me, it has been a long, long time—all I needed as a yardstick by which to measure anything wonderful or potentially wonderful was one single word: "Paris." It's my code word.

Which is a crazy way to live, needless to say. But ever since that day when the stars lined up and I felt "transparent to transcendence" (thank you, Joe Campbell), my one surefire way to settle down and not get too carried away was to whisper: "Paris."

That's all. Just the word itself. It signified to me that no matter how excited I might be getting about something or someone, it'd be a mistake to try to force anything.

Because nothing for me in Paris on August 28, 1944, was arranged, scheduled, choreographed, scripted, planned, outlined or legislated. It all just happened. Nothing was officially "on the agenda." And, moment by moment, bliss was mine.

Meeting Jerry again in the vicinity of the Eiffel Tower was not nearly as impossible as it sounds. Untold numbers of soldiers and sailors crossed paths and overlapped and met again in those years. Coincidences were so common, hardly anyone noticed. I do recall a second or two of disbelief on my part. But then life took over in a hurry.

Before I even had a chance to tell him that I thought his snazzy-jazzy hat was quite right for the occasion (the atmosphere in Paris was more than festive; more than celebratory; it was like Mardi Gras and New Year's Eve and one thousand weddings and a million new births all at once, with such overflowing goodwill and generosity of spirit that even the *gendarmes* were embraced left and right, and Parisians were never noted for their love of the police), I was startled by his change of appearance.

He was slim when first we met in New York, but now he was rail-thin. Back in Manhattan, he'd been clean-shaven and Brylcreemed so well that his hair was slicked back like a matinee idol. Now I could see the remnant of a regulation moustache he'd recently shaved. And his eyes had changed. He had seen things. Darkness. I knew without asking that he'd already escaped death a dozen times.

When he saw me, during a lull in his obviously friendly conversation with some French civilians (for a moment I remembered fondly how much he enjoyed it when I explained to him at the Stork Club that all of my high school classes in French and then my night school studies in French and German had given me an edge when I enlisted in the WAC; his own ability to speak German and French was what made him a natural for the Counter Intelligence Corps, and they were happy to have him), he blinked fast a few times and grinned as he nodded, asking me a quick question.

"I'm so sorry, " I had to say. "But I can hardly hear you. W*hat* was that?"

He asked again. "Did you sit through Judy's movie that day?" In fact, I had. Why not? Seeing *Presenting Lily Mars* was a great way to pass the time. And I'd happily discovered that not only was Tommy Dorsey's band in the picture, but that Bob Crosby's band was also prominently featured. I almost blurted out that I'd not only seen the movie on that day he stood me up, but that I fell in love with Van Heflin, too. Van was Judy's co-star in *Presenting Lily Mars*. He was my new crush.

But I said nothing of the sort. The change in Jerry's voice startled me. It was even more pronounced than the way his eyes had changed. Something was missing. I'd thought about him, now and then, during the nine or ten months that'd zoomed by between the night we met and the hectic, ever-changing, manic following months. And the echoes in my mind conjured his spirited, exuberant speaking.

Now it was all changed. He spoke with more than a softer tone. It was distant. Even though he was standing right there, I felt as if he were somehow far and away. But at the same time, it was clear that he was happy to see me again.

Women can always tell about that. And what gave it away that day in Paris was the effortless way that Jerry casually ended his dialogue with the French civilians, which seemed to be as comfortable a conclusion for them as it was for him. Embraces all around. Hearty handshakes all around (for the life of me I never understood how the French got their reputation for being aloof or cold or haughty; they're natural-born handshake artists and even if you mangle their language, a good-faith show of interest in just a few words—a few expressions—makes them smile).

Boundless and heartfelt gratitude, as well. You could feel their respect for this French-speaking GI standing there so tall and lean in his quirky hat, and also so clearly identifiable as a soldier with the 4th Infantry Division. We heard explosions.

Of course we heard explosions. All day long. Throughout the heart of Paris. There was no doubt that the Germans had surrendered and all sorts of information was flying about regarding the formal surrendering of the city to the Allied military authorities, but that didn't prevent plenty of they-died-with-their-boots-on Kraut holdouts from setting off their charges and explosives, hitting back at the insurrection that'd begun days before the formal surrender, and hoping to knock off some Resistance zealots. The city was mined, booby-trapped, and far from calm.

Gunfire. Grenades. Snipers. It was all the weirdest mix of the Wild West and total confusion, buoyed by celebration and rivers of alcohol. That's one point that never ceases to cause me to shake my head. And not with mirth. More like shake my head in a lifelong state of disbelief. Or disorientation. With memories of inebriation. That day in Paris—and that whole month, from all that I heard—was fueled by the endless numbers of bottles that were emptied. And I mean untold numbers. The sheer variety of liquors and liqueurs, wines and cognacs, plus all the varied brands of whiskies and Scotches and every other drink that could blow out your eyeballs . . . I never thought Champagne could be so guzzled. Everyone was utterly soaked.

You didn't even have to look for it. What happened was that geysers of alcohol erupted from every hidden source, each subterranean wine cellar, the most cleverly hidden and well-stocked caches with innumerable bottles and bottles and bottles, fifths of Courvosier, quarts of Haig & Haig, and magnums of Champagne. Add to all that the wild-eyed generosity of the French as their gratitude and pent-up anger, pride, frustration, humiliation, suppressed urges and all-consuming energies were released at last . . . oh, good Lord, God only knows how many babies were hatched nine months later. It was a dizzying kaleidoscope of Eros and libido unleashed against the backdrop of a dream-like city miraculously intact, despite the four long years of Nazi occupation. There was plenty of damage, but Paris was quite intact.

Still, the explosions near the Eiffel Tower scared the daylights out of me. For a moment I half-expected to see the Tower come tumbling down. But it didn't. I'm sure that has something to do with how, no matter what, for the rest of my life, I have felt this deeply visceral and impossibly hopeful and poignant sense of life, whenever I've seen a good photo of the Tour Eiffel. It's far more than a structure. It's a beacon.

And when I say that we were in the vicinity of the Tour Eiffel, I don't mean looking at it from afar. I mean within one hundred yards. Which is merely the length of a football field and really nothing vis-a-vis the vast spaces surrounding the Tower. There were people absolutely everywhere all over the colossal Trocadero, that enormous and well-paved, vehicle-friendly area near the Tower. And I have to admit that I wasn't all that surprised to learn that Jerry had an Army jeep and it really was at his disposal due to his rank and his work with the Counter Intelligence Corps. But the day we met again wasn't about work. The war had briefly paused.

And leave it to Irwin Shaw, the amazing short story writer and once popular novelist (and I mean truly amazing: in all my college classes as a teacher later in the 1970s and eighties, two short stories of his never failed to resonate with the students, no matter how fashions or politics or society were being revolutionized; Irwin had really tapped into some universal themes and timeless patterns with the hurts and the slights of "The Girls in Their Summer Dresses" and the collapse of the male ego in "The Eighty-Yard Run"), well, leave it to Irwin Shaw to sum up in one sentence the essence of that final week of August 1944 in Paris: "That was the week the war should have ended," he wrote. Of course he was right. It was a dream come true.

And just as the wackiest, most implausible happenings in dreams unfold naturally, the next thing I heard was Jerry saying: "There's someone we should see. Hop in!"

If I had just hopped in, I'd've had broken glass spackling my butt. The seats of his requisitioned jeep were loaded with bottles. Gifts from passersby. That never even stopped for one minute, as we slowly maneuvered our way down the Champs-Élysées. Any Allied vehicle during those days became the repository of endless offerings. Not just bottles, but also flowers and fruits and hunks of cheese. The spirit of gratitude mingled with nothing less than the triumph of . . . what *was* it? Well, it was the triumph of everything we thought our uniforms represented.

One by one, I moved the nine bottles arrayed on the passenger seat of the jeep. Gingerly. With care. The labels alone were fit for museums. Calvados brandy. Chateau de Laubade Bas Armagnac. The only sensible thing to do was to place them on the floor of the jeep, and there was hardly room for my feet by the time we took off. Funny, too. All I could think about was Pop. For as long as it took to make our way all down the boulevard to the Place de la Concorde, where my assumption was that Jerry had been tipped off on where or when to catch a glimpse of General de Gaulle, I thought about Pop and missed him terribly. Even now I remember what made me think of him so fast, so suddenly. It wasn't that I was in France and long ago Pop had been there too. It was something far smaller.

The visible bubbles in one of the bottles that I'd moved. As I rearranged things, I gave a shake or two—inadvertently—to one of the bottles and just like when I was a child, I marveled at the sight of the visible bubbles floating within. And right away I could see it all again, the way it was back home in Chicago, when I was small and Pop would sit as close as possible to the big radio in the living room, his ear glued to the Zenith speaker atop the radio, behind its circular brass design and that funny-feeling wooly-type material that covered the speaker; and if it was a Saturday he'd have a tall glass of beer on a coaster there on the table, and always and forever I'd be mesmerized by the way that the bubbles swirled about and had their choreography after his beer was poured from a Pabst bottle into what he called "a frosty glass."

There were tall glasses just for beer that ol' Mom set sideways on the tiny freezer shelf in our icebox. And Pop never seemed to mind how often I said: "The bubbles! It looks like they're running. They move all over like they're running on the football field across the street." We'd attended many football games there at St. Rita's all-boys high school.

My reverie might have struck somebody else as rudeness. I really spaced off. But I don't think Jerry was miffed at all. He was too busy trying to avoid hitting *flaneurs* and myriad gift-bearing Parisians, who from each direction radiated joy. Except for the dreadful scene that caused him to slam the brakes, leap out, and start to holler.

15

One of the women was already shorn. Her stooped shoulders spoke volumes. Her humiliation was complete, as she stood in nothing but a wretched slip.

We'd heard about such scenes through the Army grapevine. And there'd been stories not just in *Stars and Stripes* but some of the magazines too; stories about this kind of thing happening in Rome after its liberation back in the first week of June in '44, when collaborators with the fast-retreating Germans were hauled out and made into symbols in ways that were degrading and unworthy. Now it was rife in Paris.

Just before a turn that leads off the Champs-Élysées to the boulevard going right to the Hotel Ritz, a crowd had already formed and you could tell it was something ugly. A perceptible shift was in the air. A mob in the making was well along in the act of shearing the hair of women accused of bedding down with the Nazi occupiers. There was more than hostility in all this. But even before sorting out varied thoughts and feelings, there was the shock of the visual.

Seeing a bald woman is usually startling. Or distressing. Maybe less so now, thanks to the contemporary efforts to raise funds or offer moral support for chemotherapy patients and cancer survivors (or sometimes simply due to quirky fashion trends). But this was *then*. And a bald-headed woman was shocking enough, compounded by the deliberate effort to shame and to mortify by stripping away her clothes. In my view—and I may be wrong, but I doubt it—I think it was the degrading act of forcing these women to stand half naked in broad daylight, in the middle of a horde of angry, bitter, contemptuous, vengeance-seeking fellow citizens . . . I think it was *that*, even more than the shorn heads, which caused Jerry to unleash his fury.

So much happened so fast that it scared me. One minute we're

slowly making our way in the jeep amid this wonderland of history and
architecture (such balconies and trellises and endless glorious terraces
boggled the mind of this Chicago girl), and the next minute I'm standing
up in the jeep but afraid to exit because the whole scene was so damn
confusing. And orders to all WACs were simple: Absolutely *not* to
"engage with or interfere or involve oneself" (as we were told a thousand
times) with any elements of "civilian discord" or "social unrest." The
usual rules and regs.

Doubtless the guys were told much the same. But Jerry was out of that
jeep and in the fray before I could even ask him what in the world he
intended to do. Turns out there was no need to ask. All I had to do was
watch.

First things first: Believe you me, his demeanor changed. It started
with the way he *stomped* that brake pedal. I'm surprised the jeep didn't
jackknife.

And it was a short walk—maybe thirty yards—to the public square and
the madness underway, but you could see by the way his walk changed
as Jerry approached the red-hot center of all this crap that he was in no
mood for anyone's interference. Seated in the jeep, I watched from behind
as he picked up his pace. The casual, relaxed, friendly mien that I'd seen
on him back near the Eiffel Tower as he spoke with the bespectacled and
diminutive civilians quickly altered. Now he was ramrod straight and
in a few seconds both his posture and the power of his voice demanded
total attention.

After a few deep breaths I exited the jeep and got close enough to the
square to at least be able to hear him clearly. He spoke mostly in French,
but also used a few German words and as he repeated himself he threw
in some English slang as well.

This particular scene involved two Frenchwomen obviously accused
of sleeping with the enemy and enjoying privileges galore vis-à-vis
consorting with German officers. But of course there'd been no trial by
jury or any due process. You could feel how it was all in the heat of the
moment. Maybe it was true. But maybe not.

"I don't care, goddammit!" is what Jerry kept shouting. And then he yelled some more in French and once again bellowed: "This is *not* acceptable. You will *stop!*"

What mattered most was not that he said anything at all. Half of his words were drowned out by the crowd's yelling and all sorts of cacophony. There were noisy vehicles rumbling nearby. Occasional explosions turned heads. It was bedlam.

What mattered most was that he never stopped moving. As he hollered and waved his arms all around, gesticulating with vehemence and getting results (again, his height was an asset here: when he ordered some of the crowd to step away or to step back, and his six-foot-two frame towered above them, they backed off); at the same time he got right up close to the woman standing there ashamed and bald, with her legs and her breasts mostly on display as her slip clung to her in the wind. Without ceasing to give orders, and while imposing on the whole scene the authority of his presence and his uniform, he took that dehumanized woman by the elbow and walked her away from several screaming Frenchmen. That's when it hit me that most of the crowd was male, although some women were also in there. Raging. But infuriated men made up the vast majority involved in this ritual punishment of suspected collaborators (I was naïve enough to feel twinges of guilt about the possibility that they were being falsely accused; everything was happening too fast and anything resembling judicious deliberation was entirely absent). It occurred to me that shaving their heads and stripping them down to their slips and brassieres was a surefire way to inflict sexual degradation upon those women, who had in the eyes of the mob committed a different kind of sexual degradation by taking German lovers. Making the women ugly by shaving their heads and treating their bodies like disposable waste was revenge for the emasculation felt by the men, in particular.

My own fear spiked when Jerry briefly let go of the first woman's elbow and for a moment she no longer had his implied protection. But it took only a few moments for Jerry to grasp the hand of the other woman about to be shorn. She was sitting in a rickety old wooden chair that someone had brought out from a nearby café and she still had most of her hair. The glowering man ready to scissor away on her was livid about being ordered to stop. The crowd demanded that he continue. Jerry made it indisputably clear that the whole damned show was over by taking a hold of the man's wrist and fiercely twisting it with such vigor that the scissors fell away. The crowd booed and Jerry was already onto his next priority. He took the sitting, sad woman by the hand (with her free hand she finger-combed what was left of her long hair, which had been chopped but not shaved off, and the expression of relief on her face was heartrending; you could see how bad she felt for the other woman, whose bald head made her look like Curly of The Three Stooges, but nothing was funny at all).

And in short order he once again took hold of the other woman's elbow and quickly he looked from side to side, again and again, as he held his posture ramrod straight and with military precision walked those two women to the jeep. Actually, that's not quite right. He escorted those two women. Straight to the jeep. I was flummoxed.

The mob had already begun to disperse, but then there were some really nasty and resentful hangers-on. The cutter had retrieved his fallen scissors. Tempers flared. You could tell that more than a few had the notion that by outnumbering one GI, they could easily snatch back both women and carry on with the degradations.

But something was there, in Jerry's eyes . . . something ultimate was manifest in the way he moved. The authority he exerted. Nobody risked messing with him.

He told the two women to sit in the jeep's backseats. Crossing their arms over their chests (their clothes had been ripped to shreds; sitting in their slips and bras was inevitable; there was no time to spare), they listened and nodded as Jerry then pointed at me and I could tell that my female presence was a comfort to them. Ten minutes later, we handed them over to a Red Cross station and went on our way.

The whole episode unfolded in fifteen minutes. But it felt like hell. To witness the civilians just liberated now choosing to brutalize others; it made for sick feelings.

"How did you know?" I finally managed to ask. "I mean, how could you be sure?" He understood the gist of my questions. We all had leftover, sweeping, romantic, silly, naïve, and even glorified fantasies about the grandeur of France and its storied history and our textbooks in school had reinforced all that. But we weren't naïve to the point of being stupid. We knew that collaborators were a major problem; just as we knew that throughout the Nazi occupation, there'd been somewhere between fifty and seventy thousand babies born to Frenchwomen who'd allied themselves in the ultimate way with the Germans. We called them "horizontal collaborators." Hell. Come on. Let's not be shy here. Coyness—at this point? There's no point anymore. I was mightily impressed that day with Jerry's willingness to stick his neck out and intervene and put a stop to what was obviously a foul episode of public humiliation.

But I had to ask my questions. Confusion demanded it of me. You see, we were loaded with up-to-the-minute information, those of us whose duties involved any sort of communications or Army PR. So we knew full well that back in Sicily in the summer of '43 and then later in Rome, especially, in June of '44 and throughout Northern France in the summer of '44, there'd been untold numbers of such scenes. It was weird, but somehow we just accepted our knowledge of it. Like it *had* to be. It seemed predictable. The angry locals often reacted to liberation by turning against the female collaborators in a hurry. They'd been known to live with or fuck with or somehow consort with the occupying Germans, and enjoyed privileges left and right thanks to that. More food, most of all. The Krauts made an art form out of emptying the occupied countries of extreme bulks of food; all of it sent back to the Fatherland. We knew about that, too. It's something else that's never really gotten across as time goes by, that scabrous near-starvation plaguing the occupied cities.

Anyway, even though I felt awkward about asking (spasms of guilt over seeming to be unsympathetic afflicted me; another display of Catholic guilt), I repeated my two questions to Jerry as he slowly drove in the direction of the Ritz Hotel. "How did you know?" I asked again. "How could you be so sure?" That's what I was mulling over. Because somehow he sensed that those two women were being falsely accused. Yet, all of France, and Paris, in particular, was known to be plagued by collaborationists.

"Chalk it up to this," Jerry said: "One third Counter Intelligence training. One third instinct. And one third X-ray vision. Fact is, I could see that they were innocent."

It sounded like a quip. Like a whimsical crack. For a second I flashed back to our patter at the Stork Club. Of course it was all dizzying to me. Not only the memory of that one night's chatter at the Stork Club but the Ripley's Believe It or Not reunion that suddenly found us driving across the boulevards of Paris just one day before that massive formation of the 28th Infantry Division came marching down the Champs-Élysées and provided for one perfect snapshot moment an exalted image.

If I'm any example whatsoever, believe you me: Most of us spent the rest of our lives silently amazed and forever wondering how we ever managed to process all of those staggering events, those life-jolting transitions, and those implausible coincidences. It happened all the time. Except for those whose duty was so static that somehow they rode out the war being stationed in one or two places far from the real deals. But even those GIs and even those officers—the ones who never left the States or who maybe just landed duty in some remote outback and action-free locations— even those folks had been uprooted from their hometowns; hauled out of their first or second jobs; extricated from college or somehow thrust into a whole new world.

That's another thing—an important thing—that never really got across. Contrary to all the gung-ho "Remember Pearl Harbor!" patriotic fervor that supposedly made it a dour necessity for so many to put on those uniforms, the thing is like this: For way more folks than ever admitted it, the whole shebang could not have happened at a better time. Nobody *ever* wanted to articulate that. I just did. There were massive numbers of GI Joes and GI Marys who were secretly thrilled by FDR's declaration of war against Japan and the other declarations that followed against Germany, most of all, after that bastard Hitler declared war on us. Sure it was awful and scary.

But it was also exciting. Way down deep. In the bones. For innumerable young folks (what I still can't get over is how young we were; most of us barely in our twenties), who had learned long before high school ended that the drudgery of a boring job killed the spirit or wounded the soul right off the bat (and I later learned that more than half the folks in the service after America entered the war had not completed high school), the sudden chance to be yanked out of everything familiar and sent far way to another state for basic training—I mean, most everybody had never been away from the town or the city they grew up in—felt like getting a brand new life. Even if they didn't ship out overseas. Most of the millions who spent those years in uniform were not ever sent overseas. But still, their lives were upended. Geographically. And for millions, their military time raised their living standards. New clothes. New shoes. Free food. Medical care and dental attention. For many, the draft was a boon.

In my case, by the time our communications team made its way from New York to Southern England to Northern France to Paris, feeling surreal was how I knew I was awake. It was all *so* unreal. My dreams, by comparison, were dull. Paris was beyond category.

Why so? Everything was there to be seen. To be touched. Smelled. Apprehended. As our jeep made its way slowly across one Paris signpost after another (every one hundred yards offered up more extraordinary elements than I could keep track of: architecture from centuries gone by and lampposts and balconies that were designed as exquisitely as Rodin's sculptures; plus the sheer majesty of landmarks with the power to induce dizziness; I nearly gave myself whiplash by quickly turning my head again and again to see the Eiffel Tower recede in the distance, but then I'd crane my neck to try to take in the expansive, extraordinary Champ de Mars, that vast expansive area adjacent to the Tour Eiffel, and suddenly Jerry maneuvered us onto Rue Saint-Dominique and then before I knew it my heart melted at the glorious Alexandre III Bridge—the Pont Alexandre III sign made me tearfully think of Pop), the goofy remark that Jerry had made about his "X-ray vision" segued to what he knew.

"I knew from the bony shoulders and how thin their arms were," he explained. "The likelihood of a true collaborator being so skinny is minimal. Food is now everything. No kidding. The goddam Fritzes have been vicious about food. Sending more than half of everything back to the Fatherland. We learned that milk consumption here is down seventy percent since 1940."

I knew he had the right dope. It was true in every country that the Germans put the clouts on. Poland. France. Holland. Belgium. Norway. You name it. They stole all they could and food, most of all, was confiscated and shipped back home. Along with clothing, currency, art, and every type of resource. Bastards.

"Most collaborators will have meat on their bones," he said. "Some girth. Not fat necessarily. But definitely some pounds in the middle. Some muscles on the arms. Those two caught up in that scene back there? Did you notice their necks or legs?"

I thought hard for a moment. "Too thin," I said. "Their necks were much too thin. And no fat on the gams either." He had noted those visual details at a distance. I was too distracted by the mayhem in general, the vile catcalls in particular (seeing those women stripped to their undergarments brought out the beasts), and most of all the sheer cacophony that assaulted all of our senses on that rambunctious day.

"So how do you think they got fingered as collaborators? What happened?"

"If we've learned one thing town by town, village by village, and city by city," Jerry said, "it's that there's a thin red line between actual collaboration and just trying to somehow get by. To be left alone. To stay below the radar. Everything is dicey."

He'd already had plenty of practice. His job with the Counter Intelligence Corps involved interviewing French civilians in each liberated village, town and city. It had to happen quickly. Right away. The local population was most likely to offer useful, helpful information in the first flush of newfound freedom. And for a while, at least, as the Allies moved deeper and deeper into France and the occupying Germans were all of a sudden pulling out, on the run, retreating like hell, the big job for Jerry's outfit (his CIC cadre was part of the Fourth Infantry Division, to which our communications team was assigned by summer's end) was to get information. To get details. To get as much useful knowledge as possible about everything: Where the Germans had done this or that? What Krauts had been the last to make tracks? How many different directions did they flee in? When Germans who had straggled for any reason were rounded up as prisoners of war, he then interrogated them in a hurry. It was the captured Krauts who often had the most important information to share, and knowing that all was lost it was those POWs who usually sang like birds.

"Something else," he added. "Actual collaborators usually finger each other in big numbers. Hoping for leniency. Maybe amnesia on the part of the locals. So most of the time there's a larger number being rounded together and sheared like sheep. If you see just one or two being put on display, it's likely a false accusation. For sure. Because real Fritz fuckers would finger a dozen others to try to get a break. Right?"

I was so startled by hearing "Fritz fuckers" that for a while I did not say a word.

16

I guess you could say I'm set for the weekend. Today is Friday. It's almost noon. And after she finished helping me with every little thing, the amazing Lorena (or I should say my Beloved Beansy, she of the Rena-Bena-Bean-now-Beansy persuasion) doubled back to my tidy little suite here and surprised the daylights out of me. That generous and ridiculously beautiful girl (I don't care if she's forty now; she's still a girl to me; I've got earrings older than her) brought me a box of new cassette tapes.

And she suggested something smart. I think so, anyway. She left the small TV in the corner on. I mean, it's still on, but the volume is turned down all the way. It's my preference most of the time anyhow. I can't stand the hyper-loud and stupid chatter-chatter-chatter of today's awful commercials. And whether it's CNN or Sky News, in recent years, I have discovered that watching in silence is good for me. It helps my memory. Sharpens the mind. I swear it does. And Beansy agrees with me.

Her theory is that by concentrating my focus solely on the visuals they show on the news programs, I'm getting the heart of the story anyhow. As for the words recited by the talking heads? Come on. With the constant flow of what Beansy calls "visual aids" (you know, the flow of alternating photographs, film clips, big maps, charts, and every other kind of illustration scrolling on the screen), the story is transmitted. The heart of the story anyway. Or the core information. "Anything is better than just staring at the ceiling when you're not recording yourself," Beansy said. "You may not be able to move anything at all, but you can still fill your mind up."

It figures that she'd be the one to say that. I've expressed my frustration to several of the staffers here. They nod. They make notes. But nothing changes. They walk off. Only Lorena-Rena-Bean-my Beloved Beansy *really* hears me. And knowing full well that I'm what she calls "a news junkie," she made the most obvious suggestion about letting Sky News play on and on, but in silence. Which suits me fine. It helps me just to see so many worldwide images. It calms my anxiety to have my mind distracted.

But it's not like dumbbell distractions. There's a minimum of stupid stuff on Sky News. It's mostly serious stories from all over the world. Not celebrity trash. A few hours ago, with the television playing silently and Beansy washing my back, we both saw a special segment about a final gathering in Memphis. It was heartrending. The story was all about the last reunion get-together for the 30th Infantry Division, which has been having reunions ever since the first one down in Memphis back in 1947. It was astounding to Rena-Bena that such a thing had been going on that long. Close-ups on the handful of old soldiers who were present at this last reunion really got the point across. They reminded me of the sepia-toned old-time photographs of the last living Civil War veterans, who faded away back in the 1950s. I can still recall how one of the big magazines took their pictures back in 1955 to mark the 90th anniversary of the end of the America's Civil War. Tiny little wizened old men. All gone.

That's what the ex-GIs looked like when the news story played over and over again. One of the things that I swear helps me not get lost in a fog is that when Sky News or CNN is on my screen over there, and I don't have to listen to all the advertising junk but just see what I see, they recycle and rerun the big stories time after time. Just like they're doing today with the repeating of the Memphis story about the 30th Infantry Division's last reunion down there in Memphis. Then I see the guys.

When they rerun the story, I can't help but see the resemblance between the diminished, small, frail ex-GIs who are so obviously moved and emotional and upset and grateful to be part of this final get-together, and yet . . . they all know it means the end of something. And they're as withered and frail as the last living Civil War vets turned out to be when they were photographed in their twilight time. It's all over. But something else had the full attention of Beansy. It's April 24th today and now that the last week of the month is here, the news is filled with something closer to her heart. "Closer to home," as she puts it. Echoing a song I recall my son loving.

The same news programs are loading up on special features vis-à-vis the 40th anniversary of the end of America's war in Vietnam. The stories are abundant. On the news we keep seeing the replays of the exodus from South Vietnam at the very end of April, forty years ago. Those images of the American helicopters taking off from the roof of our embassy in Saigon, making a desperate effort to escape. That's something that hits her hard, because the father she says she's hardly ever known or seen was drafted back in 1971, and according to her family lore he was a mess when he came back. I'm not surprised. By that late stage in the war, it was a morass and a disaster in so many ways. Big and small. From the top to the bottom. But on and on it dragged until the middle of the 1970s. I asked her if she knew when he got back to the States. "Not sure," she said. "But he must have got back here by '73 because he and my mother were married in the summer of 1973. All she ever talks about is how their wedding weekend coincided with the release of *American Graffiti,* and she's been obsessed with that movie ever since. I was weaned on that soundtrack."

"They were in search of their lost youth," I said. "And I don't mean to sound cute."

"Lost youth? They were barely in their twenties. They were in the prime of youth."

"No, dear. Maybe in terms of numbers they were. But not in terms of their lives."

I could tell that she was a bit confused. After she sat me up again, I tried to explain.

"You see, it's impossible now, that's what it is. You just can't imagine how the whole society was torn to bits in those years. Especially as the country crawled out of the 1960s and into the 1970s. I was teaching college in those years. Believe you me, the changes in everything— especially the spirit of optimism that'd been a mainstay in America for as long as I could remember—really were spooky. It was a dark time."

"Tell me something," she interrupted. Usually I hate interruptions, but not this time. "Do you think the antiwar movement was at fault for that 'dark time,' as you put it."

In the privacy of my mind, I swear, I had dozens of flashbacks all at once. From one extreme to another. Images of burning Buddhist monks and Mothers for Peace and clergy marching against the war along with students and proud men who identified themselves (by their banners) as Veterans for Peace and by their suits and hats and ties I could tell they were part of my crowd, but it was extremely different in every way, six and seven and eight years later, when the first antiwar marches in 1965 were long forgotten and by the opening years of the 1970s the movement was not only misdirected but derailed by the mayhem created by the Weather Underground and all the other violent, dangerous, anti-everything screamers and shouters who thought nothing of not just burning flags, but bombing buildings. And not just the federal buildings they targeted, but even university libraries and science labs. My mind was like a slide-projector with a rapid-fire sequence of still-life photographs that all signified plenty to me, but which were all snapped before she was even born.

It was weird. The soldiers in the news photos marching off to Vietnam in the middle of the 1960s looked somewhat similar to the GIs who came marching home in 1945 or after the Korean War in the early part of the Fifties. You could see similarities. But by the time *Life* Magazine was running special photo-essays on the Vietnam War in the early 1970s, something happened. Those GIs looked like runaways from rock bands. Their longer hair and moustaches and peace buttons were all at odds with anything resembling the guys who had gone off to that war in the beginning. It was a sea change. Then: Suddenly I heard Beansy again. (I'd really drifted for a minute.)

"My mother tells me that in our family the protestors were hated as much as the war was. That never made any sense to me. But she hardly says anything about those years. Except that he was drafted in '71. And they got married in 1973. Then I was born in '75, and all I ever heard for ten years were her *American Graffiti* records."

"That's right," I recalled. "There were two discs. It was a double-album set. And make no mistake about it. That film and those records were like time machines for their generation. All of those early rock 'n' roll hits.

One-hit wonders and favorite ballads. The whole movie was designed around its soundtrack songs. Did you ever see the film?"

"She made me watch it with her when I was a kid," Beansy recalled. "But I wasn't into it. All I saw were people driving old cars. I was more into *Star Wars* movies."

"Bingo!" I yelped. "The same man *made* all of those movies."

"What?" Beansy actually stopped moving, for once, and stared at me. "George *Lu*cas? No way. There's no way that George Lucas made anything like . . ."

Then it was my turn to interrupt her. "Google it, sweetie! You'll see. *American Graffiti* was the first hit film George Lucas ever had. It was *his* baby. And it was all about much more than people driving cars. It was a lamentation for lost youth."

17

That's been the story of my life. Lamentations for lost youth. Not just mine. But that of others. Lots, too. It's not only just what I'm about these days. It's been the dominant, uppermost, always-on-my-mind way of thinking, ever since whenever.

Sharing thoughts with Beansy about her parents and all put a spotlight on it. By the time she was done in here earlier today we'd more or less figured out the timetable of her own little family's evolution. As best as we could figure it, her long lost father was drafted in 1971 and probably was back from Vietnam later in '72. Then, like so many other veterans in all the wars, he married fast and furious after his discharge, thinking that a wife and a family would put him on track. And the poor bastard and Beansy's mother got married in '73 and she was born two years later and he was out the door and long gone before she was a toddler. She says she barely recalls him.

But the loss is there. The hole in the heart. The aching absence. Yearning. Grief.

Just the brief conversation about all that stuff this morning brought into focus for me the lifetime I've spent lamenting lost youths. Starting with Pop's. Ages ago. I realized long before I was a teenager that Pop was prone to deep mourning. Even though he worked his job and did not disappear from the house and hide out in bars or wherever else men disappear to when they're incapable of sitting still, which is most of the time of course. Pop's quiet ways were actually like textbook melancholy.

And it all made more sense to me, as my own growing up shifted into gear.

That year he spent giving me clarinet lessons at home—*that* was a giveaway. For me, in the beginning, it was exciting. Like a domestic adventure in the arts. After a while, though, the sadness that overcame him sometimes really got to me. Usually it was when we were well into some aspect of yours truly producing a better tone on the clarinet. On *his* clarinet, I should say. Our once-weekly lesson swiftly turned into a twice-or-even thrice-weekly at-home workshop. We *really* got into it. And we'd sit there in the living room, with ol' Mom out in the kitchen either reading the latest issues of *Time* or *Life* (with fresh-baked brownies warm in the oven), and we'd take turns passing the clarinet back and forth to each other, practicing melodic lines or playing the simple exercises from the old How-To booklet Pop had saved. There were two mouthpieces stored in his clarinet case and we each had one. I was just fascinated by the subtleties and the delicate details of the reeds and their effects. Sometimes a certain reed made for a harsher sound. Or a gentler shade. It's what Pop would call "the timbre" of the sound. He wanted "a round sound," he'd always say, during the brief lull when we'd be changing mouthpieces and talking just a bit.

"That's one of the other benefits of proper breathing," he'd remind me. "When the inhalation is deep and proper, and your tummy expands, it not only guarantees a longer breath, which allows you to play more, but it helps to create a round sound."

That's when I'd see it. That look of melancholy. A shift in his focus. A sadness in his eyes. It was right then and there, when he'd be softly speaking about round sounds. It was always at those times that I wanted to ask him more questions about, well, about everything. Especially his time in France in 1918. Back in the Great War.

Even now, it seems odd to again use that original expression. But for the longest time we never called it World War One or the First World War. Only later on did those terms come into being. For Pop and his crowd, it was the Great War. And it was all of a sudden remote and then quickly diminished and forever packed away into the distant past after the 1930s, because everything else took over. *Every*thing.

I'm sure that had something to do with the faraway look—almost like he was a little lost in some strange place and trying to see through the mist and the fog—that Pop had on his face when I'd see him looking that way. It was 1935 when we started that routine of the clarinet lessons, while I maneuvered my way through eighth grade, and by the time I graduated high school in 1939 the twentieth anniversary of the end of the Great War had come and gone. What happened? *Nothing.* That's the truth. The world had so many new problems in 1938 that there was hardly anything in the way of major acknowledgements about that twentieth anniversary.

"Much to my own surprise," I said to Jerry, when I tried to share with him how deeply I was pierced by my inner awareness of Pop's lamentations for his own lost youth, "when November 11th rolled around back in '38, and I was expecting time to stop and for there to be some kind of high and mighty moment, some sort of grand national salute in honor of the Doughboys who turned the tide back in 1918—"

Jerry interrupted me as he parked the jeep and yanked the clutch. "Lesson learned right then and there, I imagine," he said. "The word 'grand' ought to be abolished."

"Duly noted," I replied. "But I was a naïve high school senior. And thanks to all the questions that ol' Mom had tried to answer, because Pop would not talk about his time over there or I should say: over *here*—my appreciation for the immensity of it all was at a peak. Did you know that throughout all that year, back in 1918, the Yanks were landing ten thousand soldiers per day in France? Every damn day! That was phenomenal. We're talking 1918! One year after America entered the war."

"And twenty years later it was like it'd never, ever happened." Jerry looked morose. "Even though Armistice Day was then made into a national holiday."

"That's right. That's precisely my point. Even as a high school kid back in '38, I couldn't get over how ancient it all seemed to almost everyone else, even though it had all been happening only twenty years earlier. Pop's generation dissolved into history. But that week of November 11, 1938, when that twentieth anniversary—"

Jerry interrupted me again, but not rudely. He quickly interjected: "That was the same week of the Night of the Broken Glass throughout Germany and Austria. I'd scooted back to America right before that onslaught—"

Now it was my turn to interrupt: "*Kristallnacht!*" I bellowed. "Of course. The week of that twentieth anniversary of the end of the First War was also the week that the news was all about *Kristallnacht.* Jesus, that explains Pop's memorial display. That week he did this unusual thing, where he lit candles every night and placed them in a specific formation—four candles on this antique circular table in our living room—and on the table he placed all these books from the basement cabinet. They were his books about the Great War. Mostly the novels he loved, but history books too."

"Like an altar?" Jerry asked. "Something like an altar?" He nailed it.

"It was," I said. "It reminded me of the chapel at St. Rita's. But I didn't realize it until just this second . . . in addition to *Three Soldiers* by John Dos Passos and *A Farewell to Arms* by Hemingway and *The Enormous Room* by e.e. cummings and of course Remarque's *All Quiet on the Western Front*, there was something else. A photo of Pop's one brother. Killed at Chateau-Thierry. His body was dismembered."

"Hold that thought," Jerry said. We were parked across the way from the Ritz.

18

Right. As *if.* I wanted to hold my thought about as much as I wanted to hold my bowels. Which is how I feel now. There's no time left to hold my thoughts. And most of my time—when awake, that is—in this blessed yet cursed locale (come on, it's a hospice and I'm here to die and I'm not ready, yet, but I haven't a choice; this kind of illness has its own timetable) there's far too much time squandered on my bowels and my bladder (an indwelling catheter is not for the meek or mild of heart) and the goddam way my thoughts are so often redirected—or in my much less than humble opinion, *mis*directed—to the most basic of hygiene issues and whatnot, well, all I can say is that what I live for now is getting my story told. At long last.

"There were a few practical things to be said," as Hemingway put it so well. OK.

As if things weren't already surreal enough, it all then spiraled into fantasyland. I mean, me and my girls were merely a small communications team attached at varied times to different Army divisions, distinct regiments, particular companies, specific stations, and that's that. No one could have been more startled than we were to be suddenly in the middle of the City of Light as it awoke after four suffocating years of miserable, frightening, murky darkness under the intimidating and authoritarian boot of German occupation. But, after our brief stay in England, our orders put us right in line behind the forward-moving Fourth Infantry Division, and the guys were out in front and fast moving in and around Paris and we were following behind them. With a detour vis-à-vis Paris and our all-important twenty-four hour pass. It was a last-minute pass that gave us the freedom to roam for one day and one night: the dates still singe my memory (August 28 through August 29, 1944). Always.

And there he sat at a table in the bar of the Hotel Ritz, looking like an old lion. But even before Jerry held me by the elbow (gently), and sort of steered me across the boulevard and toward the entrance of the Ritz, I was entranced. Who wouldn't be? Back home in Chicago, when visiting downtown years earlier or when Sunday drives with ol' Mom and Pop occurred (it's the ultimate stereotype but I swear it's true: Pop and ol' Mom had an *idée fixe* about using their car and they rarely took it out of the garage for more than the proverbial Sunday drive), we'd gone a few times on a self-styled tour of the downtown realm considered so fine. The Drake Hotel. Lovely. The Palmer House. Royally chic. Compared to the South Side of Chicago, those majestic hotels and the restaurants and shops and theaters they anchored seemed to us like a movie set. And yet, as we walked by the Place Vendome (by this time I saw Jerry was buoyant, moving with an effortless fleet-footed confidence and brio and that made me wonder if he'd been drinking, but I'm quite sure that he was one of the few GIs in Paris that day who was not bombs away with the booze), the spectacular size and the royal design and the mind-boggling architecture of the Ritz Hotel in Paris made the Chicago landmarks of my youth look like roadside motels by comparison. The marble columns in the lobby were apropos for Athens.

But it wasn't just the Ritz itself, of course. The pandemonium all around intensified every little thing. And one of the only ways I can describe the non-stop intensity of the crowds in the streets and the endless sounds of ecstatic mayhem and sheer human celebration (the ugly incidents of vengeance to the side) is to fall back on what I know sounds exaggerated and dumb. But it's true! It *is*. I was there.

All you have to do is close your eyes and think of any film clip you ever heard (forget what you were seeing, but try recalling what you *heard*) about Beatlemania. The screaming. The relentless cheering. The roaring of masses of people and their voices all exclaiming joy and freedom and tears and emotions and all in a fever. That's the way it was. Throughout Paris and all down the boulevards and right there adjacent to the Ritz, as well. People were standing atop their parked cars, craning their necks and using binoculars and pointing here and there and hoping (I suppose) to get a glimpse of General Charles de Gaulle or his fellow hero General Leclerc or any of the other distinguished figures who paraded through town in the prior few days. Those three days, from August 25th to the 26th and 27th, had been one monumental public celebration after another. And it was certainly not over yet.

Church bells never stopped ringing. Musical horns blared from out of nowhere. You never heard so many spontaneous sounds of jazzy saxophones, trombones, and trumpets and drums. From private apartments way up high and their splendid balconies, almost all of which displayed Allied flags, and I do mean Allied—it was a cinch that many folks would unfurl the French flag, but we saw American and British and Canadian flags by the score. Along with more gorgeous flowers than in heaven.

And that was another thing. It happened time after time after time. In celebration, and probably with a lot of help from the spirits being consumed by the magnum, there were exquisite moments when those Parisians standing out on their balconies grabbed handfuls of the flowers they'd displayed and tossed them with love and liberated glee down below. More than one GI caught a flower floating from above.

By the time I was more or less guided by Jerry through the Vatican-style courtyard and the front doors of the Ritz (which remained intact, like most of Paris, thanks to the astounding decision by the last Commandant of the Occupation to defy Hitler's orders and not exit Paris with a demolition orgy that was actually ready to explode: we soon learned that up to the last minute the plan was in place to detonate tens of thousands of explosives as the Germans fast retreated, with more than two hundred factories, four dozen historic bridges, innumerable buildings from the Opera House to the Louvre and all the gas lines and electrical grids meant to be blown sky-high), and by the time we were standing in the bar at the Ritz, I thought we were levitating.

There *he* sat. Calmly. Drinks lined up before him. But there was no razzle-dazzle. His demeanor was low-key. Subdued. Still, it was Hemingway. No doubt about it.

I'm not sure what was going through Jerry's mind at that moment, but I can attest to having had one thought only. Actually, I had a two-part thought. Part one was that Jerry had not known definitely or precisely or exactly that here he'd find his literary godfather, but that he'd managed by hunches and instincts to do so. That's because I could tell from the bug-eyed look on Jerry's face that he was almost as surprised as I was that sitting there amid a cadre of other correspondents in uniform (and also the inevitable gaggle of sidekicks) was the man whose books had defined our epoch.

I know that sounds over-the-top and outsized and full of hooey nowadays. But to hell with today. And to hell with the way that he's been lampooned. In 1944, the thing was like this: Most of Papa's greatest works were considered essential. And thanks to the way that millions of pocket-sized editions of his beloved books made their way into not just the pockets but the duffle-bags and musette bags of millions of American soldiers who were given the books freely as a way to pass the time on the troopships and all, he was at his absolute peak. The wartime rationing of paper and glue and everything else did not apply to those special pocket-sized paperback editions that the government allowed the publishers to provide by the ton; and not only did that wartime protocol set the stage for the postwar rise of paperbacks, but, it ensured that millions of the GIs (many of whom never completed high school, with the dread Great Depression hauling them into the work force by default as kids) at long last got the chance to read *In Our Time* and *The Sun Also Rises*. But the biggest favorites of all—for all the obvious reasons—were the pocket-size reprints of *A Farewell to Arms* and *For Whom the Bell Tolls*. One may have been about Pop's old-time Great War and the other was set during the Spanish Civil War, but no matter. It was those two novels that made the GIs in '44 think of Hemingway as "Papa." That was no cute locution. It was serious. They needed an iconic, strong, fatherly image.

You can bet your last dollar that's one of the reasons we loved Ike the way we did.

My other thought was that Papa Hemingway had really plumped out big. Our first edition hardcover of *For Whom the Bell Tolls*, which I remembered so clearly from back home in Chicago, featured a grizzled image of the author on the dust jacket. A profile shot. Hemingway typing away, looking burly yet still fit and rugged. At the Ritz that day, as Jerry and I stood there briefly staring, it wasn't the rugged face on Papa that drew my attention (although I thought it pretty damn impressive). It was his girth. Army time usually thinned people out. But he was heavier than ever. Truly. "He could almost pass for a partisan, with his scruff and all," Jerry said. "But his eyes give him away. See what I mean? He's got Francis Macomber's eyes."

Our staring could not last. Somebody had to say something. The bar at the Ritz was like a cocoon of half-lighted camaraderie, with the aromatic and mosaic woodwork and the fine accoutrements and the bartender's pristine white apron all conveying security, ease, and remoteness from the chaos of the erupting city, and the war, too.

"I recognize you," Hemingway said. And he was pointing right at Jerry.

19

One hour later, I had a better understanding of why Hemingway said that. Moving steadily once again on the crowded and hectic streets of Paris in the jeep that Jerry maneuvered like a prize-winning race car driver, my questions were answered.

"What did he mean by that? I mean, that finger-pointing 'I recognize you' remark was quite the showstopper. Did you meet before?"

"No, never," Jerry said. "But he never forgets a face. And when *Esquire* published a story of mine, they also ran a really good picture of the author who's here to tell you that he does not like *any* pictures of himself. But, the shot *Esquire* used was actually pretty damn okay. Not sure I feel that way about the story. But the old man saw the photo, and he liked the story. That's why he recognized me."

"So much for the recognitions," I said. "And then what did he say?" You see, while I stood off to the side and observed, Jerry and Hemingway spoke to each other. It was odd. They spoke so quietly. You'd think they were in cahoots. And the others there, all sitting around Hemingway like he was some potentate or some Turkish pasha, well, you could sense their annoyance at the effortless way that Jerry acquired Hemingway's attention. It wasn't just a polite howdy-do. The old man offered real attention. For a few minutes they spoke quietly and never stopped looking at each other with a serious eye-to-eye focus. Meantime, the others at the table had quizzical looks on their faces. Expressions of surprise, actually. Who the hell *was* this young kid? I think that's what they wondered. Jerry seemed oblivious to their skeptical glances.

"They probably figured I was just another guy with a crush on the old man's books. Another nobody who 'wants to write.' And they probably figured he was being nice and all. But when he asked about any new stories and I mentioned the new one in *The Saturday Evening Post*, something shifted there. Then, he asked to read it."

You see, that's how we'd ended up leaving the Ritz and using the jeep to circle around other *arrondissements* and then make a beeline back to the Ritz. Jerry had quickly excused himself from this encounter with Hemingway and explained to me on our way back to the jeep that as fast as possible he needed to find anybody-somebody-someone-somehow with a copy of the *Post* from the middle of July. When I told Jerry that a copy sent by ol' Mom was in my room at a small hotel and he could have it, we zigzagged our way there and back in a hurry. In any other place at any other time, such a coincidence would have begged disbelief. But by 1944, we were all so used to serendipitous encounters, uncanny synchronicity, and cosmic jolts that the whole thing just unfolded. Off we went. I retrieved the *Post* from my hotel room. In a jiffy, we were en route back to the Ritz. It was as if we 'd just stepped out to eat.

My questions did not surprise or seem to annoy Jerry. Which surprised me. Sort of. I mean, here he was—or *there* he was—engineering a dicey situation with a writer we all idolized. Asking the old man to read a new story wasn't even necessary for Jerry, because the old man had asked *him* first. That surprised me. Hemingway's reputation for bluster was nowhere on display. Papa had extended the invitation.

So I knew enough to know that Jerry was doubtless preoccupied and mighty pumped up (inside, that is) about his latest work being evaluated. There's no getting around that element. A reading from Hemingway was not like anybody just reading the magazine. This either would or would not be a blessing. A benediction.

I tamped down the impulse to ask about that. Instead, I asked Jerry about the crowd of hangers-on sitting there at the table with Hemingway.

"For starters, I can't figure out who that tiny woman in the uniform might be."

"Her name is Mary," Jerry said. "Mary Welsh. She's another correspondent and works for *Time*." That settled that. Her little frame was further dwarfed by the bulk of the old man, who sat beside her with a definite sense of lordly possession. "Even though he's still married to Number 3," Jerry added, "I get a sense that he's already picked out this Mary to be his Number 4."

"You think he's going to divorce Martha Gellhorn?" I asked. I felt right then and there like we were in some weird dream. A fantasia mixing up high school gossip with Ed Sullivan's syndicated entertainment column in the newspapers back home.

We'd all known for years that Hemingway's third wife, Martha Gellhorn, was publishing more than he was. Martha was *everywhere* in those days. Literally.

As a *Collier's* war correspondent, she'd made tracks from Spain to China and from Finland over to Normandy. Her audacity was already legendary. The story we heard was that because no female correspondents were permitted at the big D-Day landings on June 6 back at Normandy, she bluffed and conned and made her way somehow onto an Army hospital ship. And hid herself in a closet. Stowed away! From there she got as close to the beaches as any writer could. Then: She was *there*.

And it didn't require Freud to figure out that her guts and grit made the old man jealous. Her travels and adventures were outshining him, during most of the war.

"Do you think that he's finally over here because he's competing with Martha?"

Jerry turned the steering wheel and rounded a corner. "If we were talking about any other couple, I'd laugh," he said. Then he added: "But Martha's been all over the world with this war and you might be right. I think he's finally here to stake his claim and steal some of her thunder. They hardly see each other, is what I think."

"Well, the star eyes between that little woman in her spiffy uniform and Ernest sitting there, that looks to me like exactly what you said. Something's in the making, indeed."

I mean, really. It was all so obvious. Helen Keller could have seen it.

But I had to ask about somebody else, too. Because a husky, zesty, curly-haired dynamo who also sat at the table at the Ritz as part of Hemingway's liberation fiesta—well, he also had his eyes on the small woman with the big eyes. But before I asked about that guy, my question about something else popped out: "Why doesn't *he* wear insignia?"

It was Hemingway I asked about. I noticed he had no correspondent's badge like other writers wore. No insignia to indicate that he was a non-combatant. The Army had strict rules about all that. But the old man's insignia simply wasn't there.

"No doubt we're not supposed to ask about that," Jerry said. "Or even notice. OK?"

In other words, button it. Which I did.

The plain truth is that Papa opened fire now and then.

20

No. It's not possible. Is it? Well, it still feels impossible. No matter what it is. But the calendar on the wall doesn't lie. It's the 8th of May. The news on CNN is pretty much running and rerunning the same sort of video medleys and old newsreel clips as what I can see on Sky News or France 24 as well. I have the volume turned all the way down, of course, to guarantee that I'm spared having to listen to all those awful commercials. The visuals are enough for me. Just seeing the images chosen to illustrate any story gets the point across for me, along with the scrolls and banners and whatnot made by possible by all of today's CGI. Isn't that a good one? Beansy explained to me how CGI is shorthand for Computer Generated Images, which no doubt make up the vast majority of special effects in anything in films or on TV.

The subject came up earlier this week after she and I did something unusual. We watched a whole movie together. Right here in my hospice suite. No kidding. I told her how much I wish I could have gone out to see a new film called *Selma*, which was given lots of attention in the news a while ago, even though the dummies that run the Academy Awards kicked it to the curb. She didn't even ask me questions, she just showed up with the DVD last night and because she was off duty and not on the clock she was able to sit still for two whole hours. We watched it together from start to finish and aside from all my other observations, what I really could not get over was how the violence and mayhem at Selma Bridge was re-created with the horses and the violence and all. Beansy explained that with CGI, anything can be visually presented with extraordinary realism, from outer space to human drama.

That struck me right off the bat because in the movie the amazing actor who plays Martin Luther King uses the word "drama" with great specificity, to explain what's needed at Selma Bridge in order to keep the cameras rolling and get the attention of President Johnson, who would have much preferred that things simmer down a bit. We had no time, really, to discuss much after seeing the movie. My nighttime aide was waiting to proceed and there was no chance to talk. But the next day— it was only yesterday—when beloved ol' Lorena-Rena-Bean-Beansy was back for her usual daytime shift in here, she was full of questions.

Did I recall seeing the interruption of regularly scheduled programming when the news broke in with live footage from Selma back in 1965? Of course, I told her. My son and I were watching the Walt Disney television program and suddenly it all changed and we saw the brutal use of the horses by state troopers to trample down defenseless human beings, while the troopers beat the civil rights demonstrators mercilessly with clubs and bats and bullwhips, too. It was ghastly. My son cried. I cried too, out of rage and fury and grief and frustration. It was beyond dreadful. And for such hateful insanity to reign with state-sanctioned authority in 1965, almost exactly twenty years after the end of the war in Europe, that to me was inexplicable.

And it's just as inexplicable to me that today—May 8th, 2015—the news images are steeped in whatever they're saying about this being the 70th anniversary of the end of the war against Hitler. This morning I asked Beansy to use the calculator on her iPhone and do the math. She had it in a jiffy. Seventy years ago today adds up to 25, 550 days ago. She thought that was a royal hoot. And she double-checked on her phone's calculator. Then she said it again: "Unbelievable! Seventy years ago today was twenty-five thousand, five hundred and fifty days ago." And that's when she repeated herself by spelling out the figure numerically: "My God. That's 2-5-5-5-0. And you've lived each one of those 25,550 days? That is simply amazing to me."

I suggested that she use her calculator to learn how many days she had lived, as of her fortieth birthday earlier this year. "Go ahead," I said. "Forty times three hundred and sixty-five. And then we can figure out the rest." She looked positively stricken.

That's when she dodged me and asked more questions. Did I recall the legend of Viola Liuzzo? The movie made just enough room toward the end to include the story of Viola, the Detroit housewife and mother of five, who answered the call that Dr. King put out for all people of goodwill to go to Selma for another march after that bloodbath at Selma Bridge. And white Viola was targeted by the KKK as she drove a black civil rights activist here and there. She was shot dead. Mourned by many and vilified by others. Her story really hit a nerve. I remembered it with painful grief.

Just as I remember now what was happening seventy years ago today. Twenty-five thousand and five hundred and fifty days ago. They're not telling the whole story on CNN and Sky News isn't much better. Only France 24 has shown some of the awful 1945 newsreel footage of shattered cities, camp survivors, and other grim evidence of Europe on May 8, 1945. Of course there were wild celebrations and the joy was valid and the sense of blessed relief was valid and true. But the familiar scenes of tens of thousands (hundreds of thousands; maybe millions) dancing in the streets of London and New York make it easy to forget that sixty million had died and millions of refugees remained and an entire social order had been woefully destroyed.

I'm so glad I've still got what little strength it takes to use the TV remote sometimes. One poke and I can change channels, if I'm lucky. Everyone thinks I'm goofy for watching all the news so much and viewing it in silence. But I really cannot abide the talking heads anymore.

As for pushing the damn buttons on this cassette recorder, that's never going to be as easy as using the TV remote. So I'll just ramble on until the tape runs out . . .

Everything began making more sense as we drove from my small hotel, where I'd retrieved that copy of the *Post* for Jerry, and then returned to the Ritz Hotel. As usual, with the right questions asked in the right sequence and with a reprise of that timing and patter that served us well the night we first met, our words flowed.

And all along the way, I learned something new as every question was answered and I recalled something else—usually something about Pop and ol' Mom—as well.

"So this new story in the *Post* is not any sort of debut—right? You published in *Esquire* before this?"

We'd always subscribed to the *Post* back home in Chicago. But in those days, *Esquire* was still considered new and even a bit brazen. It was more like the kind of magazine that a man bought for himself in a train station. Not really something for the wife to see in the mail, delivered to the house. Not that it was all that risqué or tawdry. Certainly not smutty. But the agenda was clear. Back then, *Esquire* had high IQ writers (Hemingway included) working up stories and columns about the myriad ways for American men to live exciting, tantalizing lives. Think of it as a guidebook for the guys who wanted to emulate snazzy, youthful Clark Gable.

"Just a couple of years ago," Jerry said. "My first story publication was—get ready for this meticulous repetition—in *Story* Magazine. Then *Esquire* gave me a shot."

"I know that magazine!" We all knew *Story* Magazine in those days. That's no exaggeration. Pop and ol' Mom subscribed to it. Short stories were the coin of the realm for millions of readers then. And the new works highlighted by this almost famous New York editor named Whit Burnett in *Story* magazine gave us all a lot to look forward to. You see, here's another thing that never really got across. Our lives were defined in many ways by the written word. Not that most people were out there buying books all the time and reading around the clock. Of course not. For the most part, people were consumed—and sometimes devoured— by their economic needs and just earning a living was tough enough.

But the vast majority of folks who may not have been habitual book buyers or even book readers were still in there with the rest of us living by words and more words. All the magazines then—and I mean damn near every one of them: from *Time* and *LIFE* to *Redbook* and the *Ladies' Home Journal* to *Esquire* and *Harper's* and of course *The New Yorker*; and even *Good Housekeeping* and *Argosy* and others—not only featured long articles, but also really solid short stories. Not squibs. None of this cut-cut-cut to the bone minimizing of everything; that's now the norm. Juicy, fat, in-depth stories with illustrations (sometimes) and room for a writer to stretch? We loved all that. Good grief, even the ads had loads of text. And we read it! Always.

"My folks have subscribed to *Story* Magazine for years. Ol' Mom gets a little discount because she's a teacher. When did your first work appear in Burnett's chronicles?"

"Touchdown!" Jerry exclaimed. "What I've been searching for all my life. A girl who can name the editor of a distinguished short-story magazine. Will you marry me?"

"I'll go you one better," I said. "I'll make sure everyone I meet reads all your new stories. Thanks to my old folks, we're always up on the new work that's out there."

"And thanks to Whit Burnett," Jerry said, " 'The Young Folks' was my debut story."

I simply had to ask him: "What did you say? I mean, to get Hemingway to have a look at your new story." I had scrolled *The Saturday Evening Post* like a scepter.

"It was his idea," Jerry said.

He had to pause the jeep on the boulevard only scant blocks from the Ritz because a streaming parade of small French schoolchildren were attempting the impossible. Under the wings of three French Catholic nuns in traditional habits that were so Old World my former teachers at St. Rita's were Hollywood starlets by comparison, this long line of urchins did their level best to stay in "single file." The nuns kept calling out again and again with reminders to stay in single file, as the boys in one row and the girls in the row beside them trudged along en route to a day's work. How they managed not to all simply break free and run wild with glee and liberation joy is anybody's guess. Everywhere else it seemed as if all normal, daily protocols were suspended indefinitely. One could scarcely believe that anyone had the power or the control necessary to carry on with a typical school day. But the nuns reigned.

And just when Jerry braked fully and the side-by-side uniformed students (clad in dark colors vis-à-vis their trousers or skirts, but all wearing a clean white shirt or blouse, as if the wartime rations and deprivations had somehow never been), the most glorious sounding solo trombone was heard as a solitary man on a third-floor balcony played the full melody of Tommy Dorsey's famous theme song "I'm Getting Sentimental Over You." I was flabbergasted. Jerry was mesmerized. Whoever that trombone player was really had chops. This was no hobbyist. An amateur musician is always easy to spot. They crack notes like kids crack peanuts. But this man on the balcony that day knew his instrument. That "round sound" that Pop always talked about during our year of clarinet lessons? This guy had it in spades.

It's easy to be mesmerized by the opening melodic line of Tommy Dorsey's theme song. I wasn't surprised to see Jerry look as if all of a sudden he was aloft. That's the way that song hit all of us. And it's no surprise that it served TD so well as the very first musical offering that audiences would hear whenever his band performed: On radio shows or in ballrooms; in the movies he appeared in or when presenting his band on the risers that emerged from underground and rose to stage level at all the legendary theaters where he was a featured star in between the most popular films.

The song always began with solo trombone. And the way Tommy played that horn was unusual. There was nothing typical about TD's musicianship. He made the trombone sound like a choir of angels. He had a band that was stacked with great jazz players. But Tommy wasn't really a jazz master at all. He was a virtuoso on the trombone and ballads were his *forte*. We called him "The Sentimental Gentleman of Swing" for all the apropos musical reasons (even though he was a temperamental maniac in real life; the big music magazines reported about his fits and tantrums).

This tableau overwhelmed me. Nuns in their 19th-century garb leading innocent schoolchildren along the boulevard in an orderly, timely way, as the afternoon sun and the passage of time hinted at the blue of evening. And the man on the balcony played his trombone and perfectly, meticulously played the opening four notes of TD's theme song (it starts with four quarter notes evenly articulated, followed by a shimmering high note that's held for a few beats, until the release that is followed by the remainder of the melodic line). Those opening four notes and the long tone that follows always sounded like a clarion call. A real attention-getter. Just gorgeous.

It was enough to make Jerry look as if he'd swallowed wine and drifted into reverie. But in my case I was flabbergasted because the very sound of TD's theme song thrust me back in time and reminded me of the endless dialogues I shared at work in the very early 1940s, when I was out of high school but not yet in uniform.

We talked about music all the time. Our passion for the big bands defined us. And between all the radio shows, the 78 records (slightly more affordable with a steady income, as small as it was), the newfangled jukeboxes that sprang up all over, and of course the live appearances and movie spots, the great bands to many of us were as hot a topic as the best sports teams were to others. We compared them all the time.

And there's no avoiding the fact that I was flabbergasted by the intimate and private and all too predictable reaction I had to hearing that superlative trombone player on a Paris balcony play so perfectly the yearning, sensuous, caressing notes of Tommy Dorsey's famous theme song. Because it brought back in a torrid rush all of the many feelings of excitement, anxiety, hoping, confusion, pulsing, and basic desire that percolated in us when we danced the way we did to both of the Dorsey bands.

I don't mean all the athletic, acrobatic, show-off maneuvers that the hotshot Lindy Hoppers or world-class jitterbug dancers engaged in. They were like superstars. But most of us didn't have such flamboyant, high-energy, wildly choreographed feats to display. Don't get me wrong, though. We had something else going on.

That's why I used to get into the most unexpectedly intimate conversations with some of the girls at college (the first time I tried college, that is) and also at work, when the switchboards calmed down and we could talk a bit. Whenever music was on our minds and we compared bands, and I'm sure this was throughout 1940 and 1941 and certainly some of 1942, again and again, time after time, we ended up in whispers because speaking about the effects on the dance floor when either one of the Dorsey bands got going was pretty much like reading your diary aloud to friends.

The thing was like this: All of the jazzy, fast, loud instrumentals aside, what really had us all hot and bothered was the way our bodies touched when we danced.

Slow dancing.

That's what turned us on. And believe you me, we used that expression long before all the Woodstockers caught up with such a notion later in the 1960s. Slow dancing not only turned us on, but often caused the girls I knew to admit to each other: "That's the switch." You couldn't help but feel sexual desire by moving that way.

And within the space of fifteen seconds or so, as the dignified looking man alone on that Paris balcony played a fine solo trombone rendition of Tommy Dorsey's theme song (and played it with such incremental precision and instrumental grace that it reminded me of how I always thought "I'm Getting Sentimental Over You" ought to be titled "Seven Steps to Heaven," except that some other song already had such a title), my mind was filled with the echoes of both Dorsey bands, years earlier, and all the remarks made by the gals when we told each other which band we preferred.

There was Marlee, who worked with me as a switchboard operator at Korvette's downtown (the best day job I ever had after bailing out of nurses training before my second year began). I started that job in the summer of 1941, one year after the fall of France in June of 1940; and though we always had current events on our minds, we were still far from being in the war. Or so we thought. Marleee loved dancing.

"I prefer Jimmy's band," she explained to me once. "Because of the big changes in the way the music makes us move, all in the same song. That Latin flavor is really what I adore, but then his singer goes into ballad or swing stuff, and always at the end the whole band really kicks it out. It's like a three-act opera or something."

I knew what she meant. We all knew. That was the signature of Jimmy Dorsey and his band. Not just the soaring sound of his alto saxophone or the clarinet playing that he was masterly at, but something else. Jimmy's batch of all-time greatest hits was dominated by that formula that worked Marlee up into a fever. She was right. In a three-minute performance like "Green Eyes" or "Amapola" or "Star Eyes" or my own favorite, which was "Tangerine," the music was arranged in varied ways. That's why our dancing changed three times as the record played (if we were dancing at a house party) or if you were lucky enough to go out and see and hear and dance to the band in a ballroom or at a theater show.

There was a big-time Latin craze going on in those days, and now you hardly ever hear about Xavier Cugat or Carmen Miranda, but with a lot of help from Hollywood and Decca Records (good grief, I can't remember where I put my glasses, but I can clearly recall the labels like Decca and RCA and Columbia, and which band was on what label) they imported a boatload of South American and Cuban music and Jimmy Dorsey picked up on that in a great big way. His most famous records were the ones that started with a distinct Latin style. "And that makes us move in a way that's totally different," Marleee admitted. "My guy and me, we just start bumping more and more, and at the same time we're looking at each other and . . . *you know*."

Of *course* I knew. I'd seen it at the Aragon Ballroom, where I went more than once to see the different Dorsey bands between 1940 and 1943. And it was something.

So much was packed into one arrangement that if you went along and flowed with the way the song was performed, it was like a litmus test for having the hots. Come *on*! When you're dancing in our old-fashioned style, you're not just cheek to cheek. We were chest to breasts. Belly to belly. Privates to privates (let's not mince words here: a lot of radiators were overheating when all our groins were in such proximity, and, unless you were at a Catholic school dance, there was no interference from any chaperones, proctors, parents or nuns about "keeping the Holy Ghost between you" and those rules about having a space of one foot between dancers at all times).

"It's de*licious* how it all makes me feel," Marlee confided. "We move this way and that way, with our hips going side to side and all around during the Latin part of the song; and then we wrap our arms around each other and slow Fox Trot while the singers do their part." Her face used to blush a little when she added: "And if we end with a jitterbug kind of spirited finale, phew! We're squeezing hands like our lives depended on it or something. Those different moves are like passionate *prac*tice."

Of course everyone was dressed and often dressed up and that's what fooled so many people. There were plenty of preachers and teachers and Father Coughlin types who *hated* our music. And they hated how the white bands tried to adopt all they could from the black bands. And they hated the dancing when it was sexy and full of high energy. But everyone was wearing dresses and suits or sport coats, with dress shirts and nice ties and proper shoes. That camouflaged a whole hell of a lot.

"I think Tommy Dorsey knows exactly what he's doing," Barbara Corkery once said to me. She was a classmate of mine when I tried nurses training after high school. I left that after only one year. Just didn't have the brains required for those courses. But I made some real friends. And Barbara's theory was that this thing Tommy was famous for was a calculated stunt. "Think about it," Barbara once explained. "With all the other bands, when they perform a ballad for slow dancing, they give it a go and if you're lucky they play the whole song and for a few minutes— it's all lovely."

That was true. Usually a ballad was performed in between a medium-tempo song or two, then the ballad, followed by a fast one for complete contrast. Except with Tommy.

The thing was, Tommy Dorsey made a whole format out of playing at least three and sometimes four and even up to five ballads in a row. Not cut-rate short versions all crammed together in a medley. I mean the whole song. Which then guaranteed us that when ballad after ballad was fully presented (each slow song highlighted by TD's trombone playing and Frankie's singing—no one thought of him as Sinatra in those days; he was Frankie and he belonged to the Tommy Dorsey band—and the sensuous vocals of Jo Stafford and the harmonies of the Pied Pipers), we had a ten-to-twenty minute segment of slow dancing that never flipped into up-tempo swing or anything fast . . . oh, for heaven's sake, of *course* it was all deliberate. No doubt.

Even if your dance partner was a newbie or a potential boyfriend that you were auditioning, there was one revelation after another you could assess in your mind by the way he'd react to so much slow dancing. And for the couples who were really truly couples and wanted any excuse to press their bodies together, those lengthy sequences of ballads that TD's band specialized in were a godsend. You see, they weren't full of mixed tempos like the "Something Old, Something New, Something Borrowed, Something Blue" medleys that Glenn Miller arranged. Not at all like that (where the songs were cut so short and given only one or two choruses before the next one). If you think about it, the intention was obvious. Tommy Dorsey did all that because he knew what we knew and we knew what everyone knows: All that embracing and all the caressing, rubbing, squeezing, holding, and other dance moves add up to sex.

I don't mean that it automatically led to sex in a bedroom. It *was* sex, on its own.

"It's like sex with clothes on," Barbara once said. "Even better than what I've been through with*out* my clothes." She looked sheepish, but she was onto something. I knew exactly what she was getting at. And Jerry certainly had the same notion.

Years later, in his most famous book (and I doubt any work was ever as famously misunderstood as Jerry's one and only novel), poor Holden spoke for a generation of males who were bewitched, bothered, and bewildered by female anatomy, when he said all that about not even knowing what the hell he was looking for down there.

I think my tape's about to—

21

The thing about me is that I always preferred up here to down there. It's just the way it was for me. And when the man on the balcony did his thing with that gold trombone of his—and I couldn't help but wonder: Is he playing that song as a sort of lamentation? And for anyone in particular or everyone in general? Was he playing such a somber melody for the Allied dead or the occupied French? The citizens by the hundreds of thousands forcibly sent to labor in Germany? The members of the Resistance and their many risks and monumental losses? A collapsed world?—the power of music and its effect on me exerted its usual bodily impact. I firmed up.

That's the way it always was for me. Excitement about music I loved usually made my chest heave a bit and my nipples firmed up and sometimes they got really hard. It wasn't unique to me. More than once, whether I was talking with Marlee or Barbara or any other gal-pal I knew all those years ago, the consensus was that we all preferred the two-piece outfits with skirts topped off by a woman's version of a suit coat. That was better than anything else because the suit coat (no matter how much it opened up at the top) covered our breasts with material so textured that no matter how thick and juicy and hard and excited we might be when our nipples firmed up in reaction to dancing or just the music itself, we weren't worried about being seen.

Maybe that sounds idiotic or ridiculous in this new era of total abandon. Even here with some of the staff members, there are boobs spilling out and falling all over like cantaloupes on display at the Farmers' market. And of course it's due to the low-cut tops and the total disregard for modesty in any form. What're you gonna do?

The best thing, though, was that it was all to our advantage. When you were dancing in close embrace with a guy you really liked, it felt secretly sweet and truly exciting to realize that your body was so at ease with so-and-so that between the music in the air and the slow dancing chemistry and the closeness of your bodies and the sense that things were *right* . . . well, to know that he could not see or even feel the hardness of my nipples (those suit coats we wore were as warm and protective as our regulation Army uniforms) allowed me to glory in my sensuality, the desire, the Eros. But it was not right-away mandatory to suddenly let *him* be aware of that.

All that flashed through my mind as the jeep rounded yet another corner and the evanescent sounds of the solo trombone player dissolved like wisps of smoke in the air. Although the first bodily reaction I'd had to his solitary musical serenade was to feel that throb and the slightest bit of moistness down there, the bulging nipples I'd quickly acquired beneath the armor of my uniform gave the game away to me. For the first time in eons, I gloried in my body and loved the yearning and longed to be touched. I was extra sensitive up there. And usually that's what led to trouble.

It just never seemed to the few guys I'd necked with that anything really mattered up there. Except for a half-dozen hurried squeezes on each breast (usually too damn hard and much too fast), my limited forays back then into anything intimate had always been hampered by the stupid notions about everything down below. There was such a rush to shove their hands below the waist, or to slip their fingers inside the pantywaist or worst of all just to start jabbing and stabbing with fingers between our legs, getting all hot and hyper with what I always called a rutting sense of barnyard etiquette, well, it was about as sexy as a pissing toad when the guys took the lead.

At least with me. That's why it helped that our clothes allowed us to be discreet. It was astounding to me just to feel at home in my body, all warm and fine and mellow, especially if the excitement built up while slow dancing. And when I did go out once to see and hear Tommy Dorsey's band and experienced that habit of his of creating a long, long segment of four or five ballads in a row, it was heavenly to me. The guy I was with that night was a real sweetheart, and my body reacted astutely.

Not only were my nipples hard as marbles under my outfit, but, my body heat just naturally spiked and if we could have danced like that for a month, I'd've been fine.

But of course it was pretty much ruined later, in his car. He had a flask. And we were no longer dancing. And the music on the radio was too fast and always being disrupted by the yakety-yak of those damned announcers (we used to call their high-speed chatter exactly what it was: "tobacco barking" and that's because it was usually the cigarette sponsor of the show whose product they never shut up about, just hawking and huckstering over and over—like carnival barkers—for Camel or Old Gold or Raleigh). The midnight radio jive to the side, though, what really made even a sweetheart like that guy turn into a bore, a boor, and a boar (my students in later years used to enjoy how I made that one my primary example of homonyms) was, of course, the goddamned flask. Booze made even the nice guys nuts. Truly.

And I swear that one of the reasons that we gals loved to dance-dance-dance and for hours just stay put on the dance floor was that while we were dancing, the guys weren't able to elbow-bend and gas up on booze. That was the pattern. Once we'd arrived at a place like the Aragon Ballroom or the Willowbrook in Chicagoland (and doubtless it was the same at all the more famous spots: the Roseland, the Savoy, the Meadowbrook, the Palladium, the Casino Gardens, and all the others we heard about from the radio shows that were broadcast out East or out West), the usual thing was not to sit down like they did in nightclubs like the Copacabana or the Stork Club, and just sit-sit-sit and drink-drink-drink. Instead, we danced for hours.

Even now, I'm kind of amazed at our stamina and focus. But the trade-off was simple. The guys got to keep their hands on us as we danced, and for us gals it was always acknowledged that they were a lot more well-behaved when dancing kept them moving and occupied. Away from the booze. There were always bars around and you could order drinks at any of the ballrooms, but the dancing was *really* the main event and sad to say but important to admit: That's when the guys were nicer.

As Jerry shut off the jeep, after pulling on the clutch and taking a deep breath that was followed by an enormous sigh, I deliberately shook my head (just a bit, but fast, from side to side), and ejected from my mind the sour memory of the way that the guy I thought of as a real sweetheart had done what the others had tried: namely, to squeeze my tits like two softballs and then get my skirt off. It all ended with a fight.

I forced myself to put my mind on our return to the Ritz Hotel. We were there.

"Sorry to be so preoccupied," Jerry said. "I'm lost in thoughts over here."

"Fear not," I replied. "My head is spinning over here too." We entered the Ritz.

As we crossed the threshold into the otherworldly calm and ornate elegance of the most ridiculously privileged milieu we could enter (with the exception of Versailles), I handed Jerry the copy of *The Saturday Evening Post* sent to me by ol' Mom.

"This is it," Jerry said.

"I guess so," I whispered: "Now's the time."

Yes, indeed . . .

22

Their ribald hollering and raucous voices and the overlapping insights, insults, accusations, challenges, and other nonsense made it clear that while we'd been gone, the whole crowd surrounding Hemingway in the old bar at the Ritz had sopped up gallons of champagne, cognac, and Scotch.

You could tell right off the bat that everyone had tied one on. They were bombed. And it seemed like a downright relief to Hemingway to receive the copy of the *Post* that Jerry handed to him; and to excuse himself. "I'll read this in my room right now," he said. And as he rose to exit the table, all the others looked crestfallen.

The focus on Papa and the hunger for his attention was palpable; and it was even sort of pathetic. Like it or not, he was the red-hot center. And in our absence, it was easy to assume that all the weird undercurrents of competition, fawning attention, patronizing praise and sexual jealousy collided. No sooner had Hemingway risen from his chair (slowly, holding the magazine with Jerry's new story in it, and for a moment appearing to be unsteady; he wobbled just the slightest bit, but it reminded me of how Pop sometimes had to steady himself if he'd had a few too many and so the moment was all too familiar to me), when the boisterous others made noises.

They were half-kidding as they booed and feigned their theatrical chagrin, but then the gregariously loud and nearly bug-eyed curly-haired one started to riff in a way that was interesting to me but also awkward as can be. It was Irwin Shaw acting up and his goal (no need for Sherlock Holmes to solve this) was baiting Hemingway.

"Another disciple in the making? Will this kid be your next wife, Papa?"

That's how drunk they were. In those days, homosexual jokes –or what most people called "fag jokes"—usually didn't burst forth until all the vats were loaded and booze liberated the idiocies within. I could see that no one thought Irwin's crack was all that funny. It flopped on too many levels. First, it drew unwanted attention to the reason that Hemingway was leaving the party. Second, when Jerry twitched as Hemingway used the rolled-up copy of the *Post* to smack Irwin Shaw on one of his broad shoulders, the feeling wasn't fun. It was a bit sour. "At least I'm capable of cultivating disciples, Mr. Shaw. If you're lucky, someday you'll do the same. But I have my doubts, junior."

And, right then and there, a look of open hostility flashed across Irwin Shaw's no-longer-jovial face. Which made the look on Mary Welsh's face even more awkward. She'd been sitting right in between the two men, and both of the guys were vying for her attention like boys at a prom mutually swooning over the prettiest girl in the room. But it lacked that kind of innocence. They were snarling at each other, with phony smiles on display. "Time is all I need," Shaw said. "And yours might be up."

Holy Moses, believe you me, *that* zinger went over like shit on toast. Hemingway shot a glance at Mary Welsh, and he caught her staring with star eyes at Irwin Shaw. She and Hemingway had been circling around each other for the shortest time, but they were all in heat (despite being married to others) and at the same time she was doubtless enjoying Irwin's crush on her. My eyes could scarcely take in all the varied signals, cues, hints, and non-verbal fury. Soap opera!

That's when Jerry piped in with his own put-down and it was directed right at Irwin Shaw: "Any chance you'll ever get a first novel done?" Jerry inquired. Sardonically. And as he pointed at Hemingway, Jerry added: "His wife has published two already."

Ouch! That couldn't mean all that much to the tanked-up Maquis hanging out with Hemingway at that time, and even I had to mentally calculate in a jiffy to figure out the depth of that insult. But insult it was. It was a quip that cut to the quick, all across the board. Jerry had needled Irwin most of all, but also Mary Welsh right there. And this was before all of that "Miss Mary" *LIFE* Magazine PR years later.

"So she did," Irwin weakly replied, "but who read them. Did *you*?"

Hemingway knew what he meant by that, and said: "The work was done and her books are out there, for all the world to see. Maybe someday they'll get their due. Meantime, fuck off." Everybody was so drunk that they exploded with guffaws. But just as there's a spooky silence after anything from firecrackers to artillery fire going off, there was then an immediate and discomforting silence. Dead air time. A really heavy sag in the room. Briefly.

"I read them," I said. "Both of them. And Martha's two novels are worth rereading."
"On a first-name basis, are we?" That was how Mary Welsh knocked me down a peg. But I didn't care. I really had read and I truly admired Martha Gellhorn's two novels.

She published more and more (of everything) in the many decades that she lived after the war. But no matter what, she was always pigeonholed and usually referred to as "Hemingway's third wife." And as former wife Number Three, her own work and her own identity were terribly discounted. A real shame. She was a trailblazer.

"Give her the credit she earned," I said, looking at Mary Welsh and Irwin, one after the other. "Her articles about the Spanish Civil War probably educated millions of Americans. And when that first novel of hers came out in 1940, I know that folks like my parents and several people I worked with considered it a revelation."

That sounds overblown, but it was true. Martha Gellhorn had made her way out of Spain after 1937 and into Prague later in 1938. She was in Czechoslovakia right on time for its October collapse, shortly after Chamberlain and the others sold out the world with the Munich Pact that October. Martha didn't read all about it or visit briefly as a correspondent. She lived there. And took it all in. Living there as she did for many months on end allowed her to witness the horrendous suddenness of the Gestapo's takeover there. Somehow, while still pounding out reams of articles, Martha Gellhorn also wrote her debut novel and it dovetailed with the history in the making, right in our time. She called it *A Stricken Field* and the gist of the novel was the main character's dangerous ways of allying herself with refugees and others who were on the run, day in and day out, being hunted by the Nazis and their spies.

I recalled how moved and provoked my parents were by that novel in 1940. But of course it was all overshadowed by the massive success of *For Whom the Bell Tolls*.

As Hemingway excused himself from the crowd of sloshed companions in the bar at the Ritz, he looked directly at me and asked: "Did you read her second one? Gellhorn's?"

I nodded. Vigorously. Martha Gellhorn's second novel was then almost brand new. God only knows how she found the time to write that one, while also dispatching her wartime correspondence from here, there, and everywhere. Its title was *Liana* and it broke new ground. There were scant few novels about interracial romances. And there was nothing *Guess Who's Coming to Dinner*-ish about *Liana*.

"I liked it very much," I said. Hemingway squeezed my shoulder and walked away.

Jerry and I declined invitations to sit and drink with the others. We went to the main lobby at the Ritz, wondering what to do for the hour that Hemingway said he'd need to look "truly" at Jerry's new story in the *Post*.

"Tell me about *Liana*," he suggested.

"Forget Martha," I said. "But brace yourself. I think Irwin's making one of his eighty-yard runs and this time it's to take a poke at you." Irwin Shaw was huffing and puffing. He'd found us in the lobby and was still smarting from Jerry's remark.

"For a kid with a few published stories in the slicks, you've got a big mouth," Irwin said. And that was another shot to the head. The "slicks" were the magazines that were popular and printed on a kind of, well, slick and almost shiny paper. But, for writers, more was at stake. What was really being said was that Jerry had not been published in *The New Yorker*. That's the real deal. It was the Holy Grail for all the writers to appear in *The New Yorker* and Shaw had become one of their stars.

"Am I wrong or am I right?" Irwin demanded to know. As if. He was full of zest and brio and male dynamite in his writing (and his personality), but he was also drunk. So I should not have been surprised that his competitive furies swirled about Jerry. And though it wasn't just about being writers, that's what Irwin hammered at.

"A couple of stories in *Story*, a nice *Esquire* debut, and now *The Saturday Evening Post*. Oh, boy! Have you had any plays produced? Funny. I never saw *that* one. Have you written any scripts for Hollywood or radio? Must have slipped me. But then you mouth off about who the hell has a novel on the way! What about you?"

It was the most peculiar thing. Normally writer-guys love to bitch and moan and compare sales. What they're doing of course is in lieu of unzipping and comparing. But despite Irwin's slew of provocative questions, Jerry just pointed at the vase full of lilacs on the nearby table. And smiled. The fresh-cut lilacs smelled beautiful. At that moment, I could not get over the ways in which the two of them differed. Sure, both were rising stars and Shaw had already breached *The New Yorker's* parapets.

But in every other way, at least as far as I saw, they were a pair of opposites.

I sat there in a royally upholstered old chair in the comely lobby of the Ritz, my sense of smell repeatedly piqued by the efflorescence of the lilacs in a becoming vase on the table beside me, witnessing those guys convert the lobby into their private demesne. It was no longer a hotel lobby. It was an arena for male egos.

But clearly there'd be no real fighting. Nothing physical, I mean. You could just tell that Shaw was full of bluster (the booze was at work) and Jerry was detached. That was all the more reason for me to note their contrasts. Shaw was short, with really broad shoulders. Husky. Squat. A football player's build. Jerry was extra-tall. Slim. Wiry. Like he belonged on a basketball court. Shaw's hair was thick and curly. The straight dark hair on Jerry just lay down and stayed there. Both were in uniform. But in Irwin's case, his Signal Corps identity signified that he was behind cameras. In Jerry's case, his 4th Infantry Division patch spoke for itself. He was steeped in the war. The guys in the Signal Corps were in it to record it. Not so for Jerry's guys.

Out of the bar and into the lobby then came Mary Welsh. Looking for Hemingway. She was also high on more than a few of the dozens of Martinis that Hemingway had ordered for all those hours that they spent in the bar. I'm not kidding at all. Legend has it that upon arriving with his raggedy band of hangers-on, plus a loyal cadre of Maquis fighters (they were mostly rural guerrillas who fought the Nazis on their own terms), and, eventually, all the others, not only was Ernest greeted as a long-lost friend by the Ritz's lifelong manager, who remembered young Hemingway well from the 1920s, but he was asked one question. What would he like? "Eighty-one Martinis," Papa said. He was serious.

That's that. His mystique prevailed. Everyone around him was in his aura. And all day long those dozens of Martinis fueled libidos from left to right. Now Mary Welsh had her eyes on Shaw, and ol' Irwin didn't have Hemingway's glare to contend with.

Clearly she was attracted to Shaw. But back in the bar, it was brazenly clear that Hemingway had star eyes for her. And of course all three were married to others.

But instead of chiming in with a trivial question or a dumb provocation on the fly (as a *Time* magazine correspondent, Mary Welsh had a healthy ego of her own), a question was popped that shifted the focus. She directed her question to Irwin.

"What's the scoop on tomorrow's parade? We haven't heard about the time."

"When they get here," Shaw replied. "They're sleeping outside tonight. Nearby. They're bivouacked in the Bois de Boulogne."

It took a while to sort things out, but "they" were the 28th Infantry Division. A decision had been arrived at to parade the 28th ID straight through Paris on the following day. There had been a lot of uncertainty about whether or not General Eisenhower would release a Division to participate in the Liberation parades. In the end, to make a massive show of support for de Gaulle and to further tamp down the threat of the infighting and political chaos all knew would ensue if the Communist party succeeded at taking charge of the new French government, Ike cut the order.

And that's how I ended up standing with Jerry beside me, when the most beautiful sight in the Western world was to see the GIs of the 28th Infantry Division of the U. S. Army, marching as though representing the sword of St. Michael, moving in untold numbers of massively choreographed units (companies, battalions, and regiments) and doing so down the Champs-Élysées, witb the Arc de Triomphe in the background, erasing the footprints of the Germans who'd marched there daily (with their military bands blaring away) for the four long years of the dreadful occupation.

But all that was the next day. In the lobby of the Hotel Ritz, we sat and smoked.

Waiting. Still waiting . . .

23

Jesus H. Christ and 23 skidoo, without my *Mad Men* what'll I do? Crazy but true: Here I am, personifying the bluntness of Faulkner's title *As I Lay Dying*, and all I can think about is how the finale of *Mad Men* last night seems like another nail in my you know what. The TV news covered it aplenty and I've seen reminders left and right about the last episode and the marathon rerunning of the whole series (all 91 of the prior episodes!) over the days and nights leading up to the Sunday night conclusion.

And, now, today is Monday. I've asked a few of the staff members (over the past weekend, in particular) if they were excited about seeing the final episode of *Mad Men*. Wasted words. Most had never looked at the show. Not even once. Except Beansy, of course, who used to watch because "I want to be like Joan," she says.

Don't we all? But good grief, I didn't realize what a tiny audience that show had. I lived for it for all those seasons. For lots of reasons. Right now, the thing that keeps going through my mind is all about the smoking and the drinking we indulged in.

Just thinking about that interlude in the lobby of the Hotel Ritz, as we awaited the return of Hemingway and his verdict, I swear I can still smell the Chesterfields. We all smoked in those days the way they did on *Mad Men*, and the sour truth is that on more than a million occasions, I'm sure, every damn one of us wanted to cut it out. I cannot believe how we went on not just for years, but, for many decades, doing that.

Believe you me, the war had everything to do with creating in us a generation of chain-smoking coughers. Hollywood certainly did its part. And the advertising biz so perfectly recapitulated during the seven seasons of *Mad Men* stirred the witches' brew more than anything else. And yet, all along the way, even as we smoked more and more and fired up carton after carton by the ton, we all knew it made us sick.

I'm not kidding at all. How the hell could we *not* know? The awful smell and the wretched taste and the need to pick tobacco flakes off of our tongues, at least until later on when the crooks making their fortunes off tobacco realized that filtered cigarettes aimed at "the ladies" would eliminate that sloppy and indelicate problem.

No wonder filtered cigarettes caught on like wildfire. They got rid of the tobacco-flake grossness and also promised "smoother" and "better tasting" smoking bliss. It was all crap all the time, of course. We got hooked. And our thinking that it looked sophisticated and hip and Hollywood and all, well, it's just what we bought for every stupid reason that we conned ourselves into. Nervous or tense? Have a cigarette. Just waking up? Light up with that first cup of coffee. Lacking energy? Smoke away.

I remember ol' Mom telling me that when Pop came back from World War One, a woman on the downtown streets of Chicago (even in a major city) would likely be arrested if she smoked in public. That was in 1919! Ten years later, thanks to the roar of the Twenties, and certainly by the end of the 1930s (courtesy of Hollywood), women and men smoking together had been popularized, glamorized, and patented as a mating ritual for a whole new generation. My generation. We bought it all. And by the time the war was in full gear, our smoking and boozing all went hand in hand.

Which is why Jerry surprised me yet again. He puffed away and sparked up again and crushed out one cigarette after another, out there in that lobby at the Ritz, as did just about everyone else. Looking back, I see more than ever that the old Army riff about "Hurry up and wait" had much to do with how often we just sat and smoked.

Somehow, though, he was unaffected by the pressure to drink. Nobody then used the expression "peer pressure," but it was in the air when it came to boozing up. I can't get over how typical it was to hear "Let's have a drink" or "Another drink?"

And all that added up to nothing but trouble, more than half the time.

But the same malarkey about being grown-ups who of course aspired to sophistication made the drinking and the smoking a double act. Combined rituals. We were so snookered.

Needless to say, we simply got so used to it that we didn't realize how we stunk. And I mean *really* stunk. Stink-stank-stunk. Our clothes were ruined by tobacco's stench. And cheap booze or basic beer, most of all, made our mouths cesspools. At the time, though, the thing we did was smoke more and quaff by the quart. That's *every*where, by the way. You could smoke in a hospital room until way later in the 1980s and the chronic puffing and sloshing on *Mad Men* accurately represented us.

But no movie or TV show could ever get across the awful smell of it all. No wonder it could be pitched as classy and sophisticated. The fetid ghastliness went missing, unless you were standing or sitting in the middle of it. But it could not be avoided.

I was no angel. For the longest time—even though my own coughing or my own awareness of the way it stank—I couldn't even imagine not smoking all of my life.

But now and then, an epiphany would strike. One did when Hemingway returned.

I could smell him as he lumbered across the lobby of the Ritz. And lumber he did do. I felt sad. He seemed to be straining. Only in his mid-40s, he looked exhausted.

But at least he could do that much. Lumbering, I mean. Yet he seemed sluggish, heavy-footed, and definitely overweight. He looked bloated, if you know what I mean. Though he could still carry himself. And given what I've learned in the past thirty years, that means everything. Or it means *al*most everything. Who am I kidding? The biggest lesson of this illness for me is not that every separate case of MS is different. It's that no matter what losses result from the progression of the illness (and my case has been dubbed "extreme" by the doctors, who otherwise have little to say, knowing that when it comes to multiple sclerosis they know next to nothing), the end result is the same: Piece by piece, phase after phase, one limb at a time and so incrementally that it's like watching clouds dissolve while sitting on a hilltop . . . but in the end the paralysis wins and yet I'm reminded always: We are *not* our bodies. I'm quadriplegic now, but my body isn't *me*. Not the *essence* of me. Ego be damned, we're not our bodies.

We *think* we are. All of our lives. For as long as I can remember, I was told and I was taught and certainly I always thought and felt that the ultimate key issue to life was the full functioning of a healthy body. We never got that memo on what to do or how to think or what to say when the body betrays us. But that's how I have learned what untold others apprehended elsewhere: We are *not* our bodies. Consciousness thrives, even as it's harbored in this defunct physique of mine. As Beansy likes to say: "From the neck up, you're all-in. From the neck down, your body's checked out."

Still. Until this happened to me over the course of 30 years, I'd've never-ever once believed that I'd ever say that we are not our bodies. But *ever*ything's been revised.

Anyway, like I was saying, after the better part of an hour in that smoke-filled lobby at the Ritz in Paris, as the non-stop celebrations continued all throughout the City of Light and before Jerry and Irwin ended up bickering even more, Hemingway came back down from his room and I watched him as he lumbered in our direction.

That's when I realized that not only was he carrying way too much weight on his frame, but also that his crimson face had to be the result of skyrocketing blood pressure that had to be exacerbated by not just all that fat he'd packed on, but also the two-fisted boozing he soaked himself in. And he was soaked. But not just due to the two canteens that hung from his web belt, one full of cognac and the other full of brandy. His weight and everything else (his blood pressure must have been off the charts) made him not just perspire, but sweat like a pudding at a June picnic. And in the middle of August or especially at the end of August, with nothing like the usual air conditioning that Americans are used to (even then, when AC was scarce, we all knew that if we escaped to the theater to watch movies all day—for a quarter!—we'd be cooled for the duration, and sometimes we'd watch the same film three or four times just to wait until after dark when the heat finally abated), to say the least, Paris was a broiler. Add it all up and there you go: It was already hotter than at any other time of year and no air conditioning was the norm in Paris and Hemingway's sweating like that really resulted from a combination of his poundage, his blood pressure, days on end of overly excited and highly stressed circumstances, plus his hypersensitivity to the spectacle happening all around him and God only knows the degree to which his inner life was being affected by all of that. We all knew he was by then in his mid-forties. The math was easy. His works imprinted it on everyone's memory. Young Hemingway had been eighteen or nineteen when he was wounded in the First War back in 1918. So, in 1944, he had to be going on forty-five.

That's why I wasn't surprised to see how much grey was in that scruffy beard he'd grown out. It was way more salt than pepper. But the old man wore it with a regal sense of self. No doubt about that. He knew he was then the champ. He *knew* it.

And he also knew that Jerry's new work had proved yet again that there was a new guy in town, so to speak. Jerry had gone back into the bar to use the men's room tucked away in there, and Hemingway's eyes darted all over the lobby for a few seconds before he addressed me: "Any idea where he is?"

I nodded and said: "He'll be right out." That seemed like the thing to say. Irwin had a different idea (again, the alcohol) and quipped: "Nervous in the service? Gone to the head to jerk it off while he can? Maybe you're making the kid scared, Papa."

For the second time, with effortless power and precise accuracy, Hemingway rolled up *The Saturday Evening Post* into a tightly scrolled baton and whacked Shaw right on the shoulder, saying: "Nothing to be scared of. Jesus, he has a hell of a talent."

Jerry returned. Irwin Shaw shut up. Mary Welsh dragged on her Old Gold cigarette and kept eyeballing both Shaw and Hemingway. Measuring each man. My sense of it was that Jerry would have preferred to speak privately with the old man. But like everything else that happened in that surreal episode of August 1944, it all unfolded with no one having the ability to do more than witness all the mystery. It was beyond surreal, all of the time. Three months earlier, the Normandy landings were still being delayed and brooded over. Only one year earlier, the speedy liberation of Sicily had yet to lead to the Allied landings at Salerno, Italy, which soon enough became one of the most doggedly frustrating, bloody campaigns of the war.

Now all of a sudden Paris was free. Not organized. Still dangerous. That's the other thing that never gets across: before, during, and after the Liberation Days in Paris in August 1944, there were relentless bursts of small arms fire from hibernating Nazi snipers; endless explosions as pockets of fighting continued between the retreating Germans and the advancing Allies; truly a miracle that most of the city was spared by that general's decision to ignore Hitler's mandate to leave Paris burning, but, still, even as the series of parades unfolded, folks were wounded and panic erupted each time grenades exploded or machine guns opened fire, which happened a lot. For us, though, the respite at the Hotel Ritz was like visiting another world. Another planet. When Hemingway and Jerry were again eye to eye, the old man spoke: "I'd like to keep this," he said, grasping the *Post* like a scepter. "I want to remember you."

24

I shivered. For a moment or two—what I thought was a moment or two—I looked downward and quietly repeated in the privacy of my mind what Hemingway had said about Jerry ("He has a hell of a talent") and then, what he said right to him: "I want to remember you." It became the mantra by which I lived.

Wanting to remember. Not straining to, either. Just recognizing that within my mind the natural pattern leans toward remembering. For others, it is forgetting.

I thought only a moment or two had passed but perhaps it was longer. All I know is that by the time I again looked up and around, both Mary Welsh and Irwin Shaw had gone. Maybe they'd retuned to the bar. Maybe they went outside to witness more of the non-stop fiesta-like liberation celebrations that were sure to go on all night.

It wasn't yet dark. Not exactly. But the early evening light was already affecting the interiors of the Ritz. The light was subdued. The lobby oddly quiet. And Jerry and Hemingway were not standing there. They were sitting. Maybe fifty feet away or so. That's when I realized that I'd really drifted with my mental flight as I committed to memory the old man's words: "I want to remember you." It must have been when I stared at my feet and committed those words to memory that the others dispersed.

Chances are, Irwin was annoyed by the affirmation Hemingway had offered to Jerry. All those guys were so competitive, so gladiator-like about writing. Good grief, it had to be exhausting. But that's the way they were. Somehow, though, Hemingway sensed that Jerry was cut from another cloth. No doubt he was as competitive as can be in some ways. That fixation he had on leaving "the slicks" behind and publishing in *The*

New Yorker, exclusively, wasn't derived from modesty. But, nonetheless, he had something going on that differed from the guys whose writing was their substitute for boxing.

I could see this clearly, even then. Because when I focused again and truly observed the two of them—older Hemingway and young Jerry—conversing on the edge of an antique couch that was off in a corner of the Ritz lobby, there was no posturing of any kind. No stances. No hierarchy. What we later on began to call "body language" told me plenty, even though we didn't yet use that expression. But I could see it all.

"Jesus, he has a hell of a talent," the old man had said. Asking to keep my copy of the *Post* was yet another way of saying that. It didn't even bother me at the time that my copy of the *Post* had just been claimed for the duration. I was happy to let it go.

And I was more than happy when I saw the way that Hemingway tapped Jerry on his shoulder with the rolled-up copy of the *Post*. Earlier, when he'd scrolled up the *Post* and used it to smack Irwin Shaw (not once but twice) on the shoulders, the old man made it clear that Irwin's high-energy, verbose persona was grating on him. Which is funny, because Shaw was indeed very charming and witty and bright, but boozed up and all he came on too strong. Just like Hemingway did, much of the time. That's a fact. Most of the time, once he stoked himself with his brandy and cognac, then his Martinis (with a patented recipe that'd destroy brain cells fast, even if you were used to drinking), there's no getting around it, most of the time Hemingway carried on very much like Irwin had. Challenging. Pugnacious. Having to be champ.

Nobody needed Freud to explain that Irwin had actually modeled himself on the old man. Innumerable writers would do that.

But something there was about Jerry . . . something rare. Instead of being smacked by the old man, Jerry was knighted. The way Hemingway tapped his shoulder with the scrolled magazine *was* a benediction.

And the way that they simultaneously looked over at me was a surprise. But they did. The others were gone. I was still there. Hemingway and

Jerry beckoned me.

Even though they'd both gestured for me to walk over (Jerry with a single wave of his left hand and Hemingway with a nod and a smile), I felt like an intruder. But in less than a minute, I was an honored guest. "You come too," the old man insisted.

Of course the old boy knew what he was saying. Nobody of his vintage would cap off an invitation with the words "You come too" and not be deliberately echoing that line from the Robert Frost poem. No wonder Hemingway had such a twinkle in his eye. But that didn't ameliorate how his newfound hulking overweight appearance also made him sweat and stink. But who cared? Nobody was about to sound off and tell him to take a wash and start over. We were too busy following his directions.

He may have had a towering reputation and a competitive streak as long as the Burma Road, not to mention a sense of command presence to rival any bona-fide general in the Army of the United States, but much to my own surprise Hemingway insisted on sitting in the back seat of Jerry's requisitioned jeep. He ordered me to sit up front on the passenger side and from the rear he gave Jerry specific directions.

His familiarity with Paris was palpable. You could tell how at home he was. Even as the hectic and noisy hurly-burly all around us unfolded (believe you me, for each one hundred yards we drove, there had to be five, six, seven, eight noteworthy sites and specific encounters to see and absorb in rapid fire sequence: some people embraced with joy but only twenty yards further on there was another suspected collaborator or another accused woman being harshly confronted, pulled with vehemence into a seething crowd emanating commotion, fury, and a hunger for vengeance, and wherever you looked all the human drama on the streets was in the vicinity of innumerable historical and architectural wonders, all of which loomed over the impassioned and almost frightening intensity of the liberated Parisians), there sat Hemingway in the jeep's rear seat: He observed it all like a visiting king.

And then we sat for the next few hours in a vast loft to which he'd been invited and where his arrival with two acquaintances unknown to anyone else was never once questioned—instead, we were made to feel most welcome, as the others all cried out: "Papa! You have made it here to enjoy our little effort? A fine welcome to your friends as well!" It hardly mattered to me that I was so unaware of the Who's Who and other issues, because there was *no* question about who had invited Hemingway.

Just a few years after the war, others in that motley collective of theatrical novices would gradually become famous (or at last well-known) and quite tendentious. But as we three sat there like visiting cousins, the well-dressed and seriously business-like rehearsal of theirs proceeded. All the rampant joy and freewheeling mayhem and the violent undercurrent of boiling recriminations throughout greater Paris stopped outside of Picasso's apartment. It was a loft unlike any I'd ever seen.

But even this yokel from the South Side of Chicago recognized *him* immediately.

Thanks largely to the photos of him that'd appeared in *LIFE* or *Time* Magazine, especially at the height of the Spanish Civil War, when his "Guernica" painting illustrated chillingly how the bombing of civilians was a newfound horror unlike any past war crimes, Pablo's Napoleonic stance, barrel chest, shiny pate, and laser-like eyes (which beamed at you like searchlights) were as familiar as a big movie star.

"It's her play." With those few words, Hemingway summed up why we were there.

There were a few ladies that night at Picasso's apartment, but Hemingway looked toward, nodded at, and half-signaled with his meaty left hand in the direction of a particularly well-dressed and seriously intent woman who stood by a mantle atop which there were four or five small original Picasso paintings arrayed in a row. The whole apartment was an admixture of studio, museum, warehouse, repository, and, most of all, boundless creative energy. The air sizzled from the August heat as well as from the colliding spirits, inflamed libidos (liberation was a tonic to everyone's hormones) and sheer artistic brio that made me feel like I was breathing helium. "A group reading of a new play is always a good thing," Hemingway said. "I'm sure it is," Jerry replied: "If you have the right group." Jerry looked morose. Brooding . . .

25

Simone. Herself.

I'm not even sure if Papa knew all that much about her. At that time, I mean. Later on, everyone would know something about her. But Jerry and I were brought along by Hemingway because he'd been invited by Picasso to sit and listen to a reading of a play by someone or another. Well, that someone turned out to be Simone.

From the bits of dialogue and snatches of conversation I was able to put together, it seemed that in the past year or two this cadre of writers and artists had managed to be unmolested by the authorities during the German Occupation, and just a few months earlier Picasso had roped them all in to read aloud and sort of perform for his own amusement— right there in his apartment—a play that he had written. Now a similar workshop reading was underway for a play recently written by Simone.

I'm not sure what was thicker: the omnipresent haze of smoke in the room (pipe smoke emanated from one man's nervous puffing and others fired up one cigarette after another; thick hand-rolled cigarettes that Jerry referred to as "tailor-mades") or the barely contained egos. It was more than a lion's den; it was Minotaur's lair.

Nonetheless, I was struck by her composure. Simone, I mean. She may have been insecure on the inside or secretly worried about what others would think, but to me her self-possession was remarkable. She looked everyone in the eye. And I mean all those guys, no matter their reputation. She wasn't about to be intimidated. No sir.

But still, there was no getting around it. The charismatic overflow of lordly male authority was spilling over between Hemingway and Picasso.

All the other men who were there were definitely in the shadows, so to speak, and seemed a bit smaller. It was therefore even more remarkable that Simone was the one to finally call out and clap twice to gain the attention of one and all. The reading commenced at her cue.

Jerry sat to the right of Hemingway and I opted not to sit at all. That surprised me. But with a limited number of chairs and more than a few others who'd been invited to hear the reading that night, it was easy for me to step away and just take it all in.

It was also easy to admire the primary choice that Simone had made as a writer. Her play was steeped in the distress and deprivations of recent years, yet she set it all centuries earlier in Vaucelles, which is a town in Flanders. But there was no possibility of anyone missing the analogies to the German Occupation. She spoke briefly before the reading began, and said that her play's title, *The Useless Mouths,* required no further explanation. With the chronic hunger that plagued all of Paris and France at large throughout the Occupation, her theme of useless mouths and disposable citizens too old or too weak to work for the invaders was lacerating.

However, none of it seemed cloyingly ripped from the daily newspapers, thanks to her decision to set the scenes back in the 1300s, I think. My memory is fogging up.

But I do recall with certainty (and admiration) that her play was dialogue-driven, as most plays are. Yet it never bogged down due to windy monologues. A play can be so easily weighed down and fast submerged by characters giving speeches. Instead, she had her characters speaking mostly in rapid succession, never spiraling or going off on tangents, and through their quick exchanges her ideas were boldly filtered. Sartre sat there behind his heavy-rimmed glasses, sucking his pipe.

Believe you me, her ideas were blunt. Hunger was her play's main theme. All of the historical background and whatnot created a necessary backdrop, but the dialogues and ideas driving the play's content boiled down to the ravages created by hunger and how its devastating effect on the human spirit made conquest easier for brutes.

Like I was saying, the analogy to Nazi occupation didn't have to be spelled out. That's something else I don't think has ever gotten across. And it still bugs me.

Many years later, when I was patching together my income as an itinerant college instructor (now they're called Adjuncts, but then we were Instructors and that signified everything right off the bat: anyone dubbed an Instructor was thereby known not to have a doctorate and thus no chance of a permanent position; we had to be reviewed annually and sometimes reapply all over again for the same job, even after we'd been on staff for several years), the ignorance on this subject appalled me.

I'd assign a few short stories to my students later on in the Sixties or the Seventies or the Eighties, and the stories were set during the war and to my mind tailor made for opportunities to generate discussions and papers about literature and history.

Ha! What a silly dope I turned out to be. The kids in my college classes ceaselessly reminded me that "it all happened before we were born," and they were downright offended (even furious) when I reminded them that in my less than humble opinion, nothing was less significant than the year that any single one of us was born. They were befuddled by my insistence that everything important came before we did.

And all I needed to do as the years rolled by was keep assigning certain short stories that were set during World War Two, and boy oh boy did I get reminded year in and year out that lousy history classes in elementary and high school (along with all the crap on television), compounded by the idiocies of Hollywood, well, it all added up to creating one generation after another with no clue about what *really* occurred. A million French civilians slave laboring in Germany? Nobody cared.

In the middle or late 1960s, when I asked my students what they thought about how the near starvation of Paris during the German Occupation might have affected the ways in which French morale collapsed, they were mute. And not because the new war in Vietnam consumed their thoughts. I was teaching at that small Catholic college in Chicago, which wasn't even co-ed until later in the 1970s. And the awful truth is that during those years a favorite television show for all those kids was that rotten nonsense "Hogan's Heroes," which made the Nazis into bald, fat, "funny" caricatures.

By that time, of course, Simone was no longer an obscure Paris-based author who surrounded herself with powerful male mentors. By the time I was teaching decades later, her major claim to fame was *The Second Sex*, a gospel and a definite cornerstone for the Women's Movement that emerged out of the 1960s. Even that book was largely unknown to the students in my classes. None of which surprised me. Contrary to all of the myth-makers who have created the delusion that young Americans all across the board were "radicalized" or "transformed" by the 1960s, the truth is that the majority were content to watch TV, marry, and be "traditional."

But as I sat there on that night when Simone's play *The Useless Mouths* had its workshop reading in Picasso's apartment as Liberation Week approached its peak, all those future years and inevitable disappointments were unknown. Which made it even easier to admire the incisive, radiant intelligence permeating Simone's play.

Jerry agreed. He had risen from his chair and wandered over to me in between the play's two acts. Everyone had agreed that a break should be had. Not just to smoke but also to look over pages and retrieve some energy.

"Each line *says* something," Jerry observed, "but every other line also suggests what's *not* being said. Her mind is not just stating a theme, but it's beyond subtle in connecting the past to the present."

That's when it hit me right over the head that what Jerry was noting about Simone's play was pretty much exactly why we'd all admired and sometimes adored those short stories that'd made Hemingway the best of the best, in our time. That subtle and oftentimes seductive restraint. Indirect writing. Allusive flourishes. Leaving *out* what other writers would pile on about. Never opting for saturation. Jerry had it right. Throughout the rehearsal reading of Simone's *Useless Mouths*, which added up to three tableaux in Act One and five tableaux in Act Two, it was discernible to me that a slew of ideas and mighty themes were being articulated between the lines. "Not too much of it is *on the nose*," Jerry concluded. "It really appeals to the ear."

I envied his ability to instantly ascertain why he liked her play. There was plenty of commotion in the studio that night, what with Picasso's swaggering hurly-burly at the center of the whole shebang, and everyone there being inevitably a bit cowed yet also galvanized and magnetized by not just Picasso's self-conscious theatricality but also by the looming presence of Hemingway. Yet, the damnedest thing of all was that, in a funny way, it also felt ridiculously normal. The paradox was beyond me.

And even now, damn near seventy-one years later, the paradox still stumps me. I mean, I'm trying to get this across . . . but I can't. Ob*viously* I've been talking about all this, but nothing I say comes close to even hinting at its dizzying momentousness.

It was then and there, as I stood and listened to the remainder of the rehearsal reading of Simone's play that night at Picasso's studio at 21, Rue La Boetie, right there and then it finally hit me that every little thing about each of our lives in that summer, that year, that ineffable period... it was surreal enough to silence all of us.

That was my hunch. And the oddity was omnipresent: I mean, there I stood in a realm of words, words, and more words . . . but in my gut I had the sense that in the future neither Jerry nor Hemingway would ever find the language required to bring to their pages anything direct or fully evoked about that whole panorama. Which is pretty much how it evolved, years later. After the war. Both of them published important books and their new works were always under the spotlights, but never did either writer ever manage to directly convey or detail in his fiction the sheer immensity of what he had seen between Normandy and the liberation of Paris. All that somehow remained out of reach. Merely hinted at in elusive, indirect ways.

The same with the big parade. The one the following day, I mean. There wasn't a chance that any of us would miss witnessing the march of the 28th Infantry Division down the Champs-Élysées on August 29th,

1944. But by the time it happened, there was such a sense of everything being so beyond category, so outsized, so incredibly unmoored from anything even remotely normal or typical or mundane, that in the end all we could do was be present, see it, and acknowledge the passage of time.

That's all we were able to do in the moment, as such immense moments occurred, and I swear I've been grinding my teeth ever since because that's all we've ever been able to do ever since. Seventy years? No. Now it's seventy-one years. Make that seventy-one fucking years. Good God, *where* did the time go? Where *does* the time go? How could such a majestic episode be reduced to the size of a postage stamp? Literally.

That was accomplished in record time. Only a year later, the famous Army photo of the guys in the 28th Infantry Division boldly striding forward as the Arc de Triomphe stood in the background . . . of *course* it was chosen to be on a Victory Stamp. There was no image more apropos. Yet, it was misleading. It made everything . . . let me put it this way: There were 19,000 French civilians killed by Allied air forces during the relentless bombing runs that occurred before, during, and after D-Day. Whole towns on the Normandy coast were wiped off the map. And long before I had clueless students, what it *really* took to beat Hitler was forgotten.

26

I've said it before and I'll say it again: *Time's up*. I can feel how little time is left. My energy is more diminished than ever. And if not for my beloved Lorena-Rena-Bena-Bean-Beansy's savvy way of making it easier than ever to record all this, I'd've called it quits long ago. But now that amazing girl of mine (Girl! At forty! Why the hell not? She's unmarried and besides, she's the closest thing I've ever had to a daughter . . .), well, she's going way above and beyond the call of duty. Now she visits for a minute each night, at the tail end of Visiting Hours, and she places her tiny micro-cassette recorder on my pillow. Adjacent to my face. It's perfect. The gizmo has a one-hour tape ready to go and it automatically shuts itself off when the tape runs out. It's like magic. I can whisper my words, and it still picks up everything. And then I slumber. I've been talking myself to sleep. And nobody has to push a button or poke anything.

Not that sleeping tonight will be easy. Too many major anniversaries.

It's been going on for days now. Even for an old-time news junkie like me, it's too much. Now it's Saturday night. I can try to sort things out a bit. Today is (or maybe I should say "today was") June 6, 2015. You know what that means. Anytime I was on my side (either for my weekly bath or just to get off my back and my butt) there they were again: the images on CNN and the news reports on France 24 and Sky News of course, rerunning and recapitulating pretty much the same images and all about this being the 71st anniversary of the D-Day landings at Normandy back on June 6, 1944. How odd and weird and old and funny we must seem to be.

Leading up to this weekend, the media's usual annual bonanza about this D-Day anniversary stuff wasn't all that subdued. You'd think that after last year's big-time 70th anniversary hurrahs, there'd be some dialing down on this business. Not so, as far as I can see. And seeing as I'm landlocked, bedridden, squared away, and easily fixated on whatever the tube is showing when I glance at the news programs, I do think I'm a fairly good judge of what's going on there. As usual, it's all ridiculously selective. Maybe re*ductive* is the right word. But, always it's the same milestones.

I can't imagine what the youngsters make of all this. If anything. When Annie the Wonderful gave me my shampoo in bed the other day (I've been settling for a once-weekly shampoo because only Annie knows just how to get things done right, with this old girl being permanently supine), she appeared confused by the portraits and news clips and even the names scrolling across the Sky News screen. "I thought all that happened in November," she said. "Like, right around Thanksgiving time."

Then she went on to say, in her Annie way: "Doesn't really *look* like JFK, either."
"You're thinking of the first Kennedy assassination," I said. "They're recalling the *second* Kennedy murder. Robert's assassination. It happened in June 1968."

That was news to her. And she's no dummy. She's in her mid-thirties and passed her way through all the required grades in the public education system here. But somehow she'd never learned that RFK met the same fate as JFK. And the other day, as June 4th gradually shifted over to June 5th, a slew of the usual annual repeat tales about Bobby's doomed 1968 presidential campaign all boiled down to again seeing those highly selected moments: RFK standing and waving from an open convertible making its way through the streets of this or that city; and then RFK finger-combing his hair at the podium in Los Angeles, after claiming victory in the crucial California primary during the first hour of June 5th, 1968, a primary election so critical that, if he hadn't won it, then his Quixotic effort to reclaim his martyred brother's throne would have been abandoned. And then the obliteration of Bobby's quest as shots were fired and not only the candidate but five others were hit by bullets flying every which way in that cursed pantry behind the stage where RFK last spoke. CNN was particularly relentless in repeating and rerunning the horrendous news footage of Bob Kennedy sprawled on the pantry floor, his head in a crimson pool of blood. I told Annie to turn off the TV, because they kept rerunning the same awful images.

That was then.

Within the next twenty-four hours, you could not only feel the shift—you could see it right there on the screen. As usual, with the sound down, and as the hours rolled away with me, myself, and I spending far too much time gazing at the ever-changing, cascading, revolving, repetitious, and sometimes all-too-predictable TV images on CNN or Sky News, the visuals alone pretty much got the job done. All those 1968 images of frenzied campaign crowds and Bobby in twilight out there in Los Angeles, followed by the grim portraits of despair that the Kennedy Family became (again) in the aftermath of Bobby's assassination . . . those sorrowful profiles shifted to this latest round of D-Day flashbacks and the news coverage about the goings-on here, there, and everywhere to commemorate the 1944 Normandy landings, all those years ago.

I'm beginning to think it's all quite weird. The relentless focus that the media time after time after time pummels us with. These anniversaries. The backward gazing. I can assure you, the president, and the Pope, that back in 1944 the last thing on our minds was the notion of constantly looking into the rear-view mirror and making a big deal out of whatever had happened fifty or sixty or seventy-five years earlier. I may be a quadriplegic at long last (funny but true: I still catch myself thinking that I'm a semi-quadriplegic because with concerted effort it's possible for me to move my fingers the slightest bit; not that I can make them functional or anything), but from the neck up my faculties are intact. Why? *I* don't know. *No*body knows. Each case of multiple sclerosis—even one as extreme as mine—is unique and without the type of textbook templates that cancer patients or others can learn from. But that's not my point. My point is that I'm not hallucinating when I say that I clearly recall the year 1940. That's when I turned eighteen. And that's when America slightly acknowledged the seventy-fifth anniversary of the end of our Civil War back in 1865. And I do mean "slightly." Sure, it was acknowledged. Some ceremonies of remembrance occurred. Books were brought out to explore the subject with fresh ideas. And *Gone with the*

Wind remained ridiculously popular (as it still does). But, there was nothing resembling this newfangled media saturation that yammers and hammers and pounds away at all these milestone anniversaries nowadays.

It would have struck most of us as borderline psychotic to be harping and hollering about 1865 and Appomattox and Lee's surrender or even Lincoln's assassination throughout 1940, seventy-fifth anniversary or not. We were much more consumed by the daily news that made 1940 a series of catastrophes (and believe you me, from the Battle of Britain and Hitler's chronic bombing of the civilian centers in England to the fall of France and the awful newsreel images of those conquering black-booted Nazi bastards lording it all over the streets of Paris), and though today's news is always top-heavy with the never-ending miseries of Syria, for example, I get the damnedest feeling that none of it makes much of an impression on anyone. How can that be? How could over a quarter of a million Syrian civilians be slaughtered by their own so-called "government" in recent years (and millions made into refugees), but, somehow nothing is done by the West or at least America? Instead, we see here on the cable news shows a non-stop flashback focus on the Normandy landings, which again covered the screen this past weekend simply because the calendar hit June 6. Right on schedule. All this chronic focus on selected "glory days" is wrong. It's all about selling images.

Not that I'm opposed to invoking memory. My God, it's all I do in the privacy of my mind. But this media madness is not memory. It's selling. And the commodity is my generation's sacrifices. And the way that it's sold is through a Hollywood format of editing. All the complexities are cut. Ambiguities dissolve. Hollywood endings rule. No wonder that the only thing guaranteed to make me happy then (before, during, and after 1940) was any new musical I could go see with Judy Garland and Mickey Rooney. They made four musicals. And each one made me smile for days on end.

Again and again and again, this past weekend, it splashed across the screen. After all the obligatory images of the vast naval armada and the Normandy beaches and the exploding shells and the cliffs that the Army Rangers climbed at Pointe du Hoc, the damned news report cut to the mandatory few seconds of the GIs marching down the Champs-Élysées with the Arc de Triomphe in the background. End of story. No context. Just the staggering "visuals" suggesting total victory and an easy triumph. It comes across that way, no matter what. Like the guys waltzed from the beaches of Normandy right on over to Paris. The truth was infinitely more complicated.

Even the night before that amazing march down the Champs-Élysées by the 28th Infantry Division of the U.S. Army, there was some doubt about it all. The word that we'd all received through one Army channel or another was that Eisenhower had finally relented and given the go-ahead for two American combat divisions to make a show of support for General de Gaulle and his newly formed government in the making, because if Uncle Sam didn't offer a big fat symbolic show of support for de Gaulle it would inspire further insurrectionary efforts by the Communists, most of all, as well as other competing political factions who didn't think de Gaulle was God.

"But it could all change at the last minute," Hemingway repeated. He was still holding court at Picasso's studio, nursing another cognac as midnight approached and basking in the glow of those who remained after the rehearsal reading of the play Simone de Beauvoir had written. "Logistics alone," he added, "probably *do* guarantee the march. At least that's what I hear from my true and noble colonel."

He sounded like he was talking gibberish, but it wasn't delusional on his part. A deep friendship between Hemingway and a career officer in the U.S. Army was the real deal. And that officer was Colonel Lanham, whose 22nd Infantry Regiment of the Fourth Infantry Division was linked to the 12th Infantry Regiment, which happened to be the outfit to which Jerry was assigned with the Counter Intelligence Corps. It was all as complicated as the human brain, and yet also as simple as a brick. What mattered was that everyone and everything was connected. *Some*how. "Logistics," Hemingway repeated. "If the 28th doesn't march straight through, they're stalled."

The old bastard may have been ten days drunk and sweaty to a fault (inside Picasso's studio the stink caused by Hemingway was almost— but not quite—eradicated by the overwhelming amount of smoke in the air; my eyes burned that night like never before), but his information was quite correct. In addition to all the other difficult, unpredictable, complex, political, and dangerous issues determining events (and from incorrigible German snipers to clogged roads, everything was in a state of tumult) the plain truth was that a march right through the center of Paris was without a doubt the safest, surest, most convenient way to get the 28th Infantry Division around all of the otherwise impassable roads. They were damn near stuck and the overloaded, overpopulated, overwhelmed French infrastructure was never intended or built to accommodate tens of thousands of vehicles and more than a million men in an Allied juggernaut tearing across the nation's landscape.

In the end, the decision to march the 28th ID right on down the Champs-Élysées was due to the fact that such a direct route was the only convenient and feasible way to swiftly transfer approximately fifteen thousand fighting men to the other side of the city.

But the newsreels framed it all differently of course. Like it was a great big party. And it *was* celebratory and wildly exciting and all. But, logistics called the shots. Still, I would not have dared to miss it. Something sacred was in the air.

27

It took twenty-seven years for me to once again feel that way. Alas, I digress.

It's easy to remember because it happened on the first of the month: August 1st, 1971, to be exact. And it made my son not just happy, too, but downright ecstatic. But even if my son and I were not there together, it'd be something never forgotten.

I'm talking about that long-ago Sunday when a month-long summertime holiday adventure shared between my son and me peaked in a way that neither of us ever expected. We'd gone on a four-week bona-fide Kerouac-inspired "on the road" type odyssey, driving from Chicago to Boston, stopping in New York on our return. It was there that a former colleague of mine from Ignatius College (where I'd begun to teach the freshman composition regimen in 1956 and stayed until the 1980s) not just invited us to stay the final long weekend of our journey, but to do so as a major favor to her. My old-timey colleague was Carol Kyle and she desperately needed someone reliable to housesit for that weekend because of her two dogs. That's how my son and I ended up staying for free in Brooklyn at the tail end of our trip. Carol had a conference to attend at UCLA (she was presenting) and could not miss it. Every other arrangement she made fell through. But our long drive back to Chicago allowed us geographically to end our hiatus with a pit stop in New York.

And that's how her beloved dogs (aptly named Simon and Garfunkel) and her spacious Brooklyn apartment hosted us and became our base for the weekend that peaked on Sunday, August 1st, when Jimmy and I attended an extraordinary concert.

Part of the lure of accepting Carol's offer had everything to do with her assurance that waiting for us as the ultimate bribe were two tickets that she'd received from a guy who had some kind of professional connection to the top editor at *Rolling Stone* magazine. Earlier in July she'd had a hot and heavy fling with that guy, who used his clout to finagle two tickets to what came to be known as the Concert for Bangladesh. Only it wasn't called that yet. At the time, it was dubbed "George Harrison & Friends in a Benefit Concert." We saw the original posters all over the place that month.

Yet the craziest thing is that Carol scored the tickets knowing full well that she'd be presenting at UCLA that weekend and unable to attend. But she was savvy enough (or conniving enough) to get her hands on those tickets, correctly believing that to offer them as the ultimate payoff to a responsible house-sitter (or at least a reliable pet-sitter) would make for an offer no one could refuse. The poor schmuck who handed over the tickets assumed that they'd attend the show together, and he let her keep the tickets at her place after she told him that she wanted such rare artifacts in her home as talismans. "They're two cosmic good luck charms!" she said. He was brain damaged from too much of a good thing with Carol, and he mindlessly let her hold on to the tickets. Then he fumed when she admitted that she'd be flying west that weekend and had somehow managed to misplace or even lose the damn things.

Of course he thought she'd sold them, because a small fortune could then be had for the hottest ticket of the year. It all happened so fast and it was announced and mounted and rehearsed and publicized all in the space of one month—July 1971—and nobody knew who might show up, but a Beatles reunion was the wet dream. "I'm not worried about him" she assured me. "He's got a backstage pass from the grand wizard at *Rolling Stone*. Believe me, he'll be in the red-hot center of it all."

Her confidence both impressed me and appalled me. She was way more at home in the spirit of the age than I was. I felt anxious about being seen at Ignatius College with my new copy of Germaine Greer's feminist gospel *The Female Eunuch* back in 1971. However, a couple of years earlier, in the same summer as the moon landing, the Chappaquiddick debacle and Woodstock (in other words, back in 1969), Carol had hauled out of Ignatius College and Chicago and transplanted herself to

Brooklyn. Sure enough, she landed a teaching position at City Colleges in New York and with Brooklyn as her base she plunged headlong (pun intended) into the Zeitgeist.

When I asked her to tell me truly-madly-deeply how she'd brought the hotshot to heel so quickly and got her mitts on those priceless tickets (I cannot possibly now express how wildly excited and full of expectations people were about a big benefit concert being led by a beloved ex-Beatle, with "mystery guests" galore), she said: "It wasn't that hard. Even though *he* was hard. But I swallowed. A lot. Putty in my mouth, that's what he was." Fortunately, the concert itself was on a higher level.

Seriously. Magically. There was something sacred in the air. All night long.

I know, I know, I *know*. It sounds kooky to be speaking on the one hand of some legendary parade in liberated Paris on August 29th, 1944, and at the same time to be detouring and riffing about the Concert for Bangladesh on August 1st, 1971. I'm not sounding off in a fit of dementia, though. Believe you me. It all connects and it is astounding to me how both events (no matter how different or disparate or distinct) generated similar feelings. Transmitted a similarly glorious and transcendent hope.

It's probably a good thing that people here aren't sitting around taking notes on what I say and then judging me to be nutty for making such analogies. But I've got a right to sing the blues (thank you, Sarah Vaughan) and I also have the right to own my memories. I was a wide-eyed witness at both events. Trust me: Bliss *is* bliss.

That's the word that Jerry used the morning after the night before, when we woke on the 29th of August to the sad fact that the seconds were ticking away, the minutes were dissolving, and after just a few more hours our passes were set to expire. We knew time was running out. So that morning, we ran.

How we ended up waking together is a story for another day. Or maybe never. I've got a feeling, a feeling deep inside, that giving voice to that is not as essential as this.

What's essential is that in the aftermath of the reading workshop at Picasso's studio, later on toward midnight the night before, we ended August 28th, 1944, with a most remarkable form of communing. And it had nothing to do with body parts or filling holes or genital gymnastics or any sticky fingers. It was something silent. Ethereal.

A search for silence is what galvanized us. I mean, *really*. Just think of the amount of chatter and the high spirits and the rhetorical flights and verbal jousting unfolding in Picasso's apartment-cum-studio after Simone's experimental play was given its rehearsal reading, during that night's workshop. Simone's pendulum swung from one extreme to the other. Before and during the rehearsal reading, she sat intently and silently. Her posture was exquisite. She carried herself with regal confidence. That hair of hers was stacked high and pulled back tight. Her dark eyes glistened. And when she joined the fray as the workshop gave way from a rehearsal reading to a wide-ranging discussion of every little thing, her voluble contributions were not just spoken with high volume and rapid precision, but also with relentless energy. She looks reserved in those old turban-clad photos, but she was a dynamo.

My God, could that woman *talk*! But, she had to keep up with all of the chattering and competitive others. Everyone spoke freely and quickly. Words ricocheted. The French I thought I knew was not useless, but I scrambled to understand *any*thing. And then it occurred to Jerry and to me that we didn't, in fact, have to comprehend or strive to understand. The gist of everything was that opinions and ideas about her play were as encyclopedic as the varied thoughts you might hear in any all-American creative writing workshop. We had those back then, too. Jerry did, I mean. "They may be speaking French," he groused, "but it's pretty much the same nonsense that made me flee from Burnett's workshops back at Columbia."

I knew he meant Whit Burnett, the famed Manhattan teacher who'd founded *Story* Magazine and also created a niche for himself as a creative writing guru long before the MFA cottage industry mushroomed in the decades after the war. I remembered that Jerry had mentioned that Burnett had selected "The Young Folks" to be Jerry's first-ever published story back in 1940. Then: In a flash of crimson accuracy, the memory of that issue flickered in my mind like a Westinghouse light bulb.

Ol' Mom's subscription to *Story* Magazine was merely one of the dozen reasons that I loved being able to open the closet in the front hallway of the house and retrieve the mail. It was always a mystery to me how two folks as quiet and private as my parents could somehow receive *so* much mail. But we lived by snail mail then. In all life areas, from bills to cards and ads and communications of all kinds, mail ruled. In my mind's eye, all of a sudden, right after he said "Columbia," it flashed before me.

"That was the issue with a red cover!" No doubt in my mind. It all came back. "That 1940 issue with your debut," I quickly sputtered to Jerry. "Of course! It was not too long after Valentine's Day and the cover was all red. With a special banner in the top right corner that read: 'A Love Story Issue!' All of those relationship stories. Right?"

"And don't forget the heart that was drawn around the words 'A Love Story Issue.' I thought that was phony as hell. But it helped to sell copies off the newsstands."

"Well," I said, "it didn't hurt that the issue offered up a dozen or more stories for the whopping cost of forty cents. Were any of you paid to be published by him?"

"Five bucks and free copies of *Story*," Jerry said. "The prestige of Whit and the fact that we all knew publishers had their eyes on each issue made us feel boundless."

"I can remember feeling many things back in 1940," I said, "but boundless was not one of them." Even now, I can easily recall the miseries of being eighteen and lost.

"But you gave it the good old college try," Jerry said. "I tried three times."

"Nurses' training," I replied. "But it wasn't for me. One year in. And then out."

Gunfire exploded. Nobody knew what to think. Hemingway and others stopped their competing monologues long enough to move *en masse* across the studio and peer out the largest of the picture windows. German snipers holding out? No one could be sure. Resistance stalwarts raising hell and firing away? Possibly. The atmosphere by that time was equal parts New Year's Eve, Bastille Day, and mayhem.

"Probably drunken fools." That was Jerry's verdict. But he showed no interest in announcing it to others. He said it only to me. Quietly. But his expression spoke volumes. He was disconcerted. Not just sad, either. More like mad and also sad, but most of all he was disenchanted.

"Keep looking around," he softly muttered. "Everything here indicates chumminess with the Germans. Abundant booze. Plenty of food. Unopened packages and lots of mail on that table over there." He was pointing to a sizable wood table. "But the rationing and the usual restraints and the standard deprivations? No indications of that here." He looked perturbed.

The roar of the music startled us. I flinched. Jerry did too. It was a brassy and bold and total blast of a big band record that someone tossed onto an RCA Victrola, which had a speaker working at peak volume. The room was instantly abuzz.

All it took was three or four bars of the record's opening and I recognized it right off the bat. It had been a minor hit back in '41 for those of us who dug big band jazz that really soaked itself in the blues. Not the usual swing band with vocals stuff. This was different. It came from the stack of charts Sy Oliver wrote for Tommy. No wonder the record was one of dozens that were piled on a "jazz shelf" near the wall.

"Dance me time!" Simone hollered in her quirky effort at English. She needn't have hollered. The music alone caused everyone to begin moving. It was what we all used to call a "dirty blues." Slow yet pulsating. Sexy as hell. Strictly instrumental.

But it was a Tommy Dorsey record. I knew that in a Manhattan minute. It was "Loose Lid Special" and back in '41 it'd been a particularly hot example of how arranger Sy Oliver redefined the Tommy Dorsey band. *DownBeat* wrote a lot about him, and *Metronome* made a big deal out of this too. You see, for all those years in the late 1930s and crossing right over into 1940 and '41, the TD band was always associated with "The Sentimental Gentleman of Swing." Fair enough. Everybody agreed that

Tommy's band made the playing of ballads into an eroticized art form.

But then, something happened. Tommy was so in love with the sound and style and the blazing jazz integrity pouring forth from Jimmie Lunceford's band (and Jimmie is like the forgotten man of the Big Band Era), he just went right after Lunceford's star arranger. In *Metronome* I read that TD asked Sy what his annual salary was with the Lunceford jazz orchestra. He named a figure. And then Dorsey promised: "I'll pay you ten thousand more a year!" And history was made. Sy Oliver was a black guy who along with TD helped break the color line in big-time music. Just like back in the mid-to-late 1930s, when Benny Goodman flipped his middle finger to agents, managers, hotel owners, and theater operators, not to mention ballroom bosses, and featured Lionel Hampton and Teddy Wilson despite the raging morons mandating that no integrated ensembles were allowed. Benny told 'em all to go fuck off. And within a few years it wasn't just the BG Trio or Quartet making waves, you also had the Benny Goodman Sextet featuring Charlie Christian and his revolutionary guitar playing, followed soon enough by the arrival in BG's band of a refugee from Planet Ellington. Trumpet-master Cootie Williams left Duke and joined Benny for a while.

Damn it all, this is something else that managed to fall between the cracks. Somehow it never got across. But long before Jackie Robinson and the postwar busting of the color line in sports, the music makers were *way* ahead of the curve.

Sometimes it didn't work out so well, and we all knew how Billie Holiday had stayed so briefly with Artie Shaw's band due to some audiences being ass-backwards about a so-called "white band" with a black singer out front. And the magazines had some stories about equally distressing crap when genius trumpeter Roy Eldridge became a star member of Gene Krupa's outfit in the very early Forties and then Artie Shaw's 1945 aggregation. All the cats in the band adored him. Always. But it was a rotten fact of life that while Roy's name was up in lights, he used to be barred from downtown hotels.

Given the shittiness of the policies then in effect about race relations, it was kind of a miracle that such high-profile bandleaders challenged the culture the way that they did. But some of those guys were trailblazers. Tommy Dorsey picked up where Benny and Artie had left off. He not only hired Sy Oliver to add a whole new angle to the Dorsey "book," but he also recruited the black trumpet player Charlie Shavers, whose musical powers knew no limits. Overnight, TD had a much jazzier big band.

Chorus after chorus, solo after solo, that spinning 78 of "Loose Lid Special" worked its magic. Even those of us standing off on our own could not help but sway a bit, find our heads nodding in tempo with the growling, sassy, hip-thrusting blues that made that record a three-minute exercise in libido. It just dripped with carnality.

The truth is I wasn't all that surprised when Jerry and I sort of floated into the middle of the studio, joining the others in the open space where dancing had become the one and only sensible thing to do. Someone played the record again.

It was one of those records that dancers craved because the tempo was just *so* right. Not too fast and not too slow. I heard that Louis Armstrong used to call such a tempo "half-fast." The key issue was that any movement seemed right in reaction to the tune, but it wasn't speedy or hectic. The arrangement was languid. Nobody would end up huffing and puffing trying to keep up with it. So we played it time after time.

Years later, the hit record that came closest to having that kind of perfect "half-fast" tempo that everyone loved to dance to (also a record that folks would play over and over at a party) was the Beatles' version of "Twist and Shout." There were some real jerks (the holier-than-thou faux-Beatnik "White Negro" crowd) who said that it was all wrong for the Beatles to be recording stuff by the Isley Brothers or Chuck Berry, but then one of the Isley Brothers came right out and insisted that he loved what the Beatles did with their "Twist and Shout." Why? Because the Beatles slowed it down.

Just like with "Loose Lid Special," the slower groove made magic.

Somebody played the record over and over again. "Loose Lid Special," that is. Now and then someone managed to make a switch and suddenly we'd hear the highly spirited acoustic guitar virtuosity of Django Reinhardt and that, too, sent a jolt of electricity throughout the room. Or I should say "rooms," because the spaciousness of Picasso's apartment and studio had as much to do with what evolved, at least as much to do with it as the dancing that was induced by the repeated replaying of "Loose Lid Special" on that loud and reliable Victrola of his. Now that I think of it, it reminds me of the way that twenty or thirty years later you'd hear certain songs being played over and over and over again when young people gathered. My son always called them "make-out songs," and though I loved when the young folks would gather to listen to their music and to hang out at our place (at least then I knew exactly where my boy was), it sure didn't take Dear Abby to figure out that by the fourth replay of "Wild Horses" or "Colour My World," some exploring usually had to be interrupted.

In a funny way, though, that kind of intervention was easy. Contrary to all of the nonsense about rebellious youth and radical behavior and sexual revolutions in the air and all, the truth was that if you turned up the lights and showed your face in the midst of pretty much any group of young people in the late Sixties or in the 1970s, there'd be an immediate reduction in the room's temperature. Whenever I knew in my bones that a fifth repeat of certain records signified raging boners and possible trouble, I'd just walk right in and ignore their awkward tumbling back into place. I'd also ignore their whining about curfew and having to clean things up before leaving.

Chances are, my intrusions prevented an accidental pregnancy. Or a few. Maybe.

But it was a whole different tableau that night as "Loose Lid Special" was once again spun around and around that blaring Victrola. No one of any rank (not parental, not military, and certainly not clergy) could have or would have had any influence *there*. The dancing that immediately arose each time that record was played was the very definition of Eros. Absolutely nobody griped about the repetition of the record. My sense right off the bat was that the music was perfectly attuned to all the unleashed moods of desire and freedom and pent-up hormones and that nameless, all-consuming desire to break out and just *be*, simply to erupt with eroticized joyful movement. All night long.

And it wasn't just the music, although whoever kept picking up the needle-arm on the Victrola and repeatedly letting that half-fast "dirty blues" fill the room as much as all the smoke and whispers and furtive caresses . . . I never knew if it was a man or a woman playing "Loose Lid Special" one more time, and then again one more once, but he or she knew exactly what was up. That repetition was as blunt as any penetration and in its three-minute replays as glorious as any perfect stroking.

Further inspiration for the volcanic steam overheating that milieu came right off the canvas of Pablo's latest painting. One of them, that is. So many new works (sketches, sculptures, prints and paintings) were arrayed all around on easels, shelves, tables, and whatnot. But there was no getting around the impact of the larger canvas that he proudly pointed to throughout the night. Time and again, he drew others' attention to what he was calling "The Triumph of Pan," which illustrated the impassioned and unbound madness of Liberation in Paris that night, that week, and the whole past month for that matter. Of course it wasn't anything pornographic or exceedingly blatant or explicit. But it was truly a vivid and celebratory and sensually overloaded painting. Truly soaked with desire. Which added to the desires that all the leaking libidos spilled over with that night.

Mine included. It seemed inevitable, for everyone. The dancing space was like a magnetic field, and once anyone entered it there was a point of no return. Not that clothes came off all the way or that there was anything like an orgy. But amidst the music and the flowing wine and the uncorked champagnes and cognac, couple after couple eased their way into one of the apartment's several rooms, or simply settled into the shadows of a dark private corner and created their own zones of intimacy.

Damn it, I don't want anything here to sound smarmy or dirty. So here's my truth.

I'd never had an orgasm. Hell, plenty of gals my age didn't even know that we *could* have them. And most women of my vintage who assumed that banging away would lead to great pleasure and joy were sorely disappointed. And I mean it: *Sorely.* God bless the guys who did their best to be patient and gentle and understanding. I'll bet there were ten of them to go around. All right, that's harsh. But, it's all I ever heard about in our after-hours Girl Talk and, in my experience, it was a fact.

But that's the way it was (and our movies back then made everything seem so easy and effortless, from winning the war to falling in love to falling into bed together). Most of the time, the guys mistook their pricks for pistons and too often we gals got pounded on mechanically. That's not me being harsh. It was biology running amok. I can't tell you how relieved I was a million years later, when some publisher issued a collection of Martha Gellhorn's letters, and in her usual brazen and outspoken way she repeatedly highlighted the same shortcomings. The same disappointments. In one of her letters, Martha admitted to her confidante that sex with Hemingway more or less amounted to him leaping on her because he needed something to copulate *on*, not someone to copulate *with*. She spoke for a whole generation with that line.

But Jerry was different.

We danced to "Loose Lid Special" at least four or five times. And with every repetition, we loosened up a bit more. Of course we did. It was Eros in the air. And even the smog of all those fat Gitanes (I'd never seen any cigarette so thick) mixed in with our Chesterfields and Old Golds somehow added to the hefty, increasing ardor.

"It's like being lost in a fog," I said to Jerry, as we held each other tight enough to know we were aroused. I spotted the craziest scene of all right about then, when out of the corner of my eye I saw Hemingway in all of his sweaty and brandy-soaked glory, actually arm-wrestling with Picasso on the other side of the room. They were surrounded by their acolytes and everyone was cheering on their *mano-a-mano* bit of theater. I swear I even saw bets being made and money exchanged. It was nuts.

And speaking of nuts: Pablo and Papa should have just unzipped and compared.

Anyway, Jerry liked what I'd said. "Lost in a fog," he remarked. "Isn't that a song?"

"I think it is," I said. "If not, it should be. That's a perfect title."

"Reminds me of 'I Cover the Waterfront' or something like that," he whispered. We got into a sweet thing about song titles, and softly conversed that way as we danced.

"I love 'I Cover the Waterfront,' especially 'In the Blue of Evening,' " he said.

"In that case," I replied, " 'I'll Be Seeing You,' and I hope there is 'Moonglow.' "

"Maybe just maybe just maybe tonight," he riffed, "some 'Stardust' too. Then again, as you may have guessed since D-Day, we 'Don't Get Around Much Anymore.' "

Quickly I riffed back, saying: "And that's why they do say that 'Saturday Night is the Loneliest Night of the Week.'" This was easy to sustain because the tempo of "Loose Lid Special" made talking while dancing a cinch. Besides, we needed a diversion like this to avoid undressing right on the spot.

Then: Jerry tried a detour, by saying: "Well, yes, if it's true that 'Saturday Night is the Loneliest Night of the Week,' then at least we know why we fight. *What* are we all fighting for? Why, for the safe and sound return of 'Jukebox Saturday Night.' Right?"

"Aye-aye, sir," I joked. "When I get home, my plan is to ride the 'Chattanooga Choo Choo' right past 'Tuxedo Junction' and never-ever stop until 'Blue Skies' reappear."

And Jerry up and riffed right back by half-speaking and half-singing: "I'll tell you this . . . 'I'll Never Smile Again' until you finally holler out 'Let Me Off Uptown.' Got that?"

"'I Got a Right to Sing the Blues," I answered back. "Because, like it or not, 'I Let a Song Go Out of My Heart.'" And then, I couldn't help but add: " ' How About You?'"

He caught my Gershwin curve, two beats on a bat, and not only squeezed my hand extra hard but also let his other hand drop down and caress my bottom with a flourish. It happened so fast and his touch was so deft—unthreatening; not a grope but instead a kind of classy flirtatious dare—that it startled me. I missed whatever he said or sang at that point, and simply exhaled one more Gershwin title: "'S'Wonderful!"

And damn if he didn't chime in with that song's well-known first line, before then steering us anew with an immediate switch hit: "All of which is 'Too Marvelous for Words' in my opinion."

"Well, then," I answered back, "I'm wondering what 'Embraceable You' happens to think at this moment regarding the only question on my mind: 'What'll I Do?'"

That's when "Loose Lid Special" ended again.

And if they played it more, we weren't there to hear it.

It wasn't too long before we were sitting by the Seine.

Enthralled.

28

I'm too sickened by the news to say much of anything now. Last night the images flashed and the CNN scroll offered up drib after drab and slowly the details emerged about this crazy incident in South Carolina. Racism. Religious persecution. Sheer lunacy. And what do we know? Some kid—and I mean a real *kid*; I think he's barely twenty—went berserk and talked his way into a Bible Study class at a legendary black church down there, and then the little bastard shot dead nine human beings, including the pastor. This kind of murderous madness? Again and again.

And yes, absolutely *any*one can get a gun. In*sane*!

It's the night of June 18th and my favorite caregivers have been on vacation. But the newbies are quite competent and I have no complaints. I just miss my usual girls.

And I really miss my boy. All that talk about "Loose Lid Special" and how that record made for such a spontaneous dance party on that long-ago night in August 1944, when for a brief few hours I thought the axis of the earth went straight through the studio apartment where Picasso had more or less been left alone to do his work in the midst of the German Occupation of Paris for years (and the Krauts were no less seduced by the old scoundrel than anyone else; they really did not harass him or in any way interfere in his life, despite his having created crates of the "degenerate art" that Adolf and his minions loved to denigrate, to ban, and to sometimes destroy), and all I end up wondering about is my boy. His face. His heart. His love for music.

Remembering all that jazz about "Loose Lid Special" easily reminds me of how my boy and the kids like him glommed onto their music and certain favorite songs and performers later on in the Sixties and Seventies. That's how I learned so much by asking questions the night of the Concert for Bangladesh in 1971, when I sat there at Madison Square Garden and marveled at everyone. It was in*cred*ibly exultant.

Of course I knew a little bit about Ravi Shankar and his transcendent Indian music. He'd been on significant television shows for years, and PBS back then had a way of reinforcing his reputation. It seemed that they needed content to fill the time now and then, and I swear they used to re-run the documentary *Monterey Pop* at least a few times each year. I can remember watching it late at night, when I'd be up on my own and grading essays for the next day's classes. And also on weekend afternoons. That documentary featured plenty of excellent music, but nothing compared to the finale as the filmmakers caught and preserved an extended Ravi Shankar episode.

"It's called a *raga*," my son informed me that night at the Concert for Bangladesh. "It's a form of classical Indian composition. Highly structured, but it still allows for improvisation. And get this: They *never* write down a note. It's all sung out at first."

I was awe-struck by the magnificence of the long, intricate, seemingly endless and glorious performance that Ravi Shankar and his fellow musicians generated on the stage at the Garden that night. They were the sole performers for almost an hour. And the amazing thing to me was that the audience was *for* them all the way. When the album and the movie came out early the following year, they edited everything down and Ravi's mind-boggling long-form *raga* was cut to ten minutes or so. But as it actually happened, it was very much like the exalted, technically flamboyant, ever-escalating and ultimately phenomenal spontaneous magic seen in *Monterey Pop*.

And nobody seemed bored or annoyed, even though they were all waiting for George and his special "mystery guests" to fill the stage with a slew of rock stars.

But thanks to my boy, I was reminded that for quite a while there had been such a highly regarded rapport between Harrison and Shankar, well, it all just fit so well.

The sounds of Ravi's sitar. Long incense sticks burning on stage. Those hand drums. The droning instrument played with such focus by a woman with royal posture. All of it created such an atmosphere of prayerful intensity and spiritual yearning, mixed in with the gradually intensifying musical peaks of that lengthy *raga* that they played into infinity. Mesmerizing.

My son was then sixteen. I'd given birth to him in 1955. And if I'm able to speak of that without bringing on a stroke, I'll get to it, I'm sure. But the thing is like this: He was sixteen in the summer of '71, and he knew *his* music they way we'd known *ours*.

During a lull after Ravi's ensemble left the stage and right before the rock stars took over the show, I asked him to remind me of when it was that George first bridged East and West with his love for the sitar's unique sound. The kid took the bait. "When I was ten," he replied. He took it *all* so personally. But that's how he framed things. Chronologically. Even in elementary school, he made order out of the chaos in the world by relating things to his personal calendar, as well as the one on the wall. "When they released *Rubber Soul*, when I was ten, back in 1965, that started it all. 'Norwegian Wood' was on Side One and the first thing you hear is the sitar George played in the instrumental introduction." Good Lord, he was like a teacher. And he loved Elvis, no matter what. He always called him "Mr. Presley."

Certainly I recalled how much we played *Rubber Soul* on our Hi-Fi back then. But to me (and I fear to most folks my age) we played that album time after time to listen to "Michelle" all of the time. Overnight, "Michelle" was being recorded by *everyone*.

"But the real impact was felt the following year," my little professor further explained. "A song on *Rubber Soul* was one thing, but George's Indian music thing was stamped all over the *Revolver* album from when I was eleven, back in 1966."

On the night of the Concert for Bangladesh on August 1st, 1971, it seemed like five years earlier was another century. Too much of everything had happened. All bad.

But we knew joy that day in the Garden. There were two shows: afternoon and evening. Our tickets were for the afternoon performance. And it wasn't just Ravi Shankar's blissful opening set that helped to create a sacred sense of magic. There were other elements. Intangibles. Much like Paris on August 29th, 1944 . . .

It was just the two of us on that Tuesday morning when we decided to stand as closely as we could to the Arc de Triomphe. That's where the big parade was set to begin. Hemingway had made his own way from Picasso's studio back to the Hotel Ritz and given the way all his hangers-on clung to him, I'm sure he had no trouble carrying on all through the night and holding court until the wee small hours. Jerry and I made our own way all through the night, but it wasn't the way anybody might have assumed. Anyhow, for us the key issue was to position ourselves as near to the Arch as we could get, because such a spot offered advantages. It all made sense to me.

"You'll be able to see the eternal flame," Jerry said. "Last Saturday when de Gaulle reignited the eternal flame, the four of us all felt like we were witnessing a miracle."

Jerry's remark was something he sort of repeated in a variety of ways through the night just passed. He was always working as part of a four-man team. And though he and his "fellow musketeers," as he called them, were very much attached to the 12th Infantry Regiment of the 4th Infantry Division, they were also on their own a lot. You see, as a four-man team with the Counter Intelligence Corps they had unique duties. They were steeped in and surrounded by all things combat. But they did not function as riflemen or artillerymen. Instead, they were like uniformed detective-soldiers. In every military sector where the 4th ID had to go, within the realm of all aspects of the Allied campaigns in which the 4th Infantry Division was up to its ears, the role of Jerry and his three cohorts was to interview as many townspeople as possible; then interrogate as many captured Germans as they could find; and then pool information about the issues at play in the combat zones the GIs had to survive.

Investigating local populations for any useful information about Resistance efforts, saboteurs, and of course most of all the presence (or sudden absence) of French collaborators? It all demanded critical thinking. The science of deduction. "But none of that," Jerry told me, "none of it in any way prepped us for the feelings we admitted to just a few days ago. To see de Gaulle reignite that eternal flame . . ."

I got the basic gist of what he was saying. Only three days earlier, on August 26th, a Saturday, there had been the ultimate grand parade down the Champs-Élysées. It was no routine event. The symbolism was beyond category. Jerry and his guys and other elements of the 4th Infantry Division were already present in Paris, but what made it different for Jerry's guys was that they could be off on their own. Most of the time. They weren't hamstrung like typical GIs. They were autonomous, really.

That's how they were able to witness the pinnacle of Liberation Week. Ever since August 19th, there had been gradual uprisings and suddenly the Resistance went into overdrive and barricades mushroomed on all the great boulevards. Gunfire and explosives were heard everywhere. The Germans who were not retreating were in varied ways still wreaking havoc. Thousands of Parisians were wounded and many hundreds were killed in street battles and firefights all throughout those long days.

"And even as de Gaulle stood there at the Tomb of the Unknown Soldier and saluted the eternal flame," Jerry said, "sniper fire crackled. He didn't flinch."

I could sense Jerry's respect for the man who had made himself into a Lincoln-like figure for the French. And the instantly published photos in *Stars and Stripes* and the instantly distributed newsreels from our Signal Corps as well as British Pathé, every kind of report bore out what Jerry had witnessed only three days earlier.

That legendary parade led by General Charles de Gaulle *had* to commence with the honoring anew of the eternal flame at the Tomb of the Unknown Soldier. Back in 1940, that was a German target. Those bastards extinguished the flame as they entered Paris and then they marched as conquerors down the Champs-Élysées.

And they repeated that march *every* day of the Occupation. Each day. Right on schedule. Rain or shine. Salt in the wounds, like clockwork. Marching and smiling.

"Remember those UPI photos of France's fall?" Jerry was staring at the Arch. "The crying man in the pin-striped suit, with his bald head and his stricken face? Or the Krauts and their goddamned pageantry? The black boots and the brass bands? And let's not forget Uncle Adolf picking his nose at the Eiffel Tower. Vulgar little shit."

It was easy to remember those pictures. They'd been reprinted everywhere. A million times. It's still easy to recall them. They've appeared in textbooks all over.

"If June of 1940 finally and really and totally ended that nonsense about 'the phony war,' then you can bet your Decca records that *this* signals the end for Germany."

Of course he was right and the Germans knew it most of all. Militarily, their loss was signalled by their exodus from Paris, precisely four years and two months after they marched in, back in June 1940. Still, another nine months of grim fighting remained.

"Today's bound to be sweet," Jerry said. "But last Saturday, when it was de Gaulle and Leclerc out front together, even we cried. All four of us. That was a first."

The minutes were ticking away and Jerry's references to the "Four Musketeers" made me sad. I knew that his pass was set to expire that afternoon and then he'd rendezvous with his three fellow CIC officers at a time and place they'd already agreed upon. Witnessing the march of the American soldiers would be our finale.

It was supposed to be, that is. That was the assumption. Mine, anyway.

29

I think I realized today that I'm finally ready to fly away. That is, I'm truly ready to pick the date, have all the necessary approvals and orders in place, and stop eating.

A slew of bedside consultations in recent weeks have merely confirmed again and again and again what we've always known all along, anyway. This is not cancer. It isn't lymphoma. Nor is it Hodgkin's disease or anything else that goes its own way. The one thing everyone knows about MS is that there's no way of knowing much at all. No definitive proof of origin. No reliable timetable for anyone's demise. And in an extreme case like mine, the thing is like this: From the neck up, all's well. From the neck down, I'm utterly dependent for every little thing on all these others. All these amazing and well-meaning, dutiful caregivers. But while I can still think with true clarity (that "being of sound mind and body" bit), I've resolved to let go soon.

Meantime, I'm right back where I started. Thinking of Hemingway's line at the end of *Death in the Afternoon*. Indeed, there *are* a few practical things to be said. Now I feel more than ever before that there is so little time left to say them. OK. Let's do it.

I need to get back to the night before that hypnotizing parade in Paris on August 29th, 1944, when the 28th Infantry Division of the U. S. Army had its day in the sun. Because the fact is, the night before it rained like hell and those poor bastards were all sleeping outside, just a scant mile or two from the heart of Paris. Not that sleeping outside would have been much of a shock to them.

Those of us in communications and plenty of others all knew that the 28th ID had found its way to the Normandy beaches just one month earlier, in July. They weren't ordered into action for the D-Day landings on June 6, but like so many others they got in on the action later in July and had already endured multiple battles, clashes, and every kind of baptism of fire between the fighting in the hedgerows and the crucible at St. Lo and eventually the breakthroughs and breakouts that led to the Germans rapidly retreating from France.

On balance, I have no doubt that for the GIs sleeping outside in the rain on that night before their glorious march down the Champs-Élysées, such a night was infinitely superior (the rain be damned) to anything that'd happened to their dead. As for those of us who were briefly on passes that gave us the illusion of freedom for a couple of days and a couple of nights, we were highly aware of our lucky stars.

One of the reasons that we stayed so long in the aftermath of the rehearsal reading of Simone's play at Picasso's studio apartment was the rain. It was briefly torrential. And that just made it easier to stay put, smoke even more, hear the records played over and over and over again as the moments of being were musically sustained with the melodies, harmonies, and rhythms everyone loved . . . and all of that art!

It was unlike any environment I'd ever seen. No Chicago museum was loaded with the sheer variety and abundance characterizing Picasso's studio apartment. That's the thing to remember. It was definitely an apartment, with chairs, tables, and rooms for sleeping and all other aspects of domestic comfort.

But it was also a studio that in every way was simultaneously a mind-boggling museum. There were alabaster life-size sculptures adjacent to long wooden tables overflowing with smaller artifacts; tiny works of pottery set out in haphazard harmony with petite sculptured items that were meticulously crafted and arrayed in some kind of Pablo-quirky designs. I swear, everything in view—especially the canvasses on small, medium, and large easels that in each part of every quadrant of the largest, main room—spoke to the human capacity for creation. The human desire to communicate a vision. It was not just that being works by Picasso made them important. They were something *else*. In all of their unpredictable, effulgent, elaborately unconventional ways, they were living, breathing, vibrant, and stunningly visible manifestations of otherworldly eyes.

That night, before the rain finally diminished and the storm over Paris receded (it was right around the last time that Jerry and I danced to that Tommy Dorsey record that had everyone hooked for a while), as "Loose Lid Special" once again gave us a chance to not only dance but to caress and whisper and talk and to rub more than elbows, if you know what I mean, that's when the immensity of it all really hit me.

There was absolutely nothing in that studio apartment—not a thing, anywhere at all—that was not somehow the result of a commitment to make each moment of life creative and adventurous. Nothing in that realm was mundane. Nothing was tidy and orderly, either. "This chaos is intoxicating," I said to Jerry, as we looked around.

And then, after our last dance, with the echoes of the music still in the air, and the remarks made by those standing at the wide-open windows of Picasso's studio apartment assuring one and all that the rain had subsided, we quietly vanished.

There was no doubt about where we had to go or what we had to do.

It was after midnight. And it didn't take us long to arrive at the Seine.

30

Plenty of others had the same idea. After the rain, there was a sudden shift in the weather and I wouldn't say it cooled off, but it was certainly more pleasant. I mean, we're talking late August in Paris, which is notorious for broiling heat. And don't even think for a second that there was anything like our vaunted all-American "air-conditioned comfort" to be had *any*where. Not a chance. However, instead of more hot and humid pressure after the rain, there rose instead a light breeze as the skies cleared and, for us and so many others, the Seine worked its magnetic magic. The stars above were infinitely wondrous as the clouds cleared. Shooting stars fell. You didn't have to wait long to see one. Every other moment, a falling star descended.

It was all public and private at the same time. Small groups of Parisians and couples by the score and individuals of every type (well-dressed and raggedy; elderly and young; wicked thin and corpulent, too) wandered by, but it wasn't too difficult to set ourselves off and though we could hear snippets of conversation and the occasional remarks from passersby, we still enjoyed a feeling of isolation. *Ours.* However illusory.

It reminded me of the hottest summer nights back home in Chicago. "We did this a few times in different spots," I explained to Jerry. "Once it was just around July 4th, but the other times were definitely in August. The heat could be so bad that you'd find out from the radio that even before sunset people were showing up in Grant Park and bringing their overnight stuff, because sleeping outside was a blessing compared to staying indoors. There'd be dozens scouting for their families."

"Same thing in Central Park," Jerry said. "Very much a hot August night kind of thing. Fire escapes, too. Amazingly cool spots compared to being stuck inside."

Of course we didn't have even the barest of essentials for such an overnight outing by the Seine. "My folks never wanted to make the trip downtown to Grant Park," I told Jerry. "They didn't want to leave the car out overnight anywhere at all, and it wasn't appealing to think of carrying pillows or blankets or a cooler or anything else on the streetcar. So, on those nights when it was insufferably hot after dusk, we'd carry some essentials to one of the smaller parks nearby. Gage or Marquette Park."

"Well, some variations on a theme here. If we have any luck and there's no more rain, that'll be great. And we can fold up odds and ends to rest our heads on. Most of all we can hear the river flow. If that's not a sedative, I don't know what." By the time he'd said just those words, Jerry had stripped down to his tee-shirt and pants.

"Monkey see, monkey do" I joked. A minute later, I was as slightly disrobed as I'd ever be in that time. That place. Just as he still had his regulation pants on, I still wore my uniform skirt. But with nothing but a chemise and bra on, I felt glorious.

That's how we ended up entwined by the Seine. And our plan was that we had no plan. I'm not kidding. We just *had* to be there. It wasn't possible to be elsewhere. Of course we both knew full well that we were expected to be somewhere else. I had no doubt that my fellow WACs at that small hotel were pulling their hair out and wondering what had become of me. And doubtless Jerry was causing a fair amount of headaches for the other three-fourths of his "Four Musketeers." We didn't care.

As inevitably as a snake sheds its skin or as a moon sheds its shadow, we sloughed off all other associations, expectations, duties, identities, and fear. For one night.

Just one night. For that blessed and limited interval, we reacted with unspoken understanding and ineffable gratitude for the wonders all around us. More than a few of the passersby could be heard saying, time after time, the word: *Liberation.*

It defined everything that night. It explained everything. Why was there such a sense of human ecstasy in the air? Simple. It was the

Liberation. Why did total strangers all of a sudden feel safe being out after midnight and lounging by the river and for the first time in years not feel terror at the footfalls of others? Liberation. Why did music pour forth from open windows near and far, long after what used to be the dread curfew? Liberation. Just as surely as the lights glowing from untold numbers of apartments indicated that the draconian German curfews were kaput, the freedom of movement atop all the great stones of each Parisian boulevard had the effect of generating an atmosphere of dizzying intoxication and transcendence.

The damnedest thing is that we never said a word. That's the truth. Once we had ourselves comfortably situated, side by side beneath God's starry panorama, our unscripted, uncalculated, unexpected, and utterly perfect impulse was to breathe together. In silence. Neither one of us suggested anything. It happened *to* us.

For three hours. That's no exaggeration. Miraculously, we were never once spoken to directly by the varied and invariably chatty passersby. Nobody bothered us. We used our folded tunics as tiny pillows to sit upon, and watched the river flow. That was effortless. So many lights were glowing nearby, from innumerable rooms that held deliriously happy and curfew-free people, that the Seine was illuminated. All we wanted to do was sit there in silence. And that's all we did for three hours.

We communed without conversation. We shared without saying a word. We kept our gaze on the waters of the Seine, and I swear our hearts beat in unison.

And of course there were the bells. The church bells. They'd been ringing almost non-stop since August 25th, and even after four days the churches throughout all of Paris kept ringing their bells with total abandon. It began as the word got around on August 25th that Liberation was at hand, with General Leclerc's imminent arrival at the helm of the Second Armored Division (the one Free French division to play a key role in the Normandy campaign, as part of the D-Day follow-up). As we all knew, Ike had made a generous (and controversial) decision to let the first Allied liberators in Paris be the Free French, whose tanks, guns, uniforms, and everything else were all provided by the U. S. Army. That was fine. It made me proud. As a schoolgirl back in Chicago, I'd loved reading all about how the French came to our aid (even to our rescue) during America's Revolutionary War against England. And I loved even more the anecdote that Pop often repeated to me, about how back in 1917, when the first Doughboys of the U. S. Army paraded through Paris in that long-ago July, before engaging in any of the First World War's ghastly battles (the French welcomed the Doughboys with a July 4th parade back in 1917, which whetted everyone's appetite for an even more rousing Bastille Day celebration), there was a magic moment when one of the officers of the American Expeditionary Force declared to the war-weary people of Paris: "Lafayette, we are here!" Even now that gives me the chills.

After three hours of silence, I whispered: "There's a book I want to share."

And that's how I more or less handed him my soul, in the form of a book that'd been on my mind, in my bag, and right before my eyes whenever time permitted. Thanks to a wartime deal undertaken by a special publishing house in Philly (an outfit we sure appreciated because they shrank and made cheaply available even the newest books on the market), I had my skinny little Blakiston Edition of a brand new novel, published by Doubleday. I beheld it, after I filched it out of my bag. It weighed less than a deck of cards, I swear. That's how effectively Blakiston shrank the books. Thinner paper. Smaller type. Far fewer pages. But still highly readable.

"Great title," Jerry said. "So-so author. Not a big fan here. Not usually."

Nonetheless, he would not—or could not—stop staring at the cover of the novel. "Look at how that typeface draws you in," he observed. "The letters alone are a lure."

I'd never given much thought to the title's appearance, but he had a point. Staring intently, in the glow that was cast by his cigarette lighter (this ought to be said, as well: During our three-hour silence, one gesture repeatedly indicated that we were very much in the groove together . . . time after time, whenever either one of us had to fire up a new smoke, each one of us automatically did the thing we loved from a Bette Davis movie everyone adored, where lighting two at one time guaranteed the experience of smoking together), it occurred to me that my eyes really did delight in the shape of the letters on the book's front cover. What we used to call a dust jacket.

"But it's not just the font," Jerry said. "And no, I don't mean anything baptismal."

"I *know* what you mean," I said. "It's one of those words I really love because of its different meanings." Anybody with a Catholic background knew the word "font" to be a sacred receptacle seen in churches, usually freestanding and beautifully carved out of stone, and filled with the holy water used for baptisms. But in French classes we also learned that a secondary definition of "font." It derived from a 16th-century word (*fonte,* which had its origin in *fondre,* meaning "to melt") that was all about the process of casting or founding. In our time, it came to mean the face and size of type.

That is, a set of type of some particular size and face. Good Lord, I do repeat myself. But it fascinated me always to ponder words that had multiple meanings. Just as it fascinated Jerry to see how the font on the book cover commanded attention. "And that symbol of his," Jerry added. "That's as distinctive as a flag or a crest. Unique."

"The book is unique," I said. "Right off the bat, he tells the readers that he's calling it a novel simply because he knows no other way to describe it. And yet, from the very first page to the last, he tells the tale in a first-person voice so autobiographical and so relaxed and casual, you end up assuming that it's all really a book of memories."

"What did you want to share with me?" Jerry asked. Lighting another Chesterfield, of course. And thanks to the light cast by his Zippo, the other words were easy to read. That was something else about the book that made it different. Right there on the front cover, below the title and the author's name and also that unique symbol, there were these words: "The Story of a Man Who Found a Faith." And *that* was it.

But that was enough. That's what hooked me from the get-go. Even more than the title. More than the author's reputation. More than the bold font or unusual symbol.

"This thing is selling back home like hot dogs on the Fourth of July," I said. "Pop sent it to me. It just came out this year. But Pop wrote that it's become the new big thing."

"Well, it's not like Maugham is a stranger. His stuff has been big since whenever."

That was true. For those of us born in the 1920s, there was never a time when we weren't aware of the towering reputation of W. Somerset Maugham. It's like the way my son always knew about Sinatra. By the time my Jimmy was born, back in 1955, Sinatra had already been a star for years. And by the time my Jimmy was growing up and listening to everyone and everything in the 1960s and 1970s, ol' Frank was like the Empire State Building. To kids, he had been around forever.

And that's how it was for us with Maugham. His books were everywhere and he was prolific. There were movies left and right based on his works. He was always *there*.

"But this is different," I insisted. "I mean, it begins with a story about a guy who was never the same again after World War One. But later it becomes all about Vedanta."

"About *what?*" Jerry's eyes burned.

31

What a surprise. What a delight. And thank goodness I'm here to say so. Today is the Fourth of July (even here I can hear the bangs and booms of local fireworks) and it's also Saturday. So, last night had to be Friday and just in the nick of time—I was feeling worse than usual; really depressed after barely swallowing a few bites of the tiny dinner brought to me by the aide who just started last week—my beloved and all-time favorite helper (Lorena-Rena-Bena-Bean-Beansy herself) stopped in for a visit. And she brought along a DVD that we watched together after she got the OK from the front desk to stay later than usual. Working here gives her some clout.

And the DVD not only appealed to me, I swear, it gave me a blood transfusion. Rena is just crazy in love with the music she likes and somehow she got hooked on this new documentary called *20 Feet From Stardom*. It's all about the female singers—and I mean the back-up singers, not the big stars—whose voices on a million hit singles from decades ago have become part of our national collective memory. It's not a long film and just seeing The Mighty Lorena actually gave me a wee bit of mental pep and once she did her techno-thing, we viewed the film together and I still can't decide who was more impressed: She was knocked out by my ability to sing along with the right words to damn near any song on the soundtrack and I was equally impressed by how quickly she could name anyone and everyone from all those years ago. Seriously! She's a culture-vulture all right. I mean, it's one thing to be able to learn to love the songs and all. Classic Rock radio still plays many of them and then she also gets into to these weekend specials that according to her replay everything under the sun on their Saturday at the Sixties or their Sunday at the Seventies programs. I don't think she ever disconnects from her phone or her iPod.

Anyway, for most of the time that we were watching *20 Feet From Stardom*, it was impossible not to hum along, sing along, and smile. All that amazing TV footage of Ray Charles and Aretha or James Brown and so many others. It took me out of my stranded, paralyzed body and allowed my mind to be wholly engaged and in the very best way possible to be distracted from what now feels like being buried alive. Of course I smiled. Just witnessing her reaction to the old music made me happy.

But she never expected me to burst into tears when one of the primary back-up singers who performed at the Concert for Bangladesh was speaking. Tears of joy and overpowering memory poured like rain. It was Claudia who spoke in the film. And as she spoke, the movie clip that played on for a full minute or more was to me the equivalent of that very special one-time performance I'd witnessed back in the day, when I heard the kid trumpet player with Glenn Miller's Army Air Force Band.

Only this was even more intense because all the mental photographs and snapshot memories in my head collided with a thousand images of my Jimmy Joe that night, when we may have been the only out-of-town mother-and-son duo at Madison Square Garden, and George Harrison and Friends all took the stage. Together.

You see, that's what made George's Concert for Bangladesh unique. Not only was it the first of the big-time benefit concerts ever staged, but, the glory of it all was enhanced by the way that all the big stars performed together. All night long. It wasn't like other famous festivals or benefits or special events, where the varied stars took turns on the stage. Instead, George created an all-star rock super-group.

And the opening song of their part of the show was my son's absolute favorite at that time. A rollicking number called "Wah-Wah," which was filled to the brim with great guitar playing and a heavy percussive pulse. My Jimmy Joe had asked for one thing and only thing only for Christmas 1970, back when he was fifteen. All he really wanted was the new three-album LP George Harrison debut solo album called *All Things Must Pass*. I fell in love with much of that album too. It was truly soul music.

But poor Lorena last night. She was genuinely startled (and I think a little spooked) by my emotional reaction to not only hearing the first part of "Wah-Wah" (which featured a lot of terrific back-up singing by Claudia and all the others in what they called the Soul Choir), but also by seeing the film footage from the documentary of the concert that was made. There they all were. Impossibly young. Almost all of them bearded or sporting mustaches. Mountains of hair and funky clothes to boot. George in the center of it all, surrounded by keyboard master Billy Preston and Eric Clapton and other great guitarists, along with Leon Russell on piano and a slew of other fine players. But in that video clip from the concert film the editors made a choice that made total sense to me. I remember it so well from that very night.

The night of the actual concert, I mean. You see, until it all unfolded, nobody knew exactly who might be up there on stage with George. It was billed only as "George Harrison and Friends," and that was that. So, when the beginning of "Wah-Wah" kicked off with its wickedly exciting guitar licks, and the spotlight hit the stage, my Jimmy Joe was already out of his seat (like most of the audience) and cheering and stomping and clapping along. A few seconds later, when the whole band burst forth like a thundering herd, I thought my son was going to levitate. He couldn't help it.

Smack dab in the middle of the stage you had Ringo Starr double-drumming with another great drummer, directly to his left. They laid down the beat for eternity. And in the video clip of that opening number highlighted in *20 Feet From Stardom,* you can see it all over again as it happened. The groove and the beat and the unifying rhythmic pulse co-created by Ringo and the other drummer caused the back-up singers in the Soul Choir to shimmy, shake, and dance impromptu as they sang their parts and made "Wah-Wah" a fanfare for every dream we had ever had.

That's why I burst into tears of joy. And lamentation. The video clip in the new DVD was more than a flashback to me. It absolutely and viscerally brought back to me the utter and total grief we felt after the 1960s collapsed into the Seventies, because for that one night at the Garden the music offered up by George and Friends was like a balm on festering wounds. For one night, they recaptured lost hopes and dreams.

And the sight of Ringo and Jim Keltner (his name just came back to me, because my Jimmy was so thrilled that they shared the same first name and he raved about that) double-drumming like Siamese twins still makes me think what it made me envision that night at the Garden: They were like polyrhythmic, multi-armed Hindu gods.

And that thought sends my mind reeling back to that night that Jerry and I spent by the Seine, when reading from *The Razor's Edge* by Maugham transported our souls.

32

"He had me hooked, well, pretty much right from the start," I said to Jerry.

"'Pretty much right from the start,' you say?" He was teasing me a bit. "Well, pretty mouth and green my eyes. Or, I should say, green your eyes." Where'd you get those eyes?" And then he added: "Those emerald eyes." I was blushing.

"From my father," I said. "They're my father's eyes. And that's what I mean about how Mr. Maugham had me hooked right from the start. With this book, anyhow. I feel like I'm reading an autobiography of my father's generation. But it's a novel."

"That's one of his gifts," Jerry said. "His own persona is amplified through his voice on the page, especially if he's writing with a first-person narrator. That's the way he bundled up his own reputation with the story he told in *The Moon and Sixpence* and recapitulated Gauguin's quest while still changing all the names—*magnifique!*"

"I haven't read that one yet," I said. "But I know what you mean. In this one, the first-person narrator takes charge on page one and not only tells you right off the bat that the whole story revolves around a young man with whom he had only the most occasional contact, but also that there will be gaps and inevitable lapses. My reaction was to yield to the author's command and just go with it. No regrets at all."

"I understand. After reading *The Moon and Sixpence*, I wanted to call him up on the phone. Tell him I thought he hit the bull's-eye with that one. Not with *Of Human Bondage*. But what does your father's generation have to do with it?" Jerry asked.

"Everything," I said. "And I think it explains why it's such a big-hit bestseller back in the States. According to ol' Mom, it's selling by the ton, budgets be damned. When Pop sent me this cheaper Blakiston edition, she wrote that she had seen four or five others reading from the Doubleday first edition on the bus or the streetcars. There is some kind of peculiar hunger for this back home. It has a depth and a texture that …"

On and on I went. I didn't mean to ramble. But I sort of did. What had me going was that I knew in my bones that Maugham had tapped into a yearning for some kind of spiritual integrity. Some kind of illumination. Elevated thinking. The folks back home sure weren't getting any of that from the radio, movies, magazines or papers.

"And the thing that makes all this so much like how I sense my father's life has been," I finally concluded, "is that ol' Mom has always hinted at the fact that when he came back from the Great War—just like the character that Maugham puts his focus on—Pop was . . . different. Utterly changed. Yet he never spoke of the war. Ever."

"All right," Jerry said. "So we have Mr. Maugham telling the tale and his focus, as you cinematically put it, is on this young man who returns from World War One. Right?"

"And to others he seems to be in a permanent state of strange," I interrupted. "He has no interest in going to work. His plans to be a stockbroker soon fizzle. All of his social connections and lifelong acquaintances are baffled. But none of that matters to Larry Darrell. That's the guy's name. He sets out on a private spiritual journey."

Then I apologized all over myself and explained to Jerry that I thought I was being much too reductive and simplifying too much and badly summarizing the novel.

"It's a vast, epic, internal journey," I said, "as well as an international jaunt. But, you see, that's just it. It's *not* a jaunt. It's not trivial. He doesn't just goof off vacationing somewhere exotic. He moves to Paris and works in a fish market. And later he visits a German monastery and other places. But the story peaks with his pilgrimage to India, where he seeks out the wisdom of what they call the Vedas, which are the philosophical and spiritual texts of the Vedantic tradition. That's a big cornerstone of the Hindu religious tradition. He goes to live in an ashram and stays for a long, long time. He recalls all this to Mr. Maugham years later, in the form of a marvelously extended dialogue that's at the end of the book. And he sums up all sorts of revelations."

"Revelations?" Jerry inquired. "Are you sure he's not just pontificating?"

"I'm sure," I said. "It's really the damnedest thing. In the book, Maugham even warns the readers in a theatrical 'aside' that they can skip this whole lengthy dialogue altogether, and pick up the remainder of the story in the subsequent chapters. But he also admits that if not for that particular dialogue, he would not have bothered to write the book."

"And somehow all this reminds you of your father?" Jerry asked.

"It does," I said. "It's *his* era. The epoch of the last war. Remember? The one that was supposed to end all wars? And it's set in Chicago, more or less, in the first part of the book. Actually, it a ritzy suburb called Lake Forest. But that's near Chicago."

"And, somehow, the protagonist reminds you of your father?" Jerry said.

"He does. Everyone else is noisy and busy. He's seeking to be calm and quiet."

"Read the pages of that dialogue you consider revelatory," Jerry said. "Read aloud." Then he added: "Can you imagine a whole family of such seekers? All levitating!"

Maybe it all sounds cornball now. Or maybe it's all too "cheeseball," as Rena says.

But there's nothing I can do about that. We were the way we were. And as the sun rose on that morning of August 29th, 1944, we were a couple of word-nerds lost for a blessed and brief reprieve in the narrative flights of Somerset Maugham. The pages I read aloud to Jerry were all contained within that section of the book that's really a series of longwinded question and answer episodes. All about God-consciousness and how to live a life of moment-to-moment God-consciousness. Vedanta.

Many of the questions are posed by Mr. Maugham, and they're all questions put to the main character: Larry Darrell. Questions about Larry's expatriate travels in France, Spain, Germany, India, and elsewhere, after the traumas of World War One.

Then even more detailed questions about Larry's immersion into Vedantic studies, which follow his efforts amid priests and monks and others; his efforts to learn what he could of Western religious traditions. His shift from West to East is revealed in the answers that Larry offers up to the narrator, whose chronicle of their vast, capacious dialogue makes for fascinating reading. I can't even begin to sum it up. But believe you me, Mr. Maugham was way ahead of his time.

He had his Larry Darrell acknowledging and exploring the ideas and notions of Hinduism, Buddhism, and meditations and levitations, not to mention the implications of reincarnation and other cosmic and ancient inquiries years before the Beats or the Beatles. Amazing. Clairvoyant. Prescient.

It certainly seized Jerry. He sat there in total silence as I read page after page out loud, but never did I see him nod off. He never looked bored. He never dozed, even though we'd more or less stayed up all night. When he did close his eyes, my sense of things was that such inward gazing allowed him to absorb more and more of the dialogue I was reading from the book. And there's no doubt that Mr. Maugham's vaunted reputation as a playwright helped in the creation of such a long colloquy.

Most of all, though, I believed then and I think now that Jerry closed his eyes to do more than further absorb and digest the myriad concepts and principles pouring off the pages of *The Razor's Edge*. I believe that Jerry's inward concentration, his inner-directed focus and such focused intention had everything to do not just with what he was hearing as I read (and the pages overflowed with queries and guesses and speculations and insights about God, life and death, love and loss, the limits of knowledge gained through texts and the glorious mysteries of Nature and its ways of affecting all aspects of human beings pursuing more than money and property), but also with accepting the inevitability of his return to the war. It was time to go.

It wasn't a matter of the minutes or the hours. It wasn't a choice at all. It was all about the day. His pass expired mid-day on the 29th. As did mine. Time was up.

And without having to say a word, I knew that whatever he had yet to face in the war would doubtless be worse than what he'd already survived. Here we go again. This is something else that's never been conveyed in anyway that's accurate. Now I'll try to lay it down as simply as I can: Much has been made in recent years of how for decades after the war, the people of my generation were "the silent generation." Much has been made about how the GIs didn't talk about the war—not to their wives or girlfriends; not to their children; usually not to anyone after the war.

But the thing is like this: The guys didn't talk about the war *even in the midst of it.*

Everyone's total focus was on getting through, moment by moment, and talking about what was happening as it all unfolded—or even during the periodic lulls or the interludes free of danger—would have been like expecting people in general conversations to talk all about their blood count or their urinations or their daily dumps or anything else related to the ineffable mystery of living in the moment. The guys who managed to survive the landings at Normandy (or anywhere else, from the shores of North Africa and Sicily to the beaches of Italy and Southern France, not to mention everywhere from Guadalcanal to Okinawa in the Pacific), well, it's not that they didn't speak of it all at that time because they thought it was fun. They *didn't.*

Nobody understood more than the GIs themselves how flawed, surreal, sometimes doomed or at best barely feasible were the "battle plans" consuming their beings.

And talking about it wasn't helpful as it unfolded. Just getting through it was more than difficult enough. Surviving. One more day. Another hour. *This* minute. *Now.*

I finished reading. We were silent.
I meant to turn to my left and try to take the measure of Jerry's reaction. His ability to sit for so long and not say anything did not mean that he wasn't reacting. When I read those passages describing the struggles of

Larry Darrell—his intellectual and emotional tussles with the essential tenets of Christianity and how Vedanta vastly differs from the West—I could tell by Jerry's body language that he was deeply engaged in the story. He leaned over closer. He listened harder. He breathed with deeper inhalations and longer exhalations. He was truly present. It was intense.

And it was intimate, too. I don't care how silly that sounds. It's true. There's an ancient and now exceedingly unpopular notion that the transmission of knowledge is, in fact, something of an erotic act. Sometimes, that is. Certainly I don't mean to say that children and their teachers ought to be engaged in hanky-panky. But I am highly aware— even now, when my own inhalations and exhalations are surely on their final rounds—that for two individuals who are mutually absorbed in a realm of ideas that touches their souls, the act of one reading to another is akin to caresses.

That was probably why I felt so airborne. I wasn't just excited by the ideas or the insights or the majestic themes in *The Razor's Edge*. What happened was a lot more than the usual mental stimulation that learning often causes. This was not mental.

This was different. For me, anyway. And I'm sure it was different for Jerry, too. In the quiet hours (at long last) that preceded sunrise on August 29th, 1944, instead of spooning by the Seine and sleeping for a brief spell or instead of going all out and just slipping off into the shadows and having our way with each other, we opted instead to stay nearest the water and to bathe ourselves in the novel's words. No matter how dark it was, reading was possible because all I needed was the glow of my cigarette (or Jerry's and between the two of us and our trusty Zippo lighters we did all right), and thanks to the glow also provided by the apartment-dwellers in the immediate vicinity who never turned their lights off all night long . . . we had it all.

We had that remarkable companionship that results from two people being tossed into each other's worlds while the larger world is seemingly coming apart. Or at the same time seemingly coming back together.

We had the shared awareness that the clocks were ticking and second by second, minute by minute, only a scant number of hours remained for us to be together. But at the same time—and the mystery of Time was the prime mover here—the words I read from Maugham's unusual, densely textured pages gave us again and again and moment by moment and time after time and passage after passage that wondrous and ethereal feeling that only "time present" consumed us. The *now* was all.

And that's what I mean by intimate. The climactic passages I'd read to Jerry (all about Larry Darrell's ultimate dialogue with an Indian guru whose sage advice and infinite patience with all the mysteries of every evanescent moment) had much to do with how to live purposefully in a world often tainted by purposelessness. And how to live quietly and with compassion in times of upheaval and chaos and war. I heard my own voice reading from the novel, but something else was involved. My sense of it was that our souls were briefly transported and we knew something like heaven. Or what others call Nirvana. Our oneness reminded me Whitman's greatest epiphanies.

So of course for a fleeting second or two I thought I'd see Jerry's face in profile, with perhaps a hint of a smile or a look of repose or at least a relaxed appearance of calm.

Instead he looked as if someone had stabbed his eyes. Before I was even able to form a question about why it was or what it was that made him look so stricken, he did something physically adroit. It's a move I don't recall seeing anyone else make, although I'm sure it's not all that impossible. But, to me, it was a genuine first.

He immediately ascended into an upright, standing position. Just like that. At once.

Unlike you, me, or the man on the moon, who would likely place a hand down on the ground in order to push ourselves upward into a standing position, he just *did it.*

His hands never hit the ground. He didn't lean on me. In fact, I distinctly recall that his hands remained on his knees. But despite his legs being crossed, and despite the lack of thrust usually gained from pushing off the ground with one's palm, what he did was just ascend into a fully erect and highly attentive posture. For a second I'm sure I was tempted to ask him how the hell his ankles and feet could facilitate that.

But all of a sudden my attention was directed by Jerry's extended index finger, which pointed with careful deliberation to the Seine. His dread still radiated.

And that's when I saw the bloated, ravaged form of a body afloat on the river.

33

That wasn't the only one. Hardly. I counted three more in the light of that new morning, which wasn't difficult to do because by the time we'd buttoned up our shirts after dusting off and gathering ourselves from what had been (however briefly) a sacred space of healing words by the Seine, all through the night, we saw more than a few Parisians hovering near the river banks and staring and pointing.

One of those we saw was the severely focused and dour-looking man who also sat amidst the inner circle of that rehearsal reading of Simone's play one night earlier, when Picasso's nearby studio apartment seemed to me like a bastion of art and Eros. Now that man looked even more severe, more focused, and downright appalled. At the time his name was scarcely known outside of Paris, but I could see by the subtle ways that several passers-by nodded, pointed, acknowledged or in some way showed attention that locally he was something of a figure. Jerry had swiftly connected dots.

"He'll be writing about this for *Combat*," Jerry said. "That's his magazine. Sort of like a newspaper and magazine combined. But he'll have the guts to acknowledge this."

And by "this" what Jerry referred to was not just the horrendous vengeance killings that led to untold numbers of bodies being dumped in the Seine in the first few days after the Liberation, with slit throats and brutalized bodies tied to stones not heavy enough to keep them submerged. "This" was also the squalor of the pandemic vengeance.

Years later, the strained, exhausted, ultra-serious expression seen that morning on the face of the man in the pin-stripe suit who only the night before had been there in the midst of Simone's rehearsal reading, his visage became the face of Existentialism as the postwar media latched onto it. But on that morning, I didn't know Camus or his name or his emerging work. Only from Jerry, that day, did I learn about *Combat*.

But in the subsequent weeks and months, sure enough, there were more than a few highly critical, outraged, deeply intelligent and lacerating articles and editorials in *Combat*, all of them exposing and lamenting the insufferable rash of revenge that made a mockery of any notions about liberty, equality, and fraternity. It wasn't just the women who were shorn and paraded half-nude in public who received the full wrath of the now liberated French. There was a spasm of staggering and lawless and wholly unpredictable mayhem, all of which went on amidst the noise and the cheers and the endless celebrations in that initial, unchecked phase of liberation.

Not just by the dozens. Not just hundreds, mind you. There were thousands of French civilians (tens of thousands) who were known to be or assumed to be or suspected of being wholly in cahoots with the Germans during the Occupation. They were located, rounded up, and sometimes after a show trial (or not) they were simply killed outright. Often after torture and beatings. And when there *were* show trials, as they later came to be called, they really were like putting on a show. Most of the time, staged outdoors with a table and a few chairs and room for the outraged citizens to congregate and vent the furies repressed and burning for over four years, the pretense of a trial was a theatrical exercise. Blood lust was omnipresent. And then, in the aftermath of the war, amnesia was induced. A case of national amnesia.

The floating bodies of murdered collaborators (I should say those who were alleged to be collaborators) were all male. "That's the difference we've known we could count on," Jerry said, as we made our way toward the Arc de Triomphe for the start of the parade and the arrival of the 28th Infantry Division of the U. S. Army.

"That was the pattern during the Spanish Civil War and we've heard nearly identical stories out of Italy. Now that three of our combat divisions are out of Italy and deployed down in the Vosges Mountains. Anecdotes about Naples and Rome: verifiable."

When I asked Jerry for a more clear-cut explanation, his speech quickly altered. He spoke in a clipped, precise, Clark Gable-style. Not at all like his old self. "Women are punished in the public square. The shearing. The jeers. Their clothes ripped off. It comes down to public humiliation, and it's almost always men punishing women. In the case of male collaborators, there's a difference. They're killed in secret. Rarely are they paraded in public. They're smoked out, usually beaten to a pulp, tortured and degraded in disgusting ways that match the methods of the bastards they all allegedly collaborated with, and then . . . when *they're* killed, it's in the shadows. As for dumping bodies in the Seine, more of that will be revealed. Because it takes more than most people know to fully weigh a body down and keep it submerged."

I didn't need to hear much more. It broke my spirit then and even now it ruins too many of my memories. But despite the decades of amnesia that followed, there is now no doubt that those first weeks and months after the Liberation at the end of August 1944, there was a dark underside to the days of celebration. And Jerry's offhanded allusion to the Spanish Civil War hit me like a sledgehammer because I remembered all too well how horribly affected ol' Mom was when we saw that film version of Hemingway's *For Whom the Bell Tolls* back in 1943, and right at the end of Part One (it was such a long movie that they had an Intermission) there was a scene of mob violence showing how one by one a handful of captured Fascist sympathizers were killed. They were forced to run a gauntlet where dozens of Loyalists furiously awaited, all of them brandishing heavy wooden bats that were specifically designed with a special hinge for a smaller club attached to the larger bat, ensuring that every strike resulted in two body blows. Thus the person using the weapon had twice the destructive power in hand. It was a weapon intended for torture, used to kill.

The fact that it was the anti-Fascists inflicting such grim punishments was one of the main points made by Hemingway that generated such enormous controversy. Atrocities were committed on *both* sides. All the time.

That scene in the movie of *For Whom the Bell Tolls* made ol' Mom sick. And I do not mean that figuratively. She didn't eat for the next two days.

And she cried all night, after we saw the film. Actually, she sobbed all the way through the second half.

Pop was upset, too. Even worse.

I didn't put it all together at the time. I guess I was more bumbling Watson that deductive Holmes. But so much else was going on at that time in 1943. So . . .

Later it was ol' Mom who clued me in. She'd connected the dots ipso-facto. And after the war, out of the blue, in the midst of another dark time, she up and asked me if I recalled that outing to the Hi-Way Theater and how the three of us saw the film version of *For Whom the Bell Tolls* and all like that. "Of course," I told her. "It was our last get-together." By instinct, I avoided mentioning her crying jag that day.

And that's when I learned that Pop's distress and his own extreme kind of grief and upset behavior mushroomed after my exit from Chicago. "He was already moody and sad, really remote after the war," ol' Mom said to me. "All the while you were gone at Fort Des Moines, in Iowa, with all that basic training you gals had to do, he was brooding and morose back at home. That silver anniversary really did him in."

It was not their wedding anniversary she referred to. They'd gotten married in 1920, so their silver anniversary didn't come around until 1945. Ol' Mom was referring instead to 1918. When Pop was steeped in his war in France. None of which he ever talked about directly, but all of which affected him body and soul.

"For him to see you in uniform in 1943," she explained, "and to have the news and the newsreels and the radio highlighting the new war every morning, noon, and night, weekends included, well, it really intensified his brooding about 1918."

"I didn't realize then that any such silver anniversary was on the calendar," I said.

Come to think of it, with what little time I have left to think, I must say that my lack of awareness in the early autumn of 1943 about anything in relation to 1918 and what a significant twenty-fifth anniversary that had to be for Pop and all the other Doughboys who were over there and in the line of fire throughout all those climactic Western Front campaigns. Well, damn it, it wasn't a personal failing on my part.

I may be lulled by Lorazepam and "chillaxed" (as Rena loves to say) by the other meds I cannot live without (the muscle relaxants scarcely work against my ever-increasing pain and paralysis, but on we go), and God knows I did not want to ask for an increase in the morphine doses now received (which almost rids me of my excruciating nerve pain, but I still feel the burning hurt beneath all the numbness).

But, nonetheless, from the neck up, I can still pass a test. I remember. I can speak.

And I am absolutely sure that in the midst of all the bad news, the chronic crises, the awful stress and the skyrocketing anxieties about the war underway in 1943, there were simply no national or noteworthy acts of remembrance regarding all that the Doughboys had suffered and endured twenty-five years earlier, back in 1918. All Pop had was our little family ritual, with the books and candles and all.

"Your father had no one to speak to," ol' Mom explained to me, after I was discharged from the WACs at the very end of 1945. "He held it all inside."

Decades later, in the aftermath of the Vietnam War, it was often said that the Vietnam vets were "the forgotten warriors." Which they were, for a long time.

And weird though it was, in those same years I'm thinking now of the late 1970s and through the 1980s it was also a cliché that the Korean War of 1950 through 1953 was "the forgotten war." Even though there was a ridiculous weekly reminder.

I never understood how the journalists and book reviewers and other media types could always cough up that "forgotten war" riff about Korea, when for well over a decade after the film *M*A*S*H* hit big in 1970, there was a beloved television series that stayed at the top of the ratings until its finale in 1983. That's how crazy it was. On the one hand, the entire nation was on a first-name basis with Hawkeye Pierce, Radar O'Reilly, Hot Lips Houlihan, Colonel Potter, Klinger, and all the others. But you couldn't find any documentaries about Inchon, Heartbreak Ridge, or Chosin.

Oh, hell, it never mattered that *M*A*S*H* was set smack dab in the middle of the Korean War. It was all seen as a metaphor for Vietnam. There's never been any doubt in my mind that the smash-hit success of all that was directly linked to the whole anti-Establishment fever that defined (and lingered after) the Vietnam Era.

But I'm drifting here and here's my point: Long before the Vietnam vets or the guys who survived the Korean War felt abandoned, forgotten, or used, the Doughboys of Pop's generation wrote the book on such grief. And the horrendous results of their Bonus Army March to Washington, D. C., back in 1933 broke a few million hearts.

They lived in silence. Unlike me.

And it's taken me all these many decades to be able to say it aloud, but the truth is that what I learned from ol' Mom about Pop's extreme reaction to the despair and the depression he was feeling in 1943, which he hid brilliantly from me while I was around . . . well, I later learned that it was right around that same time (after I was en route to the East for further training as a Field Switchboard Operator) that Pop first tried his tactic of starting their car and letting it idle, inside the closed garage.

34

Even though Jerry parked his jeep nearby the Arc de Triomphe (he drove that thing like a past master; I swear he could have parked it on a postage stamp; when I met him again—so briefly—ten years later, it didn't surprise me that he had a jeep), we weren't able to closely observe the eternal flame at the Tomb of the Unknown Soldier that day. By the time we were there, too much hectic hoopla was underway.

The plan was fairly straightforward. The 28th Infantry Division of the U. S. Army would parade right around the circular boulevard surrounding the Arc de Triomphe, and unlike the Germans four years earlier they certainly wouldn't march beneath it.

Then: The march would proceed straight on down the Champs-Élysées, which plenty of the GIs loved to deliberately mispronounce by calling it the "Champs Eloise" ("champs" rhyming with "ramps," and "Eloise" just for good measure). I thought it was funny then and even now, as my fadeout beckons, it makes me smile. It was their regional accents and dialects that made it sound especially funny: Guys from Jersey or Brooklyn or the Bronx as well as the GIs with Boston echoes (along with the endless Midwestern varieties of twang) made "Champs Eloise" into their own brand of all-American *patois*. Anyway, we got there too late to be so close.

That made me sad. I really wanted to stand up close and observe as carefully as I could the eternal flame and also the words on the plaque of the Tomb. But it was only several decades later, when visiting Paris on my own, that I had the chance to do that. And by then there was no dignity or integrity to the milieu because the whole damn space was overrun with ill-mannered, obnoxious, grinning, photo-hungry half-assed tourists from all over the world. I was appalled. You'd have thought it was Disneyland, the way they all monkeyed around and posed with their idiotic smiles and goofy gestures, as if the Tomb of the Unknown Soldier is jolly. It was almost as bad as the atrocious way I saw tourists munching Fritos and looking bored, seemingly indifferent to being on site at the concentration camp museums that I made a pilgrimage to on that tour in the 1990s. I kept pretty much to myself, even though I went on one of those discounted group tours. But on the grounds of Dachau and Buchenwald, it was almost as bad as what I saw when on that tour I finally got nearest to the Tomb of the Unknown Soldier. Arrogant, ignorant, self-absorbed and utterly lacking in manners, the behavior of international tourists was horrendous. I'm sure it's worse than ever in the Age of Selfies. Disgusting. Moronic.

So, like I was saying, on the day of the legendary parade we were late to arrive and there were already overflow crowds and closed-off areas and harried French police and other officials trying to keep things orderly. Then the 28th ID was on the march.

If I didn't know better, I'd have sworn that airplanes were swooping down from up above. That's how loud and vociferous the cheering crowds were. All I had to do was close my eyes and listen for ten seconds, and the volume and intensity and the unleashed passions and emotions of the many thousands lined up all the way down the Champs-Élysées sounded to my ears like a thousand airplanes, engines revving.

It wasn't just the GIs whose presence drove the Parisians into frenzies. The truth is that it was no normal parade in anyway. Hemingway had correctly guessed that the surest, fastest, simplest way possible for the 28th Infantry Division to maneuver its way over to the other side of Paris, there to resume chasing Krauts and fighting the war beyond the city limits, was to march the whole damn juggernaut right through the City of Light. So, a parade with a band and a regiment or two wasn't in the cards.

First came the massively impressive and innumerable two-and-a-half ton trucks and the half-tracks too. By the dozens. Also: There were tanks and artillery galore. The whole damn kit and caboodle was on display, and the untold thousands of marching infantrymen made up the latter portion of the parade. It was a vast display of mighty righteousness and after living under the boots of occupying Nazis for those four long years between 1940 and 1944, this parade of Allied fortitude was apprehended as nothing less than a miraculous deliverance. Heaven-sent.

The cacaphonous roaring and the palpable love and the unconditional joy and sheer ecstasy of the prodigious crowds—ridiculously well-dressed as they were, with summer dresses on most of the ladies and almost all the older hat-wearing men sporting suits and ties, despite the torrid late-August heat, while younger men opted for white shirts and no hats or ties—offered unto the GIs a communion of gratitude.

I kept closing my eyes for ten or twenty seconds at a time, unable to stop because not only did I wish again and again to simply "hear" the overwhelming cheers, but, I also had to do something else. I had to have moments of respite from the eyes of the GIs.

No matter how loud the cheering or how rapturous the crowds, and despite the unmistakable authenticity of this reception, what struck me most and saddened me forever were the faces on some of the soldiers marching by. Neither Jerry nor I got close to the Tomb of the Unknown Soldier that day, but we could see the GIs' faces.

Oh, sure, some were smiling and some grinning. Some were clearly enthused. But more than a few of the soldiers marching swiftly down the Champs-Élysées in what had to be for them a blur of chaotic glee and non-stop forward motion; well, it was clear to me that they were exhausted, sad, seized by grief, and probably hungry.

How could they *not* be? They'd slept outdoors the night before, when it rained for hours on end. They'd been in the field since mid-summer, living on rations. Their baptisms of fire had occurred, but now they knew the war was still waiting for them.

I couldn't help but think that despite all the adulation and the cheers and flowers, all the hugging and kissing, and most of all the omnipresent flag-waving joyful citizens, it had to be sad as hell for many of the guys who knew they were on their way to die.

So, I had to close my eyes. Time after time. When I saw one of the soldiers in the 28th ID, a guy who looked significantly older than many of the others, my memory kicked in and I recalled that we who were in communications had been briefed about the unusual history of the 28th. They were, in fact, originally the National Guard of the state of Pennsylvania. They were, indeed, the oldest Army division in the history of America. They'd been federalized and roped into the regular army as a result of the war's outbreak. Just like the Texas National Guard was federalized and transformed into the 36th Infantry Division, which paid in blood and limbs and lives for every yard of Italy they rid of the Nazis; we'd all been recently briefed on how the combat-hardened 36th had been taken out of Italy and deployed down in the South of France (for "the other D-Day" nobody ever talks about), where they were clobbering the Germans and fighting their way towards an Allied link-up.

The face of that older GI really got to me. As much as I was stunned by the boyish GIs who marched along with those prematurely sage expressions on their peach-fuzzed faces, it was the visage of the older soldier that made me close my eyes again. For the longest time. Of course he made me think of Pop. I wondered if the older GI had been in the Pennsylvania National Guard going all the way back to 1918. There was a story already going around about a kind of "Kilroy Was Here" graffiti soldier, who hailed from Chicago, and who was back in France for a second time in 1944. It wasn't as uncommon as you might think. There were guys who'd been age eighteen in 1918 and were there for the first war. And because they'd stayed in the National Guard or retained their commissions or made careers in the army, they were back over there in 1944. One of 'em had rediscovered the spot where he'd scrawled his name and added "was here in 1918" back at the end of the Great War. He now wrote his name again (that is, he carved it onto a stone using his bayonet), and added: "He was also here in 1944. He'd prefer not to come back." I had a question for Jerry.

I wanted to ask him if most of the GIs he knew were in their mid-twenties, like we were. Or if the replacement depots, along with the draft, hit younger men hardest.

I opened my eyes, ready to ask my question. But he had disappeared. Like *that*.

It wasn't possible for me to dash across the boulevard and try to see if Jerry was back at the spot where he'd parked the jeep. Police were cordoning off any of the pedestrian outlets that might've allowed for such a search, because if not held in check the throngs out there cheering and crying and exploding with long-repressed passions would have interfered with the parade. The continuous passage of dozens of colossal pieces of military hardware and mechanized weaponry and all of those jeeps (some of them weighed down with mounted machine guns; others not) and the half-tracks rolling in unison down the Champs-Élysées, followed by yet another regiment and then another one after that (thousands upon thousands of GIs smartly marching twenty-four abreast across the wide and legendary avenue), well, it made it impossible to do anything in the way of walking back around the Arc de Triomphe.

The only thing to do was walk, then trot, then jog, and finally run all the way down the Champs-Élysées and follow the parade route adjacent to the guys. For me it was involuntary. Most of those observing the parade were content to be stationary. But I had to see if I could spot Jerry. Somewhere. *Any*where. I could not help myself. As briskly as possible, I kept pace while staying on the beautifully paved and smooth stones of the Champs-Élysées as the 28th Infantry Division dominated the scene.

Each row of GIs was a curb-to-curb panorama, and believe you me when I say that twenty-four abreast in every damn row was quite a sight to behold. Equally stirring was the mere fact that despite all of the street fighting and barricades, the sniper fire and small arms fire, the last grenades and the demolitions that the German holdouts did ignite, there was a miraculously minimal amount of wreckage on the boulevard.

In no way was the heart of Paris devastated. Nothing remotely resembling the wretched damages done by the Germans to Warsaw, London, Rotterdam (or one hundred other world-class cities) had been inflicted on the Parisians. There had been a last-blast, so to speak, just a week earlier when the Luftwaffe followed its orders and dumped one thousand bombs on the City of Light in a pathetic effort to punish the

Parisians as the days of Liberation commenced. But those one thousand bombs were summarily dropped on a concentrated locale over on the other side of Paris. There was destruction and dozens were killed, but on August 29th any such detritus miles away may as well have been up on the moon. Along with Jerry.

He'd vanished. And on and on I walked and trotted and jogged and ran, believing that against all odds I'd somehow manage to find him. Hug him goodbye. Really at the time that's all I thought I wanted to do. At least hug him, kiss, and say farewell.

I never had the chance. He was gone. The war was waiting for him.

The next day, in the temporary HQ of my communications team in Paris, I saw a news article in *Stars and Stripes* that summarized a day-old story from the *New York Times*. My eyes were drawn right to the words "Chateau-Thierry" in the headline.

The day before, as the 28th Division made its way down the Champs-Élysées, other GIs with Patton's Third Army were clobbering the Krauts over in Chateau-Thierry, less than 100 miles away. The article said that the GIs were again vanquishing the Germans in the same spot where many of their Doughboy fathers had trounced the Huns in 1918. Where Pop had first fought in July 1918. Where his only brother, my Uncle Jim, was dismembered by shellfire. But somehow Pop survived.

When I wasn't crying throughout September, I was dreaming of clarinets.

35

Now in my dreams it's all more vivid than ever it was in my daytime reveries. Just this morning is a perfect example. And lucky for me that the morning aide (another new one; the revolving door here for part-timers is always going 'round and around) was okay with my insisting on setting the microphone properly on the pillow, and minimizing the routine, to allow me this time alone to record. So, today's dream . . .

Good Lord, where do I begin? They're all in color these days, which stuns me. I have always dreamed heavily, but never in my life have so many dreams been in color. It is almost funny. Echoes abound. As I admit all this, I hear the echoes of the old-time TV announcer on NBC or whatever it was, intoning: "In living color!" That was the ultimate sign of the times, when so many programs converted to color broadcasting back in the middle of the 1960s. My son was ten and eleven then. It amazed him as much as kids were amazed back in 1939, when seeing *The Wizard of Oz* in theaters for the very first time and witnessing black-and-white Kansas become colorful Oz.

In my running dreams this morning, all was Technicolor. And by running I don't mean suiting up for gym class and running laps around the track or anything like sweet and goofy Forrest Gump crisscrossing America. I mean my own running.

The immensity of the Arch was the dream's primary motif. As it was in life, so it is in my dreams. To be standing adjacent to the Arc de Triomphe is quite similar to being on the sidewalk near the Empire State Building or even Mount Rushmore. I mean, of course I'm not talking about size here. Or height. I'm talking about "immensity" and the unusual way that an individual feels both dwarfed and elevated at the same time as history reverberates the way it does around such classic landmarks. Monuments.

Like the Arch. For me, in my color dreams this morning, the essence of my awe was palpable. Just as it was back in 1944, when I stood there craning my neck to observe as closely as possible the exquisite Napoleonic sculptures adorning the Arch. Then as I began running that day—brisk walking at first, but soon trotting and then as best I could actually running down the Champs-Élysées in search of Jerry—what happened in my dreams this morning actually happened in real life. After every one hundred yards or so, as I walked, trotted, and ran, I'd stop to catch my breath a bit and instinctively I'd turn around hoping to find Jerry right behind me. He never was.

But the damnedest thing was that as I moved farther and farther away from the Arch, its size did not diminish when I turned around. Quite the other way. Logic was defied. Not to mention the laws of science. The further I traveled down the Champs-Élysées, following the exact same route as the 28th Infantry Division as their parade formation made its way down to the Place de la Concorde at the opposite end of the boulevard, each time I paused and looked back, the Arch was larger. It spooked me when it happened because it made my anxiety soar. I thought I was maybe going a little bit crazy. But I was so lost in the moment that I kept running.

In a funny way, here's the kicker. All those glorious buildings and the endless tableaux of architectural wonders that go on and on and on down the Champs-Élysées certainly retained their proper proportions: in life and in my dream. But the Arch assumed a supernatural shape-shifting power, along with the music of course.

And this is where I know it's useless to try to share all this with one of the nurses or any of the doctors. They'll make a note about dementia and order up more pills. In my experience, that's their answer for everything. Another prescription. *Oblivion.*

But I want to get this across, not matter what. In my dream this morning, the music was just as precise as the Technicolor images of the Arc de Triomphe. And just as the Arch in my dream this morning did not shrink but instead expanded in size as I periodically looked backward while running in the opposite direction, so the music that dominated the dream's soundtrack was exactly what I remember from that day.

I swear, I am not making this up. I truly do remember how it was that day, because as I walked fast and then began to trot and eventually started running for at least one hundred yards at a time (all the while remaining aware of the floodtide of the 28th Division striding in its bold, forward motion beside me as the jubilation of the Parisians reached one crescendo after another), the tempo of my movement was determined by the songs that kept going around and around in my mind.

I sang two different songs in the privacy of my mind to give me a metronome to run by. Both songs were sung by Edythe Wright in the late 1930s, when she was Tommy Dorsey's singer. And she didn't sing with only the big band, but also with the small jazz group plucked out of the band and known as "The Clambake Seven." That was a thing (as Rena likes to say, and God how I miss her; they've cut her hours here). It was a thing with a few of the big bands. Artie Shaw had "The Gramercy Five" and Bob Crosby had "The Bobcats" and of course Benny had his Trios, Quartets, Sextets.

But my favorite combo-within-the-big band crew was TD's "Clambake Seven." They had that old-time New Orleans style down pat, and Edythe Wright singing away on "The Music Goes 'Round and Around" made me as happy as a kid on Saturday morn.

So back on August 29th, 1944, when I picked up steam and shifted from trotting to running, the song in my head would switch to "The Music Goes 'Round and Around." Its bright cadence made it perfect to run with, and I could hum it aloud if I chose to.

But our chronic smoking was already doing it damage, and I couldn't run too long before having to slow down. Ease up. Settle for trotting or walking again. That's when the song I'd move to in the privacy of my mind segued to "Music, Maestro, Please," which Edythe Wright sang with TD's band during my high school era.

I don't care how flipped out this sounds, it's my truth: In this morning's dream, in all of its Technicolor wonder, the same two songs were in the air. Just like I remembered them. With one difference: The words were being sung in French by Edith Piaf.

Speaking of the damnedest things. Sheridan O'Neill is all over my dreams again. I wonder how things turned out for him. I used to audit classes at Loyola University (long ago) and I met him when auditing "Religions of India and the Far East." He never went anywhere without carrying (on his person) or usually piling (on any table) all four of the little books Jerry later published: monochromatic covers and uniform fonts on display. "Four gospels, four Beatles, and the Salinger Quartet" he used to say. It was love at first sight. Decades be damned. I was going on sixty; he was pushing thirty. We broke *all* the rules. I wish it had lasted longer. C'*est la vie*.

He was also a philatelist. No kidding. A bona-fide stamp geek. He confided to me that the famous picture of the 28th Infantry Division marching in Paris—the photo used for the three-cent Victory Stamp—made him cry because four of the soldiers in the front row of that photo were killed by Germans on the outskirts of Paris, shortly after August 29th, 1944. The war was waiting for them. Always.

36

It's after 9PM. And saints be praised, my beloved Lorena-Rena-Bena-Bean-Beansy came by to do more than set up the micro-cassette and say goodnight. She wanted to tell me that she'd finally watched the DVD of *The Concert for Bangladesh* and she agrees with Claudia Lennear (the back-up singer) that something unusual happened at those shows. In that documentary we saw called *20 Feet From Stardom*, when some of the performance of "Wah-Wah" is shown, Claudia narrates over the music and all, insisting that anyone able to witness those unique concerts knew that there was something transcendent, holy, sacred and rare about it all. Lorena wanted to tell me that after seeing the whole concert film, she "agrees with all her heart."

That reminds me of how Pop always said "I love you with all my heart." Talk about *rare*. When I shared that with some of the gals in the WACs (we always talked about family stuff and our backgrounds and all), they looked startled. Most of them didn't have fathers who said such affectionate things. Not out loud. Pop said it quite often.

Which was odd, because he hardly ever said anything. Small talk wasn't his thing. But when he spoke, either to ol' Mom or to me, he'd say the words like gospel: "I love you with all my heart." I wish that had been enough for him. But in the end, one day while I was at work, four years after the war, Pop again started his car out there in the garage and he did so without opening the garage door. That was the last time.

Ol' Mom and I agreed on a cover story. The damn church would deny him a proper Christian burial if they knew the truth. Our riff was that a massive stroke did him in. As for the garage door being closed while the car idled, we managed to dodge that. I am still awed by ol' Mom's aplomb about the tale. She had to con everyone. Claimed that of course the garage door was open when she found Pop in the car. She stood by her story: at the hospital, to the police, and to Father Gerald's face. Brave gal. I never liked Father Gerald. He looked at children like a hungry dog eyes red meat.

But I think it ate her up inside. A coronary thrombosis snatched ol' Mom in her sleep only four years later. By 1953, I was really on my own. Not an easy time.

And now's not an easy time either. But before I let go, I need to stop fuming about something I keep remembering for no good reason. Well, maybe there's a reason. When speaking this morning and recalling how those two songs sung by Edythe Wright kept going through my mind and set the tempo at which I moved that day down the Champs-Élysées, vainly in search of the invisible man, an odd recurring memory kicked in. It sounds trivial but as intrusive thoughts go, this one's a pip.

Right around 1990 or so, toward the end of my time as a college Instructor, PBS broadcast an ambitious documentary series called *Making Sense of the Sixties*. I thought much of it was done well. But when they covered the radical transition in musical taste that occurred in the middle of the 1960s, some guy they interviewed made terrible fun of what he heard when as a teenager he discovered his father's old records. This guy was a Baby Boomer hemorrhoid on the ass of Woodstock Nation.

He joked about discovering his father's old 78 record of "The Music Goes 'Round and Around" and he ridiculed everything: the lyric, Edythe Wright, the jazzy horns. *Every*thing. Full of himself and full of shit, he dumped on the popular music of his father's epoch. He sang some of the song in a half-assed way, and rolled his eyes with utter disdain.

What a smug little bastard.

Ever since this morning, when my own fond memories of that song were conjured up by my words about August 29th, 1944, I've been thinking. Too much.

I need to put a stop to any stewing or angry mulling of thoughts. It's not easy for me to do that, because just recalling how that guy in the PBS series had a field day despising what we loved, decades before he came of age . . . watch out, lady.

This is what I mean. Before I let go in a great big way, I need to let go of this thing I do. Always grinding my teeth about the idiocy of others. I don't want to die angry.

37

I wasn't the only one really on my own by 1953. There were actually some news stories (small articles but just as telling) about Jerry's move out of New York City.

Writers were in the news back then. When their books appeared, of course, or when they sold a novel to Hollywood (which Jerry vowed he'd never do again, after "Uncle Wiggily in Connecticut" was hit by a cinematic wrecking ball and turned into *My Foolish Heart* in 1949). They also made the news if they made big moves.

Besides, with a new book that he brought out in 1953, it was inevitable that the tiny bit of information that Jerry allowed for publicity would tip off the world about his migration from Manhattan to the wilds of his remote redoubt up there in Cornish. When he selected the nine stories that were gathered together for his short-story collection in 1953, he not only followed up on the peculiar success of his novel and all from 1951, but also once again, he let loose with just enough information to assuage the curiosity of readers everywhere. He wasn't the mute hermit that his PR often made him out to be. Jerry doled out crucial tidbits. And he did so deliberately.

Like on the dust jacket of his one novel, when he dispensed with most of the bio-diarrhea, or "bio-rrhea," that writers are expected to let out. True: little was said. But he made damn sure to include that he'd been with the Fourth Infantry Division during the war in Europe. That was more important to him than anything else, probably. It certainly sent a signal to anyone who chose to remember anything. I remembered.

Anyway, if you were paying attention in those years to anything from *The New Yorker* magazine (which had finally become Jerry's sanctuary;

no more "slicks") to the Book-of-the-Month Club (they'd made a Main Selection out of his novel and helped introduce the bewitched, bothered, and bewildered Holden to readers all over the world), you somehow caught the news in '53 that Jerry had moved to an isolated hamlet up in New Hampshire. "Retreated," as a few stories summed up.

Meantime, in the aftermath of Pop's demise in '49 and ol' Mom's passing in 1953, I had all I could do to hold body and soul together. But thanks to them, I at least had our home. Little was left in fiscal terms, but they'd paid off their mortgage and much to my blessed relief, they'd properly arranged for me to inherit the house. For years, I'd attended night school, summer classes, and now and then a Saturday college course at De Paul University in downtown Chicago, racking up the necessary credits for both my bachelor's degree and then my master's degree in English and American literature. With those credentials in hand, I knew I could always teach.

Maybe if I'd been away on a major campus, enrolled in a full-time traditional program of study, maybe then I'd've applied to doctoral programs. Maybe not. Women then were rarely accepted into Ph. D. programs. It happened, but they were usually exceptions. Besides, another half-decade of seminars? I decided not to. For nearly a decade after the war's end in 1945, I worked by day and schooled part-time.

Needless to say, the GI Bill did not apply to WACs and our educational goals.

Between working, finishing my master's program, grieving over ol' Mom (that really tore the scabs off the death of Pop four years earlier) and just getting by, I was not able to pay any real attention to Jerry's 1953 short-story collection.

Not until 1954, that is. That's when I kept a promise I'd made to myself to return for a visit to Paris ten years after 1944. By the spring semester in '54, my studies were almost done at De Paul. And some inherited perks from Pop and ol' Mom (small stocks and smaller bonds) were cashed out to keep that promise to myself.

So I booked a flight. When flying Pan Am was new and exotic. It made me panic.

Just the thought of it made most people dizzy. Back then, booking your passage and sailing to Europe were still status quo. But I couldn't afford to take a month off from work to spend the time it would take to comfortably travel to New York and from there embark on any ship's seven-day across-the-Atlantic odyssey. So, I thought I'd fly. But when I hit the panic button at the New York airport, I detoured.

Did I ever. Because all I could do was think of him. I'd just read all nine stories that Jerry chose for his second book. It was the one book I had with me, and after I inhaled it on the flight from Chicago to New York, panic hit me like a grenade. Instead of flying Pan Am to Paris, I rented a car and put Jerry's book by my side.

Nine Stories. That's what he called it. I didn't think of calling him. I went there.

And that in itself was an odyssey. I had to play Tic-Tac-Dough with my Pan Am ticket itinerary, but it was a cinch to do so in those days. The costly part involved renting that car to drive from New York to Cornish, New Hampshire. No bus was headed there. Nonetheless, for that one weekend in the late summer of 1954, I felt quite whole again. It required little more than a detailed map (you could get one at any service station in those years) and my own resolve to make my way to Jerry's remote property way up in Cornish. That's 240 miles due north of Manhattan.

Of course I was able to find him in that tiny hamlet (all you had to do was roll down your car window and politely ask around about the newest guy in town and it was easy to be guided toward his property's entrance). And he not only remembered me, but, he graciously received me. This was eight months before he married *her*. The passage of time had affected us both in many ways. Yet, there was little difficulty in again connecting on the mysterious levels that we had once known.

Cornish was then all new to him. No bunker yet. No wife. No children. It was pristine and as far removed from all tumult as possible. A realm with dew on it.

Of course he was surprised by me suddenly sprouting up. Yet the audacity of my solo journey appealed to him and without difficulty we got reacquainted. Maybe the smartest thing I did was repeat a few times that my reconfigured airline ticket truly mandated that I show up at LaGuardia Airport two days later. And most of that second day would be spent driving there. The clock was ticking. Two nights only.

We ended up in his bed on that first night. It was as natural as breathing. Everything was stripped down to its simplest essence with him at that time. There was a tub and I was able to bathe. And yes, we ended up in the tub together.

He had some basic food and a working fridge, so we ate without frills. No problem.

On that first night in the tub and in his bed, we cuddled and caressed.

Just as easily we shared our thoughts about the sad sweetness of yearning for Paris again. He'd been there once or twice in recent years, and he loved being back there, while at the same time feeling nothing but grief. I didn't need to ask about the rest of his time during the war. We all knew the rules. They were universal. If anyone blabbed away about the war years, chances are they'd never been in real danger and had not seen combat or worse. Thus silence was received as the ultimate testimony. And Jerry remained silent about all those things that the later revelations shone a light on in biographies and all like that. He said nothing about the slaughter suffered by the Fourth Infantry Division in the Hurtgen Forest in the autumn of 1944, three months after the joys of Liberation in Paris had given way to the miseries of Hurtgen. And he said nothing about the Bulge and how the hell of all that occurred right after the worst of the Hurtgen Forest catastrophe was barely over.

The 4th ID was fated to be flung again and again, time after time, into some of the war's worst episodes. About which Jerry remained silent. Even when I peppered our conversation with questions that easily invited more and more . . . well, he did not open up about all that madness. I remember I asked him if he'd read Martha Gellhorn's war novel *The Wine of Astonishment.* She'd written it soon after the war and it appeared amid all that stiff competition from Irwin Shaw's *The Young Lions* and Norman Mailer's *The Naked and the Dead*. But her book was unique. Truly.

Jerry nodded and quietly said: "She handled it better than Papa was able to. But no matter what, she'll always be a footnote in his biography. Unjust. Not fair."

That kind of coded remark made further dialogue unnecessary. See what I mean? It was that kind of "inside" conversation that carried us for both nights. What he really was saying was that Martha Gellhorn's novel about the war in Europe (it originally came out with *The Wine of Astonishment* as its title, but she hated that—it was the publisher's decision—and later it was reissued with her preferred title: *The Point of No Return*) went deeper, tried harder, cut to the bone. In her novel it was all on the page, in the tradition of Stephen Crane. She'd been a world-class eyewitness on-site correspondent and what she'd written for *Collier's* magazine scratched the surface.

In her novel, the dreadful waste and the squandered lives of GIs by the thousands who were chewed up and left for dead by numbskull commanders and their insane strategies in the abattoir of the Hurtgen Forest were written into a novel that also did more than any other novel at that time to try to describe the indescribable.

Martha Gellhorn also witnessed Dachau in the aftermath of its liberation by troops of the American Army on April 29, 1945, one week before the war in Europe ended.

Dachau, too, was significantly written into her text when *The Wine of Astonishment* was done. But it wasn't anything Jerry could talk about. Not even ten years after. I did not learn until decades later that he, too, had witnessed a concentration camp.

Again, *those* were the rules. The GIs who had really been in it, the guys who had gone all the way from induction to basic and advanced training and then to beach landings, savage battles, and ultimately to camp liberations, they remained silent.

But I didn't miss for a second the essence of his remark: "She handled it better than Papa was able to." I didn't need to press him on that issue.

He was not just complimenting Martha Gellhorn; he was alluding to poor old Ernest Hemingway's sole attempt to write about 1944 and . . . it didn't turn out too well. Not at all.

Five years after the war ended, Hemingway published his last full-length novel. But you hardly hear about that one now. *Across the River and Into the Trees* was the old man's one effort at capturing *some*thing about the Second World War. By and large, it caused even his biggest admirers to lower their voices.

He could not catch it. Hemingway was broken by the booze and his depression and too many other crises. When he killed himself in 1961, he was only sixty-one. But he looked ninety. That was the year that Jerry ended up on the cover of *Time*. Unlike his peers, who wrote realistic novels (for the most part) about their wartime crucibles, Jerry seemed to veer away from the war. It was a brilliant tactic. What he *re*ally did was transfer all his wartime trauma (what they now call PTSD) and transfer it he did to a fictional array of young, neurotic, postwar characters steeped in spiritual quests. Their first names alone came to define his unique oeuvre: Holden, Teddy, Franny, Zooey, and Seymour. Others, too. Many were part of the Glass family, but not all. He kept his war camouflaged, between the lines. Especially with Sergeant X and Esmé.

38

I've set a date. I've made my decision. And everything here has been approved. The protocol (how I love that word) for the palliative end of life will begin August 15th. I am at peace with all this. What it comes down to is a pain-free farewell. I'll take no more food; no more liquids. The leaving of this life ought not to take too much time.

My appetite is nonexistent. My weight's already diminished considerably, which for me is a joke because I'd already gone from lightweight to featherweight to flyweight.

Most of all, it's the daily grind of the moment-by-moment *con*stant needs . . . the never-ending series of requests. Even a couple of months ago, when I began my yammering into this gadget, I at least had a tiny bit of dexterity in one hand. It's all gone now. At its most extreme, MS is like Lou Gehrig's disease. Though I can speak.

And just in the six months that I've been here, the personnel shifts and the ever-changing ups and downs have spooked me. In the past week or so, my constant request to have my "camel pack" refilled with fresh water made some folks cranky and impatient. Not my old favorites, but the part-timers that they're hiring more of. I can detect how annoyed they are. Probably wondering why I've hung on like this.

When any of my old favorites has ever brought in a part-time rookie to observe the changing and cleaning of my ostomy bag or to irrigate my indwelling catheter or to do any of the other two dozen "essentials" I need someone else to do for me 24/7 (I love that expression, too: Lorena's taught me well), their obvious disgust irks me.

Well, to hell with all that. "Fuck them!" as Lorena says. She's also mad at the part-timers and their lack of zest. Lorena calls them "the i-Zombies." But not *all* of them.

Anyway, while I have this time and a full "camel pack" of fresh water, I'll add this.

On the second night of that brief visit I paid to Jerry's rustic hideaway up in New Hampshire, there was one spectacular exception to his Spartan milieu. And it was a film projector. I mean an honest-to-goodness, full-sized movie projector like the ones that used to clack away and screen the films in real theaters. He had one! It was right out of 1940 and the reels were nearly the size of tires, but it all worked.

I know it sounds nuts but Jerry had made some real money, thanks to the way that Holden's story caught on damn near everywhere. And then his second book had also brought him a new windfall or two. He was fine with drawing water from a stream and having to install indoor plumbing, while at the same time making sure that in his space he had the equipment required to lose himself nightly in favorite films. He'd watch favorite movies innumerable times.

That's the other thing. His 90 acres and Thoreau-like simplicity were real. But equally real was the cabinet he built with his handcrafted shelves, upon which he stacked at least one-dozen classic films that he could afford to buy copies of. We're not talking about some primitive from of Beta or VHS or DVDs here. Not at all. He'd spent whatever it took to acquire the old-time big-reel copies of his beloved movies.

I remember all too well how cumbersome and costly those things could be. When I taught for all those years at Ignatius College and did my level best to spice up my classes with audio-visual reinforcements, we had to order films from a catalogue and then hope and pray that they'd be delivered on time and that the projector's light bulb wouldn't conk out. And all like that. It was miraculous later on when all we had to do was roll in a TV-set on a portable stand and pop in a videocassette.

That became my claim to fame at Ignatius. Long before other Instructors made use of films, scenes from movies that were based on plays, or even musical scenes that illustrated all sorts of issues about characters and their conflicts, I was at work trying to hold students' attention by sharing more than sentences we underlined. I was lambasted and sometimes ridiculed by the academic purists, who thought that I was using such media as distractions. But to me it made total sense if we were all immersed in the reading of *Anna Christie* to go ahead and use scenes from the Garbo film to highlight main points. Or when I had the chance to compare and contrast the key scenes from the black-and-white 1932 Gary Cooper version of *A Farewell to Arms* with the Technicolor mid-1950s remake with Rock Hudson . . . well, on top of the novel, students loved my mixed-media syllabus. The Dean of Students? Not so.

She ridiculed me for blasting a video in class one day. I wanted to illustrate what I called "a cultural tipping point" and I showed my students some 1956 film footage of Elvis being introduced to America by Tommy and Jimmy Dorsey on their CBS-TV program *Stage Show*. Before Ed Sullivan, before Milton Berle, before Steve Allen or anyone else, it was the Dorsey Brothers who featured young "Mr. Presley" six times.

Anyhow, the craziest thing about Jerry's closet full of classics was the variety. He had everything from *The 39 Steps* to the last of the musicals with Mickey and Judy.

Believe you me, we agreed in a mighty quick minute to watch that one together.

"You stood me up when it came to *Presenting Lily Mars*," I said. Chiding him. He remembered. I could tell because he twitched. And then he placed the year.

"Apologies," he said. "But here's the other big one she did in 1943. And as you may or may not remember, this one also had Tommy Dorsey's band in a starring role." He wasn't kidding. That "other big one she did in 1943" really was Judy Garland's last major outing as a musical co-star with Mickey Rooney and yet another reason that *Girl Crazy* belongs in a Time Capsule is that Tommy Dorsey's band filmed a slew of scenes in the movie that were recorded in stereo. Times were changing.

That night, before we sank into the comfort of an antique sofa that Jerry had set in the middle of what he jokingly called his "private screening room," we spoke of the fond memories we both had about all four of the major musicals that Judy Garland and Mickey Rooney had starred in, all of which appeared over a four-year span. "Three in a row and then a hiccup," is how Jerry put it. I knew what he meant.

"I remember that, too," I said. "After *Babes in Arms* hit a grand slam in 1939, I figured they'd be in one musical per year for as long as MGM owned them."

"You were nearly right," Jerry said. "*Strike Up the Band* came out in 1940."

"And *Babes on Broadway* one year later in 1941," I said. "Right on schedule."

"I'd like to know what caused the hiccup," Jerry said. "He wasn't yet in the Army in '42, and she wasn't pregnant. But *Girl Crazy* didn't come out until '43. Who knows?"

I don't care how sappy it sounds. It's true. Some of us defined our lives by the touchstones of cultural treasures: films, books, and most of all songs. Boomers who think life didn't exist prior to the release of *Sgt. Pepper* haven't got a goddamn clue. Our lives were as bookended by beloved landmark works as theirs ever were. Jerks.

That's one thing my Jimmy picked up on in his usual sharp way. Because he was born in 1955, he always said: "I'm a second-wave Boomer, and we're stuck with the first-wave Boomers always making their speeches. But it's weird. The first-wave ones were born in the first ten years after the war. And those of us in the second wave, like, born between '55 and the early Sixties, we really got stuck in something."

There were times when Jim would explain his ideas with exquisite precision. "Take the Beatles, for example," he once riffed to me and my friend. "*Abbey Road* was their last album, even though it was released before *Let It Be* came out. Take both, in fact. I was fourteen going on fifteen when those albums were issued. To kids my age, at that time, the older hippie-artiste Beatles were *everything*. But almost all the time, all you hear about is the screaming meemies who were fourteen or fifteen when the Beatles did Sullivan's show or crisscrossed America on those tours in the mid-60s."

God, how I loved hearing him frame things according to his chronological memory.

Anyway, speaking of songs, it's a no-brainer to say that back in the day the four big musicals starring Judy and Mickey were stuffed with what's now enshrined as the Great American Songbook. The standards, I mean. Or they were standards then. Now they're classics. They're spritzed all over those four movies: "Where or When" and "How About You?" and of course "Our Love Affair." Specialty numbers, too, like "Drummer Boy" and others. But the *Girl Crazy* soundtrack really hit the bull's-eye.

To see that film again in the privacy of Jerry's nooks and crannies was to be right off the bat invited to sing, because our self-consciousness dissolved. Nobody else was around! Nothing to be embarrassed about. Of course we sang along. Out loud.

When Judy was singing "But Not for Me," we held hands and sang with her. By the time she sang "Embraceable You" we were necking and our toes were curled. It was in the middle of a spectacular five-minute instrumental performance of George Gershwin's "Fascinating Rhythm," though, that the tectonic plates shifted.

I sat on top. How could it be otherwise? It was involuntary by that time. Unstoppable. The scene in the film where Tommy Dorsey's band blows up a storm playing a full-blooded five-minute chart of "Fascinating Rhythm" (later I learned that it was one of those Sy Oliver arrangements) is in a class by itself. And it wasn't just me in heat.

It wasn't just the heat of libido, either. That five-minute segment of the movie ought to be studied at Julliard. It encapsulates the essence of the Swing Era. With a twist. By 1943, when it was filmed, TD had added a string section. Expanded ensemble and extraordinary touches by Sy Oliver from start to finish. There were brass riffs that could make the dead come to life and saxophone solos (along with two clarinet solos and then Tommy's trombone artistry) that guaranteed goose-bumps. But it was during the "trumpet battle" that the two of us went to the other side of time. I have no doubt that it was highly similar to the ways in which Boomers lost it while blasting anything from "Satisfaction" to "Light My Fire" so many years later. In our case, it was also a matter of Jerry's expertise with the projector. He had mastered that damn thing and knew how to Rewind and count slowly—really slowly—to nine, and then switch back to Play and believe you me, "Fascinating Rhythm" began anew.

When all clothes were tossed aside, we made our way through that performance at least four times. Maybe five. And each time it was during the fiery, explosive, ultra-musical high note exchange by the two dueling trumpet players that we screamed in unison.

You have to hear it to believe it. What happened was that Sy Oliver wrote right into TD's chart for this Gershwin song an extended segment where two great trumpet players took turns blowing these high-note riffs back and forth at each other. The intensity of the performance by that time is beyond category. Very much like what my Jimmy called the "dueling guitar battles" in the music he loved in the 1970s.

And I knew. In my bones. In my blood. In my cells. I just *knew*. Like women do. I was going to do this. Raise that child alone. Already I just *knew* it. The following morning, Jerry was nowhere to be found. I drove away.

I understood.

39

I can't do this anymore. This will be my last effort with the tapes and all. Or maybe one more. Tops. It's really over for me. What it takes now (I should say, what it *has* taken for more than a year) just to keep me clean daily, hydrated, fed, medicated, and "comfortable" in pretty much one or two or three positions—at best—is now beyond category. It's not a life for me. My soul's ready to exit this broken body.

Oddly, I've always been a math-impaired nincompoop, but certain sums now float through my mind with the regularity of ticker tape. One hundred thousand, for example. On average, that's the number of times that a normal human heart beats per day: 24/7, as Lorena says. Minimum, in fact. One hundred thousand heartbeats, every twenty-four hours. One hundred thousand per day. Without force of will. No effort involved that demands our attention or focus. We take it for granted, most of the time. That's a million heartbeats every ten days. Which makes me wonder how I ever spent so many years being unaware of the three million (or more) heartbeats sustaining my life each month. It stuns me. The numbers alone are startling. But it is the effortless, unwilled, uncalculated, miraculous gift of it all that I cannot in any way chalk off to the notion that it's merely the body's mechanical, clock-like functioning.

One hundred thousand heartbeats per day (rounded off), meaning an average of three million heartbeats each month. Every year! That's thirty-six million times per year (on average) that the human heart beats and thus sustains the rivers of blood flowing to the brain and galvanizing our entire body, mind, and soul. And most of the time, our brain is distracting us with anxieties, fears, regrets, and mere desires.

All that mental agitation, while the heart beats thirty-six million times each year.

Before starting to speak today, just about a half hour ago, I asked the aide who kindly placed the micro-cassette right here on my pillow, if she'd help me with her calculator. That's one thing I'll say for these kids and their gadgets. Everyone has a calculator on a moment's notice. I asked her to multiply ninety-two times three hundred and sixty-five. She briskly reported: "33,580!" Then, I said: "There it is. That's how many days I've been alive, as of my last birthday." She looked as if I'd told the world's dumbest joke. Then she tallied up her time and promptly yelped.

I wasn't through with her yet. Without saying a word about the fundamental fact that each day my heart has beat an average of one hundred thousand times, and thereby beat three million times per month for an average of thirty-six million times per year (with scarcely ever a thought from me about the miraculous mystery of it all and its sacramental, effortless, omnipresent communion with ineffable source), and without explaining why, I asked her to multiply thirty-six times ninety-two.

"Make it thirty-six million times ninety-two," I said. She figured I had gone nuts.

Proudly, however, she read straight off her iPhone's calculator: "That's three, um, wait, okay, like, that's three *bill*ion three hundred and twelve million. Ex*actly*."

That's not counting the days, weeks, and months since my last birthday. Amen.

40

One more time. This will be it. Once I stop taking liquids, no more talking for me.

And like it or not, August 15th is tomorrow. My plan is in effect. I'm going to go. I trust that all will be well. "*It won't be long,*" as Jim used to sing with the Beatles. My son. James. My Jimmy. His middle name was Joseph, so for a while in high school he went by "JJ." Later on, he settled on Jim. As for his last name, I gave him mine. Well, what I mean is, I gave him my father's last name. It all got complicated for a while.

In 1955, a single woman having a baby . . . well, that was another century. I had to manufacture little white lies. But I had the house to myself. Pop and ol' Mom were gone. There were manners and boundaries when I perennially taught core curriculum classes at Ignatius College, but gradually, if anything personal came up, I settled on the most reliable of tall tales: that his father had died overseas in an army training accident shortly after the end of the Korean War. My story was a variation on Jerry's tale of Walt Glass and his death by accident in postwar Japan.

No one questioned me. Why would they? After the Korean War, we kept tens of thousands of GIs stationed over there. And people were quite circumspect then.

All through the years, it worked. But I shouldn't have lied to our son.

41

I'm beginning to see the light.

I waited another day. For my own sentimental reasons. It's still August 15th.

In the blue of evening, I sipped enough water to allow me to talk a bit more.

Tomorrow is a long time. It'll be August 16th. That's the way it is.

It'll be the anniversary of my last encounter—my last embrace—with my Jimmy.

It'll be the anniversary of the worst decision I ever made: 38 years ago. I've never been able to forgive myself. But maybe he's forgiven me.

It was a Tuesday. August 16th, 1977. He didn't just ask. He insisted I allow him to drive my car from Chicago to Memphis to witness the vigils and funeral. Everything happened fast. "Mr. Presley" died that Tuesday afternoon. Our son adored him.

After midnight I handed over the keys. To be there Wednesday was Jim's plan.

Many thousands made the trip from all over the country. It was Jim's first-ever road trip.

And last. In southern Illinois, he was blindsided by a drunken speeder.

As Franny would surely echo: *"Lord Jesus Christ, have mercy on me."*

With or without my eyes closed, I see him with Jerry.

Father and son await me. At last.

Acknowledgments TK

Author Bio TK